A Kiss From the Past

A Kiss From the Past

A Secret Ties Romance

Kelly Cain

TULE
PUBLISHING

Dedication

To my siblings, Monique, Aharon, Senné, and Norman.
I hope you know how much I cherish you.
And to my daughters, Diamond and Kamryn, because I exist
to love them.

CHAPTER ONE

Nichelle

WHOEVER SAID SATURDAYS were meant for sleeping in obviously never belonged to a sorority.

The room was buzzing with excitement at getting together after a single month of being apart. It's not like there wasn't a whole shredding project the Saturday before; almost half the chapter of Omega Kappa Omega worked the parking lot as random folks freely dropped off their personal documents. Whew, just the memory of dragging recycling cans around on that hot day had Nichelle grabbing a cool water along with some grapes off the back table of snacks.

"Sorors, please have a seat. It's ten on the dot." Nichelle's mother slash graduate chapter president was more timely than anyone had a right to be—a constant clash with her laid-back daughter.

Everyone made it to their seats, still chattering, but at a lower rumble than before. Nichelle took a seat near the front of the classroom-style room since she'd have to present her report later. They followed the agenda to a T, including the allotted time for each item: old business, new business, adopting the previous meeting minutes, etc. Her mother was dressed to the nines, decked out in their sorority colors of navy blue and silver. Her tutu would have seemed inappropriate on any other woman of a certain age, but Betty Sampson pulled it off with her thin frame and wrinkle-free, dark reddish-brown skin—something Nichelle definitely didn't inherit from her mother. She had a more athletic build, thanks to her love of basketball. And her skin was peach-colored.

When it was time for the graduate advisor reports, Nichelle stacked the mess she'd made on the seat next to her. When she first got there, she'd collected several stapled papers, small bags of paraphernalia and trinkets from this soror and that one to pass along to the young women on campus, and her plate with what was left of her grapes.

"Soror Nichelle Sampson, please come forward." Her mother sat in her chair next to the podium. To her mom's right was Amanda, Nichelle's closest friend and fellow professor who served as the chapter vice-president and program chairman. And next to her was the secretary busy tapping on her laptop, capturing the meeting minutes.

Nichelle headed to the podium, conscious of her uncovered legs as she went. She intentionally wore a longer skirt, but they wouldn't go unnoticed. "Thank you, Madam Basilius."

Her mother looked down at Nichelle's legs and frowned.

Amanda hid a grin behind her slender fingers, rings covering almost every single one.

Nichelle knew she'd be in for it the minute she'd realized her last pair of hose had a run in them. She probably should have checked earlier in the week. She was not one for planning ahead. There was nothing she could do about it now, so she concentrated on the laptop in front of her at the podium and hit the down arrow for the next slide. "Good morning, Sorors. As you can see, Psi Gamma had a busy month. The young ladies sponsored a food drive for the local food bank, made fifty pillowcase dresses for Haiti, and visited the assisted living center close to the campus to have a sing-along with the residents." She clicked the key again to show the pictures of the co-eds with the residents, smiles all around, then clicked again to the next slide. "Five seniors will graduate next weekend, and we had their luncheon this past Sunday. Remaining sorors will begin practicing for the Labor Day Classic step show. That concludes my report. Any questions?"

The crowd murmured. She watched them expectantly, but nobody raised their hand. She turned to her mother, who probably would love to ask a question about her bare legs, but obviously couldn't. Not yet, at least.

"Thank you, Soror Nichelle. Next up is Soror Amanda Rivers with the programs report."

Nichelle sat and watched her bestie take her place behind the podium. Amanda should have been Betty's daughter instead of Nichelle because she was just as fashionable—decked-out in a chartreuse pantsuit with a blush-colored scarf draped over her shoulder. The bright pink and green colors complemented her tawny brown skin and auburn braids.

"Good morning, Sorors. Good morning."

When the crowd offered an enthusiastic but not quite roaring return greeting, Amanda raised the volume of her voice. "I said good morning, Sorors."

The response was at full volume.

"Yes, that's better. I love looking out at your beautiful faces, Sorors. You know what I would love even more? Seeing all these beautiful faces at our programs."

This was Amanda's usual spiel on the first Saturday of every month. The same forty to fifty usual suspects showed up for service projects even though there were two hundred members of the chapter. Amanda worked harder than anyone Nichelle knew, and she tried to help her friend wherever needed even though Nichelle supported the undergraduate chapter. They were extremely active, and oftentimes their activities clashed with the graduate chapter's. As grad advisor, she had no choice but to be with the younger ladies.

"Now, Sorors, I'll be sending out the activities for the week later on this evening per usual. Please ensure that you review your email carefully and update your calendars so you won't forget. We need six sorors to volunteer for the youth dance performance Friday night. Those middle and high schoolers are counting on you, Sorors. Please contact Soror Tanya if you're able to make it. Her email and number are in the chapter directory, and it'll be in the email this evening. Don't disappoint the young performers, Sorors."

She could *soror* with the best of them. As Amanda continued on with her report, Nichelle checked her phone's calendar to see if she was booked Friday. She may not be the most absolutely organized person in the world, but her phone really made it easy, as long as she remembered to update her calendar right away. She'd been in a bind too many times when she didn't. According to her phone, Friday evening was free after a staff meeting that afternoon. Who schedules a staff meeting on a Friday afternoon? Her dad, the head of the political science department, that's who. Between her father bossing her around at work and her mother bossing her around with sorority activities, you'd never know she was thirty-two years old.

She typed out a quick email to Soror Tanya volunteering. With that done, she redirected her attention to the front. Apparently, Amanda had wrapped up her report and sat down.

After everyone gave their various reports, Betty dismissed the meeting so they could sing their song and disburse. Nichelle gathered her belongings and headed to the front table to speak with her mother and her friend who were both packing up. The sorority met at the Berkeley community college and needed to right the room how they found it. Other sorors were in the back wrapping up the leftover food and drinks.

"Hi, sweetheart." Her mother pulled Nichelle in for a hug and whispered in her ear. "You know better. That's all I'm going to say."

Nichelle lifted one shoulder. She did know better. "Sorry, Mom. I'll make sure I check beforehand next time." She wouldn't mention how antiquated she thought the rule was about pantyhose. There was no point because these rules were made at the national level. It was stupid, though. They didn't even wear stockings to church—not that she attended anymore. That rule went out with the dark ages ten or twenty years before. Her mother was always decked out, with a feathered hat chic enough to put the Queen of England to shame.

Betty patted her on the back before releasing her.

Nichelle's stomach rumbled. "Where do you want to go for lunch, ladies?"

"Sorry, honey, I can't make lunch today. There's a big court case coming up, and I need to pull some documents together."

"But it's Saturday. And you're retired. Do you have to do it now?" Nichelle stuck out her bottom lip.

"Recently retired. And I hadn't checked my email in days. Richard texted me late last night because of the lack of response."

How long after someone retired were they still on the hook for unpaid work? Nichelle thanked her lucky stars again she hadn't followed her mom into the corporate world. "Can't the new CFO do it?"

"Be a big girl, Nichelle." Her mom smirked and pulled Nichelle in for another hug. "We can have dinner some time this week."

She grumbled, "Fine," then sniggered.

IT ALL STARTED with a crustacean craving. Nichelle simply planted some subtle food-related notions into the conversation with her bestie after their meeting and voila, forty-five minutes later, she was digging into a delicious Seafood Bucatini and an Ultimate Lemon Drop on the outdoor patio at Skates on the Bay. It was a good respite considering how busy Nichelle and Amanda had been. It was difficult getting her friend to slow down for a meal without Nichelle's delicate prodding. Even after sorority meetings once a month.

They walked the couple miles to Nichelle's rented one-bedroom apartment in a lovely, shaded smaller complex near the university. The breeze off the Bay was mild and the sky cloudless, and Nichelle was grateful for the shade engulfing her building, welcoming her home.

Nichelle stretched when she reached the bottom of the

stairs, her muscles still tight. "Girl, I don't know how I'm gonna make it up those stairs. I really need to get more exercise. Can you roll me?"

"Who's gonna push me?" Amanda laughed, then groaned. "Even after that walk, I'm still full. I'm ready for a nap."

Naps were fine, but Nichelle usually didn't partake. They left her feeling groggy. "Seriously though. You want to come up and watch *Island Romance*?"

"Now you're talking. I love me some Bryce. And you know he's gonna hook up with Bianca."

"No. Absolutely not. It'll be Theresa."

"You're outta line." Amanda climbed three of the stairs and looked down at Nichelle. "Team Bianca all the way."

"We'll see." Nichelle moaned as they trudged up the steps, but she stopped short and tensed at the sight of a tall man standing outside her door. "May I help you?"

The man turned, dressed in a dark-blue uniform. "Do you live here?"

Nichelle relaxed when she spotted a package in his hands, and a larger leather zipped bag near his feet. "Yes. Is that for me?"

"May I see some identification please?"

Amanda nudged her and raised a brow.

She strained to see the label on his uniform, but it was a courier service rather than a normal delivery company. "Okay, but I never have to show my ID for packages."

Nichelle walked up the final step and dug around in her purse for her driver's license.

"This is a special delivery, ma'am, and I can't release it without your identification and a signature."

She handed her ID to the man, then glanced at Amanda and shrugged. What in the world could she be receiving by courier? She couldn't remember ordering anything, certainly not something special enough to sign for.

"Here you are, ma'am." After returning her license, he handed her an electronic pad, and she scribbled her signature. Then he released the package to her.

Should I tip him? Ugh. She dug in her purse looking for money while the man waited. She rarely carried much cash around.

Amanda reached around her and handed the courier a bill.

He nodded and left Nichelle and Amanda outside the apartment door thoroughly bewildered.

"Let's go inside." Amanda was peeking around even though there was only one other apartment on the floor and the only stairwell leading up there remained empty.

Nichelle unlocked the door, and the women hurried inside. They headed straight into the kitchen which was directly to the right of the door. A short hallway led to the remainder of the apartment.

"I can't wait to see what's in here." She put the package next to her purse on the counter and searched for a box cutter in her many cluttered drawers. "I know I have something to open it with in here somewhere."

Amanda tapped her four-inch pumps impatiently on Nichelle's tiled kitchen floor. "Girl, how do you live like this?"

"What? It's in this kitchen some—Ah, here it is." She triumphantly lifted the tool, then set to work on the package.

Inside the larger box was a smaller metal box with a key. Nichelle unlocked that box with shaky hands. Next was a smaller navy velvet box along with a single sheet of ivory stationery folded in half.

She glanced at Amanda. "What the what?"

"Just open it already!"

The box gave off an ominous vibe, and Nichelle shook her head. "I don't have a great feeling about this. You look."

Amanda happily snapped the little blue box open and promptly gasped.

"What?" She peeked over Amanda's shoulder and stared at the beautiful pink ring inside. The gem was a huge pearl, like nothing Nichelle had ever seen before. Her hands trembled even more, and the paper slipped onto the floor. Instead of picking it up, Nichelle slumped into a chair. Something was wrong with this entire situation.

Amanda picked up the sheet and read aloud.

Dearest Nichelle,

This may come as a shock to you, but I am your grand-

mother. I've had to love you from afar because of decisions made by your birth parents, but I wanted you to have something to know me by even though I am gone. This is a precious family heirloom and rare gem that originally belonged to your fifth great-grandmother in Jamaica. Take care of it. I hope you'll pass it along to your daughter or son someday.

I wish circumstances were different. Try not to have any regrets in this life, dearest.

Love,
Grandmother Florence

"Is that it?" Nichelle reached for the letter and scanned it herself. The entirety of the letter was a paragraph. No other clues besides the ring.

Amanda shook the bigger metal box and peered inside again. "I guess so."

"What does it mean?" Nichelle stared at the single sheet of paper.

"Have you ever heard of a grandmother named Florence?"

Nichelle shook her head, set the paper on the table, and picked up the ring. "No. My grandparents died before I was born, but neither grandmother was named Florence. They were Josephine and Jessie. Even with all the nicknames everyone in my family uses, Florence wouldn't fit either of those." She sniffed and took a deep breath, the foreboding giving way to the harsh reality.

Amanda put her arms around Nichelle's shoulders and squeezed. "I hate to point it out, but she does say your 'birth parents.'"

The ring suddenly became heavier in Nichelle's trembling hands. "I, uh. Maybe it's a—" She was going to say joke, but who sends a family heirloom to someone in jest? Nichelle picked up the paper and studied the short prose again, and soon fat droplets splattered on it, blending the ink. Nichelle buried her head into her friend's shoulder, absorbing as much consolation as possible. There wasn't enough comfort in the world to erase what she probably should have known her entire life. She was adopted.

NICHELLE LAID HER head on the steering wheel and closed her eyes. Could she die from heartbreak? Was that a thing? Sure, she'd read about broken hearts in novels and heard of people losing the bae they'd been married to a long minute, then passing away right after. But what if it was your parents who broke your heart? She didn't know how to feel. A lie by omission was still a lie. And as far as lies go, this was a doozy.

She heard the movement before feeling the light touch. She'd nearly forgotten Francesca was in the car. "Are you okay?"

Hooboy, *okay* was such a relative term. "I'm fine."

Francesca cocked her head just the slightest.

"I'll be fine." She didn't know the first thing about researching rare gems and was grateful for her younger sorority sister's help, but she just wanted to drive back home and crawl under the covers.

"Clark's brilliant. If he can't figure out the ring's origins, he'll know who can."

Nichelle nodded. It was a blessing that Francesca overheard Nichelle talking to Amanda at the undergrad step show practice. "I'm not sure if I said anything before, but thank you for introducing me to your brother." She hiccupped a little on the word *brother*.

Her own brother had died only six months before, and the wound was still raw for her parents. Which is why she hadn't confronted them right away. She needed a couple of days to temper her fury. She missed her brother too, but they'd never been close. Besides the huge age gap, they just didn't have anything in common. He wasn't interested in education, and she was a college professor. He played tennis for exercise but wouldn't attend her basketball games because he wasn't a fan of watching sports. He ran lots of women in and out of his life, and Nichelle...well, Nichelle was friend-zoned more times than she could count. She finally made up her mind to put romantic relationships on the back burner and focus on her career, which had so far paid off.

Now Nichelle understood why she and her brother had nothing in common.

"Meet you in there?"

"Sure." Francesca hesitated a moment with her hand on the door. "One of my classmates is adopted and she goes to a group every week. They meet just off campus so let me know if you want the details."

Nichelle smiled and nodded. "Thanks. I'll let you know."

Francesca got out of Nichelle's two-seater Fiat and ran inside the building. Literally ran. Ah, to be young and run everywhere. Nichelle remembered those days well. Not that she was old, but now that she was on the other side of thirty, her running everywhere days were over. Matter of fact, her running anywhere days were gone, and she was glad about it. She'd run enough playing sports in college, although she didn't mind a pickup game here and there, just no basketball speed drills anymore. Those things were brutal.

She pulled out the dark blue box and opened it again, staring at the huge pink pearl ring. Her heart squeezed. Both box and ring were obviously ancient, and the musty smell that rose every time she opened it was testifying. It was like nothing she'd ever seen. She'd only received it a couple days before, but it was enough time for her world to be completely shattered, her identity thoroughly destroyed.

Whew, life comes at you fast.

The note that came with the box fluttered to the floor. Nichelle picked it up and read it for the hundredth time, then wiped the tear trailing down her cheek and shook her head. Couldn't the woman have given her a bit more of a clue? Nichelle snapped the box closed and put it back in her purse. Time to meet this head on.

Nichelle walked across the parking lot, and when she opened the doors to the store, a sweet mixture of jasmine and vanilla caressed her nose, comforting her. The showcase room was big, but not huge. The design spoke of ease and relaxation with low tables and plush chairs, the jewelry held in suspended boxes along the walls. There were filled bookshelves and more chairs paired with end tables. Was this a jewelry store or a library? When Francesca told her she and her brother inherited a jewelry store from their grandparents, she was expecting long glass and steel cases filled with necklaces and rings. This was not that.

There were a few customers milling about or seated in chairs being helped, sipping various colored liquids out of crystal glasses. Nichelle could use a sip of whatever they were having right about now. She spotted Francesca coming out from the back, but she was alone. Where was this brother of hers?

"He'll be right out."

Nichelle nodded. "Thanks. I sure hope he can help." She offered the girl a small smile, then turned to the back of the room where Francesca just came from.

Standing there was her brother.

It was obvious, because although his features weren't exactly the same—and he was frowning where his sister was usually smiling—he had the look of gorgeous Francesca. He was tall, at least six-one. He had the darkest brown hair, cropped close on the sides, but a little longer on top, which was mostly wavy with a slight curl at the ends. His eyes were... Even from across the room, his eyes were potent, so brown, they appeared black. His wardrobe matched his intensity with a gray sports jacket worn over a crisp white button-down shirt and pressed dark trousers. He was a whole snack. Well damn.

Francesca waved. "Clark, over here."

CHAPTER TWO

Clark

"CLARK, OVER HERE."

He turned his attention to his sister. She'd knocked on his locked door a few minutes before, interrupting his review of the sediment sample he'd just analyzed. She wouldn't be put off, so he silenced the NPR podcast he was listening to and discontinued his work.

Franny waved him over.

May as well get this over with so he could return to his lab. He rounded the table directly in front of him and crossed the room where Franny was standing with her friend.

"Finally. Clark, this is my graduate advisor, Professor Sampson, who has the ring I was telling you about."

Nichelle offered her hand and although Clark saw her hand move, he momentarily didn't recognize the gesture. "Please call me Nichelle. Hello, er, Clark, is it?" She withdrew her hand.

She was tall, standing at least three or four inches above Franny's five-foot-six. It took him a moment to register the gesture. "Oh. Yes, it is." He fumbled for her retreating hand, but it was too late, so he stuck his hand in the pockets of his trousers.

Franny glared at him. And he was reminded that he'd made a final statement before leaving his office. "Try not to be awkward, m'kay?"

It was unfortunate that the time had passed to fix his faux pas. Clark couldn't think of a single thing to say so he stood there. He closed his eyes a moment, wishing he could have ignored his sister when she disturbed his work. He was used to being ignored by everyone including his parents. But not by Franny, which is why he could never deny her anything.

His sister nudged him.

Clark cleared his throat. "I'm guessing you got engaged and want an appraisal, right? Just leave it and I'll look at it when I'm done writing my report."

"It's nothing like that at all. She needs help identifying a stone that she believes is rare." Franny rotated to Nichelle. "Tell him."

Nichelle shrugged and dug into her purse. "So, here's the ring. I'm told it's a rare heirloom."

Clark held his hand out for the stone and once she'd dropped it into his palm, he turned into the professional he prided himself on being. First, he noted the rose-gold claw setting of the ring. The pearl itself was approximately 12 millimeters which probably meant it was a cultured pearl dyed pink. The band was likely worth more than the stone. Everyone with a trinket thought they'd found a rare stone. In Clark's extensive experience, not only were the stones not rare, they weren't even real.

Without looking up from the ring, he spoke. "It could be a saltwater pearl from Akoya, which does produce pink pearls. More than likely, it's a freshwater pearl dyed pink." He shrugged.

"I was told it's a rare gem. Don't you need to run some tests or something?"

When he glanced up, the look Nichelle gave him broadcasted her displeasure. Her light-brown skin reddened considerably, and she'd narrowed those burnt-sienna eyes. He studied those eyes for longer than was socially acceptable, the port-wine color fascinating him.

Franny cleared her throat.

Right. "If this were something natural, at this size, it would be worth a fortune. Do you mind if I ask where you got it?"

"It's a long story, but I inherited it from a grandmother I didn't realize I had. She died but left a note with the ring and said it passed down through the family line."

"Oh." He tried to push down the curiosity tugging at him. Although Clark still doubted it could be anything other than a saltwater pearl at the most, he needed to be thorough. "Well, I can look at it under a microscope to at least determine it isn't an imitation. Would you want me to do that?"

She was still frowning but nodded. "If it wouldn't be too much trouble, yes please."

They kept jewel baggies under the tables, so he retreated behind the closest one and withdrew a plastic bag, dropping the ring inside.

Franny asked, "You can't look now?"

Clark walked back over to his sister and her friend. Although it was clear that she was closer to his age than Franny's. What did she call her? Right, graduate advisor. "No, I can't. As I explained to you, I'm preparing for a case, and I've allotted the next two hours for that." He'd already been out at the site and gathered samples and analyzed most of them, giving the attorneys a preliminary report, but he preferred to be completely thorough and was evaluating the samples again before finalizing his report. He'd have to testify against a chemical company soon; his reputation as an expert geochemist was unvarnished and he wanted to keep it that way. "I have a bike ride scheduled after that. I can try to look at the stone in the morning, first thing, but depending on what I find, it may require additional research."

Nichelle stepped closer to him and smiled, tentatively, but not unkindly. "I do appreciate this. I realize you're doing me a favor. Tomorrow's fine." She reached into her purse and pulled out a business card and handed it to him. "Please give me a call once you've had a chance to look at it."

"Of course." He took the card from her and pocketed it but held on to the ring inside its plastic covering. "I'll be in touch." He wanted nothing more than to reach out and try that handshake again, but he didn't chance it. Instead, he circled toward the back of the store without another word.

He passed Cathie helping a man and what looked like his young son pick out a necklace. They were in the birthstone section so probably a Mother's Day gift which was in a few days. They'd left it a bit close in his opinion. Cathie was their only full-time employee, but they employed several part-time staff who worked shifts, including Franny. Since she was majoring in management, he hoped his sister would be the business manager when she graduated, freeing him up to concentrate completely on his true love. They talked about it, of course, but she hadn't committed wholly. She'd taken an interest as a child in the "pretty rocks," so that was enough for their grandparents.

He looked at Tim next who was assisting a young couple gushing over the engagement rings. Clark thinned his lips into a tight frown. As was so often the case, seeing a couple on the brink of marriage did nothing for his disposition. Yes, he was "awkward" as Franny put it, but no different than anyone else. He wanted the same security most wanted—a gratifying job, enjoyable hobbies, a partner and children—a complete life, something that at thirty-four, he was beginning to give up on. To believe that nobody would ever completely abide him.

There was a narrow hallway leading from the showroom with a bathroom on one side and a storage room on the other. The lighting was low back there because when his grandparents were alive and ran the store, they didn't allow anyone past the counters out front. With the advent of technology and superior security, there was no need to move the gems to the back. The storage and safe inside were largely unused. He and Franny also recently redesigned the front showroom, and gone were the sterile counters, replaced with more comfortable displays and seating. All were Franny's ideas including their signature scent.

Clark unlocked the door at the end of the hallway. He'd added the lab nearly ten years before when he and Franny inherited the store from their grandparents. The lab at the local university was well-equipped and really the best place to conduct analysis, but Clark preferred this one he'd created in the backrooms of the jewelry store. It was mostly a matter of convenience, plus he could set his own hours. There was the difficulty of being interrupted though, which was not so convenient. The employees in the store knew better than to bother him when he was on a case. However, he couldn't control his little sister no matter how much he tried.

He pulled his jacket off and hung it on the back of the door.

He rubbed a hand across his brow a couple of times, then pulled the ring out of the baggie. He set it on his desk and frowned, thinking back again to what Franny said when she'd disturbed his work. "Try not to be awkward, m'kay?" He'd watched the closed door for a few moments before shaking himself. That was a low blow especially considering his sister knew he didn't care about social norms enough to be awkward. He was just him.

But he understood enough to know he hadn't made a great impression on Nichelle. That was unfortunate.

CHAPTER THREE

Nichelle

THE WALLS WERE bleeding. Seriously. Maybe it was her eyes. Or her ears. At this point so late in the day, she was having trouble remaining engaged. Lord knew she loved her father, but goodness gracious he was droning on—his usual spiel about research and publishing. It had been nearly a week since she'd found out the truth, and she still hadn't said anything to her parents.

Jamie kicked her under the table and Nichelle looked up. Everyone was staring at her. She wiped at her nose just to make sure. Nope, all good there. She pursed her lips and looked at Jamie who only bucked her eyes and nodded toward her father, his dark skin gleaming from his academic workout.

"Sorry. Did you ask me something, Professor?" There was no "Dad" within these walls. He treated her just like the other employees, which was fine with her.

"I did, Professor Sampson. I asked you if the presentation for the dean is ready?"

Shit. "I'll have it for you first thing Monday morning."

He nodded and went on to something else.

Nichelle tapped her computer to bring up the presentation she started, but it wouldn't load. Crap. When it came to technology outside basic interactions with her phone, she was definitely on the struggle bus. Even though she hadn't done a whole lot of work on it, what she did do, she wanted to preserve. She checked her phone for the time. If her father would release them, she could probably make it over to the IT department and get it looked at before she left campus. That was a big if though. It wasn't that Robert Sampson was a huge talker, he actually wasn't, but when you got him started on university stuff, he could really get going. That's what happened when he had a passion for something. Plus, burying himself in work helped ease the big hole left by the recent heartache of his son's death.

"That's all for now. Professor Sampson, I expect that presentation in my inbox first thing Monday."

"You'll have it, Professor Sampson." Yeah, it could get confusing sometimes. Especially for the students. Nichelle leaned over to Jamie. "You want to walk with me over to IT?"

"Sure, I have some time before sunset. Is something wrong with your laptop?"

Jamie could translate for Nichelle if it came to that. Plus, the IT manager was her brother-in-law. Couldn't hurt to have her along. She needed to get that presentation back.

With graduation the next day and the youth dance sorority commitment that night, she hardly had any time to work on it. "Yeah, my presentation won't come up. Do you think Noah can recover it?"

"Only one way to find out." She smiled before sliding her own laptop in a book bag, her deep dimples creasing her cheeks.

They made their way out of the political science building and headed across campus to the IT department. Students milled about, daydreams of summer vacation marking their faces. One professor held class outside in the warmth, and students were spread across the dry grass listening attentively. Gray slate buildings peeked through eucalyptus trees, bark peeling from their hairy trunks, smelling faintly of Vick's VapoRub.

As they hurried across campus, the two women took a few minutes to catch up. Although Jamie wasn't her best school friend like Amanda, they were close-ish. Nichelle asked, "How're your husband and the boys?" She'd never met Jamie's husband or kids but saw their pictures plenty considering they shared an office space.

Her face clouded over for a moment, then she quickly recovered. "They're fine."

"What's wrong? You don't have to tell me."

"It's okay. Asa's been doing some tests and needs to go in for a biopsy in a couple weeks. The doctor thinks it's just precautionary, but I can't help but be worried. He doesn't like to talk about it especially around his mother. I've told you how they're such ostriches." Jamie's mother-in-law had lived with them since they married and was the primary caretaker of the kids.

Nichelle touched her arm before pulling open the door to the IT building. "You can always talk to me whenever you want. You know that, right?"

"I do, but I also know you've had enough emotional stuff to deal with lately with your brother's long illness. I don't want to pile on. Plus, this is probably nothing."

"Right, probably nothing. But still, don't feel like you can't talk to me. You were totally there for me when my brother died."

Jamie nodded and turned to the counter running the length of the help desk to the IT department. The building was dedicated to servers and teams of people performing various functions Nichelle didn't come close to understanding. She'd never made it past this desk in all her years of teaching there.

A student assistant was standing behind the counter. "May I help you?"

Jamie spoke up. "I'm Mr. Perkins's sister. Could you ask him to come down, please?"

"Sure." He picked up the phone and dialed. When Noah answered, the student relayed Jamie's message.

"Thank you."

They sat on the nearby bench and waited for Noah to

come down. While they waited, Nichelle pulled her laptop out and turned it on so it'd be ready for inspection. Hopefully it wouldn't take long because she needed to get home and change for the performance she volunteered for later in the evening. While they waited, Nichelle's thoughts drifted again to the ring. Of who may have sent it. And why. A couple days had passed, and she still hadn't heard from Clark.

Noah rushed through the front door a few minutes later. "What's wrong?"

Jamie shook her head. "Nothing. Everything's fine. I came with Nichelle so you could check out her laptop."

He rubbed his hands across his reddened face, his blue eyes stern. "You scared me to death. I thought something happened with Asa." He leaned down and hugged Jamie with one arm.

"I didn't think about that. Sorry. He's fine. If anything is ever wrong with your brother, I'll call you instead of taking time to walk across campus to tell you." The smirk on her lips still released her dimples from their hiding place so the gesture didn't carry as much weight. "You remember Nichelle Sampson, right?"

Nichelle stood and gave him a wave with her free hand. She balanced her heavy laptop in the other. "Hi Noah. How have you been?" The exchange shook her a little. Maybe Jamie's husband was sicker than she let on. There wasn't a whole lot she could do about it though if Jamie didn't want to open up to her. Sadness rattled around in her chest, but she took a couple of breaths before it could settle there. That wouldn't help anyone.

"Great. How about you?"

"Really good, thanks. Do you have time to look at my computer? I can't get my presentation to load."

"Sure." He took the computer from her hands and set in on the counter. Nichelle saw him on campus here and there but hadn't interacted with him much. This close up, there was something familiar about him that she couldn't figure out.

After a few clicks, he handed her laptop back. "Here you go."

Once she released the breath she'd been holding, she said, "There I go. That's it? No way."

"There wasn't much to it. I can show you if you want."

She laughed under her breath. That would be a huge waste of time. Either she wouldn't understand, or if she did understand, she wouldn't remember. Appreciating her laptop's abilities wasn't on the top of her list of priorities. "That's okay but thank you so much. My goose would be cooked without that presentation. I really appreciate it."

"No problem at all. I love to help where I can."

Jamie lifted her book bag from the bench and readied herself to leave. "Is Emma coming with to Shabbat?"

His face clouded over, and he took a moment before answering. "No. Astrid called out of the blue and wanted her for the weekend. Knowing her, she'll probably bring Emma back before the night's over, but it won't be in time for dinner."

"That's too bad."

"Hopefully she'll at least make it until I come back from my run in the morning."

Jamie turned to Nichelle. "He's training for his first marathon. Isn't that exciting?"

She nodded at Noah. "That's awesome. I can't even imagine."

Jamie huffed. "Don't act like you weren't a star athlete in college."

"I think *star* is pushing it a bit. I played. That's about the extent of it."

Noah asked, "Oh, what did you play?"

"Basketball. Nothing like running twenty-something miles."

All three headed to the door, and Noah put his hand on the knob. "I don't know. You have to really be in shape to play basketball at that level."

Jamie squeezed his shoulder as they walked through the door. "We'll see you later. Got to get home before sundown."

Nichelle turned back to Noah. "Thanks again."

As they walked back across campus to the parking lot near the political science building, Nichelle ached to ask more questions about Jamie's husband, but figured that wouldn't be welcome. Instead she asked about Noah. "Is

Noah divorced?"

"Yeah. He got married before he graduated, they got pregnant right away, then his wife decided maybe that wasn't what she wanted after all."

"Jeesh. Life comes at you fast, I guess."

"It's for the best. Noah's a great dad, and he and Emma are thriving with just the two of them. She's two and doesn't even think about her mother. Then Astrid pops in and shakes everything up."

They made it to the parking lot, and Nichelle turned to the other woman. "I'm really sorry. It hurts my heart to think of a mother like that." Gratitude filled Nichelle when she thought of her own mother, who would never leave her. But had spent thirty years lying to her. She needed to get to the bottom of it, and as much as she dreaded the confrontation, it was time.

A small, sad smile wrinkled Jamie's face, then she shrugged. "What're you gonna do? Anyway, have a great weekend. I'm glad your presentation was salvageable."

"Thanks again for going with me. You have a great weekend too. See you Monday."

Nichelle sat in her car for a few minutes thinking about Noah and Emma. It really did hurt her heart so much. She couldn't understand how a mother could just abandon her baby. Her own birth mother had, but she still hadn't internalized everything that went along with that notion. She didn't need another mother, or father for that matter, but she wouldn't mind learning why her birth parents didn't want her.

CHAPTER FOUR

Nichelle

NICHELLE STOOD ON the porch of her childhood home and rang the doorbell. She looked around the front yard while waiting, observing the cedar tree where she built a playhouse with the neighbors. There were three brothers, and they'd spent a lot of time roughhousing. She learned hand-to-hand combat at an early age because they never treated her any different. More like a fourth brother. She busted her knee open more times than she could count, then limped up the stones leading from the driveway to the porch she was standing on now. Calling for her mother the entire way.

Her mom pulled the door open and gave her a quizzical look. "You lost your key?" The accusation in her voice was clear.

Nichelle couldn't blame her. She'd lost that key a bunch of times, even as an adult. "No. May I come in?"

That bit of formality caused her mother to put a hand on her skirt-covered hip. Even at home, she didn't dress casually. "What's going on, Nichelle? Why're you acting so funny?" She stood aside and allowed Nichelle to pass.

Nichelle headed to her father's study with her mother hot on her heels. "I need to speak with you and Dad."

Her father's door was open, and the man himself was seated behind his desk with his laptop open, moving the mouse around. She wasn't sure why, but somehow her father got the tech gene. Her heart stuttered. Oh, that's right. They didn't share any genes.

"Hi, honey. Everything okay?" He looked from her to her mother, concern furrowing his eyebrows.

For her mother's part, she was standing in the doorway, wringing her hands.

Nichelle sat on his comfy leather couch, worn from years of wear and tear from the many hours Nichelle spent on it exchanging political ideas with her dad. Then later, the education and teaching of it. "Am I adopted?"

Her mother sat beside her and put a hand on her knee, tears silently trekking down her face.

Her father steepled his hands and rested his chin on top.

"Why didn't you ever tell me?"

Her mother vocalized her tears but tried to tamp down the sound. It was a strangled cry.

All the way over, Nichelle knew she'd have to be gentle with her parents. She was so angry with their betrayal, but they'd just lost a son a few months before. Oh. "Was Clifton adopted too?"

Her mother sniffed but didn't answer.

"No, baby, he wasn't." Her father made to get up, but Nichelle shook her head.

Could she believe that he wasn't adopted? They'd lied to her about everything her entire life. Maybe not everything, but definitely about the important thing. "Hmmmm."

"He wasn't, Nichelle. I could get you his birth certificate." Her mother recovered and went into defensive mode. "But it doesn't matter if he was or wasn't. Just like it doesn't matter about you."

Nichelle stared at her mother, the anger rising within. "Except that it does matter. My whole identity has been blown up. And you can keep that birth certificate. Remember, I have one with your names on it too. Apparently the state of California is just handing them out like candy." Nichelle stood and went over to the window overlooking the backyard. She could almost see the swing set she had growing up. She'd begged to go to the park and get on the merry-go-round, or the high slide, but her parents made her swing at home instead. Her cousins would laugh and play and slide and swing all day long when they came to visit, and Nichelle would too with them, but when she was alone, she felt slighted somehow. The playground at the park just hit different. Now, looking back, she was just plain spoiled. But also a little put out that she was essentially an only child.

"Your birth certificate was amended when you were four, before you started school." Her father sat back in his chair, his voice faint. He was always the softer of her two parents. Always the one she went to when her mom said no. Or when her mom wouldn't drive her somewhere. Or even when she had to drink a glass of milk that she hated, and he drank it for her. He was there to cave in to her every whim.

"I don't understand why you wouldn't tell me. This is awful finding out at thirty-two years old. It's *ridiculous* actually."

Her mother shifted on the couch and sighed. "We discussed it so many times, but by the time you were old enough to understand, it didn't seem necessary. You were our child. Period. You still are. It doesn't matter."

"It matters to me, Mom. Where did I come from? Who is my birth family?"

Her mom shrugged. "It was a closed adoption. We got you from a children's home, essentially an orphanage, when you were three months old."

Tears welled in Nichelle's eyes. She'd been holding it together pretty well, using deep breaths and trying to keep her thoughts light. Remembering the fun parts of her childhood. But the thought of being in an orphanage almost broke her. What if her parents hadn't adopted her? What if she'd grown up in the system? She shuddered at the thought and wiped the tears from her cheeks. What kind of mother did she have to just abandon her and never look back? Or had she? If it was a closed adoption, that means she wouldn't know who adopted Nichelle any more than Nichelle's parents knew who her birth mother was.

"Did everyone else know? Was I the only one in the dark?"

Her mom came behind her and put an arm around her waist. She was so much shorter than Nichelle, even in her heeled strappy sandals, her head only coming to Nichelle's shoulder. "We didn't talk about it. People probably guessed, but it wasn't discussed."

Nichelle hiccupped and drew in a weary breath. "Why? Were you embarrassed?"

"No, of course not. I was more embarrassed people thought I'd given birth at forty. It wasn't like it is now. Women didn't give birth that late in life."

"So you didn't tell anyone. Not even your own sister who lives here?" She turned toward her father. "Or your sisters, Dad? What about Uncle Jameson?" Nichelle's favorite uncle died three years before.

"We didn't tell anyone, Nichelle. I doubt he even suspected. He certainly never mentioned it."

Nichelle went back to the couch and put her head in her hands.

Her mom came back and sat beside her. "How did you find out?"

The snide laugh that escaped Nichelle's mouth may have been accidental, but she felt that down in her bones. "I received a ring from my grandmother. My real grandmother."

Her mother released a choked gasp, but Nichelle couldn't bring herself to feel sorry.

"She left it to me in her will. She didn't tell me her last name so…" She left that hanging in the air. Left it for her parents to wonder.

They didn't wonder long. Her mother said, "You don't have it in your head to look for them, do you?"

Nichelle turned to her, incredulousness crinkling her face, her voice wobbly. "Yes, I'm absolutely looking for them. Why would I not?"

"We're your family, Nichelle. We're your parents. You don't need to look for people who gave you away like yesterday's trash."

Ouch. Nichelle bent over, holding her clenched stomach tight. Her mother should have just punched her in the gut. That wouldn't have hurt as much. There was so much Nichelle wanted to say. To yell and scream. "I'm going to go." She stood and headed toward the door.

Her father stood as well and followed her down the hallway until they got to the front door. Before she could open it, he stilled her hand. "I'm sorry we didn't tell you."

She nodded but didn't speak. She didn't trust her voice. Her father was sorry. She didn't doubt that. He probably wanted to tell her but went along with her mother. Her mother, who said she was embarrassed about being pregnant, but Nichelle was a hundred percent sure she was equally embarrassed about adopting. More so even. That's why she let people think she'd been pregnant. Better that than adoption.

Her dad spoke again. "You are our child. Your mother was right about that. Nothing will ever change that you are ours. Did you not feel loved?"

"Of course I did, Dad." Frustration coursed through her. Nichelle softened her voice. "And I love you both, I do. But I need to know more."

"Why?"

"I just do. I never guessed I was adopted even though there were clues right in front of my face all along. I'm going to find out who my birth family is. You made all your decisions and now I'm making mine. I need to know who I truly am. I think back on my life, of growing up with my extended family, and I really didn't fit in. I see that now. I won't bother you with the details of my search or even give you updates, but I am doing this."

Before she could second guess herself, or her rising tone, Nichelle turned away from her father's stunned face.

She walked through the door without waiting for a response. Nichelle wouldn't open wounds for them over this because they'd just lost a son. But she wouldn't go along with the farce anymore either. As a family, they could pretend nothing changed, but she would be searching, and that would be her priority.

What the hell was taking Clark so long with that ring?

CHAPTER FIVE

Clark

C LARK TRIED WORKING on his report for court. Thank goodness he had time, because he kept reading the same analysis over and over. The words wouldn't take hold in his brain, no matter how long he stared at them. He spent more time researching Nichelle's ring or cycling than actual work. Initially, he forgot about the ring, with so many tasks to accomplish, but a reminder text message and a couple of voice mail messages from the ring's owner put him on the job again. Once he got the stone under the microscope, he'd been preoccupied by it.

The gem was authentic, and he'd reached out to someone who specialized in conch pearls. He needed to call Nichelle today. He could have called her the minute he realized the ring was real days before, but he wanted something tangible when he finally did reach out.

Clark kept his lab immaculate, with specimens locked safely away to avoid compromise, and instruments put away or covered until used. He opened a drawer and pulled out the pearl ring along with Nichelle's business card.

At first, he wasn't sure how to proceed. Especially after making such a huge mistake in his initial dismissal of the stone. He wanted to correct the misstep, but there was only one way to do that. The miscalculation was embarrassing enough, but the remedy more so.

Clark looked at the card and dialed the phone number. It rang and he sat up, straightening his spine, preparing to launch into his spiel. The line stopped ringing and went to voice mail. "You've reached the office of Professor Nichelle Sampson. I'm either in a class or somewhere grading papers so please leave me a message and I'll get back with you soon."

"Um, hello, Ms...I mean Professor Sampson. This is Clark Lin-Lee. I have some important information about the ring you left with me." He hesitated a moment, not quite sure what to do, then left his phone number so she could call him back, even though she'd called and texted him several times. *Just in case.*

He turned the ring over in his hand, frowning. It was unusual and big and out of his realm of expertise, but still a stone. And stones intrigued him more than anything else in the world.

The phone chimed, and Clark snatched it off the counter. "Hello?"

There was no response, so he looked at the device. A text message, not a phone call.

He shook his head and closed his eyes, then opened them and read the text message.

Nichelle: *Hi Clark. I got your message. Can you meet me for lunch so we can talk about the ring?*

The phone nearly broke in his hand from clenching it so hard. She wanted to meet. Why? He could tell her everything he required over the phone. It wasn't necessary to meet in person. But if she wanted to meet, she must have a reason.

He tapped out a reply.

Clark: *Yes. What time? Where?*

Nichelle: *Is noon okay? How about the sandwich place between campus and your store, Ike's?*

Clark: *Yes, I'll meet you there.*

The time on his cell phone read a little after ten so he unlocked the storage and pulled out the samples to confirm against his analysis, and everything he needed for his report. He read over the first page of the analysis three times before finally giving up, throwing the papers aside, then scrubbing his face with the palms of his hands. Then he fingered the pearl again.

He sighed. What he wouldn't do for the feel of his bike pedals under his feet. The wind blowing against his face as he sliced through it, pumping faster and harder. He was a distance rider, and there's no way he could leave now and get a ride in before noon when he needed to meet Nichelle.

Clearing his head before the meeting was important. If it were up to him, he'd abscond with the ring and drive to Dallas to meet with his contact. But he didn't own the heirloom so it wasn't up to him. He only hoped he would make a convincing case for his plan. It didn't really matter, because his way was the only way. No matter that air traffic controllers had been threatening to strike for weeks. Even if that wasn't the case, Clark had no plans of flying anytime soon. Maybe never.

There was a stream nearby, not walking distance really but not too far of a drive. Clark put his reports and analysis away and placed the ring back in its pouch and inside his jacket pocket, then drove to his favorite place. Not this water exactly, but any place with an abundance of rocks.

CHAPTER SIX

Nichelle

NICHELLE WALKED DOWN the hallway to her office and placed her phone on the desk after looking at it one more time. *Hi Clark. I got your message. Can you meet me for lunch so we can talk about the ring?*

She wasn't sure what Clark was about. He seemed cold, but she thought there might be some heat in his eyes when they'd met the week before. Then again, she'd misread heat for friendship or even sympathy many times in her life. She wanted to have lunch with him to see if there was anything actually there, and this was a good excuse to meet him again without Francesca around. One-on-one hit different. Plus, he hadn't been very responsive about the ring and was finally ready to talk.

Jamie had her feet on her desk, a red pen behind her ear, glasses on top of her head, and her eyes closed. This was happening more and more lately, but Nichelle vowed not to interfere unless she was asked. She sorely wanted to though. She also wished for Jamie's opinion on this whole situation.

With the ring, and her parents, but also, Clark.

Instead of waking Jamie, she picked up her desk phone and dialed her bestie's on-campus extension.

Amanda picked up on the first ring. "This is Professor Rivers, fine arts."

Nichelle laughed to herself. Nobody would recognize Amanda's phone voice as the same person who conducted sorority events. Code switching was really a thing. "Hey, it's Nichelle. What are you doing?"

"Girl, what am I not doing? With all this sorority stuff, your mama has me running around like a chicken with their head cut off. And fall proposals for the graduate students are due so everyone wants all my time to talk about it. Whew, I'm a hot mess."

Nichelle giggled to herself because Amanda loved all of this. She lived for it. "Wow. You said that with your whole chest."

She cackled so loudly, Nichelle pulled the phone away from her ear.

"So anyhoo, I was wondering if you have a minute."

"Okey dokey. What's it about?"

"I'll tell you when I get there. I'm on my way." She hung up the phone and raced over to the fine arts building, then took the stairs up to Amanda's office. Her friend didn't have to share and had an open floor plan that also served as a small studio. There were floor-to-ceiling windows through-out with all manner of easels, paints, sculptures, and the like in various phases of completion.

Amanda wore a smock and a bright smile. Her slender fingers grasped a paint brush, rings covering almost every single one. Under the smock, she was decked out in a Kelly-green pantsuit, and her braids were wrapped in a salmon-pink scarf. She loved that color combination enough to call it her signature look.

Nichelle gave her a quick hug. "So, you know Francesca Lin-Lee, right?"

"You know I do."

She plopped in a chair next to Amanda's desk, thoroughly out of breath. "So." She held up a finger, getting her breathing under control. "Man, I'm out of shape. I need to get back on the court with a quickness. Anyway, remember last week when Francesca said she knew a guy? Turns out it was her brother."

"Uh huh?" Amanda didn't even try to hide the suspicion in her voice, nor the wariness on her face.

"Well, he offered to research the ring for me."

"Okay?"

"And he finally has some news so we're going to meet for lunch to discuss it."

Amanda was silent for a moment and the sense of her judgment traveled through the space between them. She nodded. "Okay, I'm gonna go ahead and stop you right there. I can tell from your glow you're attracted to this brother."

She raised a hand when Nichelle tried to interrupt. "But you've just found out your parents aren't really your parents. They weren't even the ones to tell you. Plus, you're the grad advisor and his sister is the undergrad Basileus. That seems like a conflict of interest."

Amanda always had a level head. Ever since undergrad. They'd been friends since meeting on the first day in orientation. Amanda was never shy, but she was far away from her family in Louisiana, so she'd seemed relieved when Nichelle introduced herself. Nichelle was a legacy to the sorority because of her mother, but she convinced her friend to join with her. Now Amanda was the vice president and programs director of the grad chapter under her mother.

Nichelle bent over and put her head in her hands. "Why won't you let me be great?"

"Girl, go somewhere and sit down with that. You know I'm right."

"Yeah, I do." She was right. Nichelle had more things on her plate than she could possibly deal with. No sense doing the thing she always did and focus on a guy when she had so much other stuff going on. "Okay, I'm going back to my office now. I plan to keep it strictly professional. Thanks for your superior insight as usual." She rose to slink back to the political science building.

"Hey, Nichelle."

"Yeah?"

"It'll all work out. Make peace with your parents, then

you'll find a guy."

"Yeah." She shrugged. There was really nothing else to say. Nichelle would never find a guy, and she'd be better off making peace with it.

She walked back to her building. When she made it to her office, she bumped the door a little too hard, and Jamie popped up, dropping her pen on the floor. "So sorry. I didn't mean to wake you."

Jamie rubbed her eyes and bent over to pick up her pen. "I'm happy you did. I didn't mean to fall asleep. I've got grades to get in."

Nichelle reached across her desk and grabbed Jamie's hand. "If you need help, I'm willing. Just let me know."

The small smile that creased Jamie's face wasn't enough to showcase her dimples, but she nodded. "I'm good. Thanks though."

"Sure." Nichelle checked the time on her cell. She still had an hour before she needed to meet Clark, but she felt trapped in their small office. She packed up her laptop and phone and waved a goodbye to Jamie. She wouldn't push her friend to let her help. All she could do was offer and hope she'd take her up on it one day. As Amanda said, Nichelle had enough on her plate as it was.

WHEN NICHELLE PULLED her car into Ike's parking lot, she

spotted Clark right away. Well, not him, but his car. There was a gray Volvo hybrid SUV and it fit him to a T. Yes, it could be someone else's, but it was his. She just knew it.

She hopped out of her car and skipped over to the Volvo. Sure enough, he was sitting behind the wheel, the sound of a news podcast seeping through his closed windows. He clearly was wrapped up in it because he didn't even notice her standing outside the driver's side door. She stood there for a moment and checked him out. He was dressed in nearly the same clothes she saw him in before. Instead of a crisp white button-down shirt, it was a crisp ivory button-down. His jacket was darker gray than the time before and his pants black. This must be some sort of uniform for him. Clark was frowning at his front window, his big eyes staring off into the middle distance. Maybe he didn't like what he'd heard on the podcast. Nichelle could relate—the news these days wasn't the greatest.

Finally, she tapped on his window.

Clark didn't jump or startle in the least. His gaze slid to hers, and there was a momentary brightness. Did that mean… It didn't matter. Amanda was right. She had other problems to concentrate on, most of all figuring out her birth family. That's why she was standing in the parking lot. He may have answers to help her on her way. That's the only reason they were there.

Clark held a finger up and turned off his podcast, picking up the cell phone from the passenger seat, and pocketing a key fob from the cup holder between the seats.

Nichelle stood back a step as he opened his car door to get out.

They stood inches from each other, and his scent brushed her nose—the same warm jasmine and vanilla she smelled in the jewelry store.

He stared at her expectantly.

Oh, she should probably say something considering she knocked on his window. "Hi. Thanks for meeting me. I wasn't expecting you to be here so early."

The heat in his irises turned liquid, and his eyes widened. "Oh, I…uh, was, um…at a stopping point at the lab." His spine straightened a bit as he rose to his full height. "Right, I thought I'd come on over early and wait. Listen to a bit of news."

If she hadn't been paying such close attention, she would have swallowed that hook, line, and sinker. But she paid extra attention, and he definitely stumbled over all those incoherent words. She wasn't sure what that meant exactly or what he wasn't saying.

"Okay well, since we're both here, you want to go in?"

He nodded and swept his arm toward the front door of the restaurant. "After you."

They entered the restaurant and were greeted by the hostess who guided them to a table near the back. Since they were so early, the place was half full and they had their pick of where to sit.

Neither said a word as they perused the menu. Nichelle had eaten at Ike's a thousand times, so she already had an idea of what she wanted. She'd have the halal chicken with grilled mushrooms, avocado, and pesto. When the waitress came over to take their order, Nichelle also asked for a lemonade. It was made fresh with a hint of lavender.

Clark ordered a tuna with avocado and a water.

"The chicken's really good here."

"I'm pescatarian."

"Oh neat. I tried that for a while, but with my packed schedule, sometimes it was hard to keep up."

"I understand. You really have to plan ahead because not everywhere has good options."

She shrugged, grinning. "I'm not much of a planner."

Clark furrowed his brows.

She imagined that he was completely the opposite. Everything about him from his clothes to his car to the mention of his schedule to Francesca when they met screamed planning and organization. He probably had a wall calendar in his bedroom and his socks were sorted by color. Nichelle shuddered just thinking about it.

"Is something wrong?"

Oops. "Not at all. You said you have some information on the ring." *Great save, you.*

Clark's demeanor grew tight again, his eyes hardening. He bit the side of his bottom lip, and it was the cutest thing ever. "Um, yes, actually." He cleared his throat and rolled his shoulders, clearly in an effort to relax.

What could he have to say that was so difficult for him? It was just a ring.

After taking a deep breath, he continued. "The ring is definitely real. I uploaded a picture of it to an online group I'm a part of, mostly geochemists, gemstone experts, and the like. I discovered a collector who believes it may be a rare conch pearl that was reported stolen in Jamaica back in the middle eighteen hundreds."

Nichelle leaned forward. "That matches the timeline, but my grandmother's note said it was a family heirloom passed down from our ancestor, who lived in Jamaica."

"Okay, that's good. That's a bit of a confirmation that we're on the right track."

"Great. What's the next step then?"

Clark grew visibly uncomfortable, rubbing his brow and frowning.

Before he could speak the waitress returned with their food and drinks.

Without so much as a *God bless*, Clark dug into his sandwich, totally ignoring her question.

Nichelle pursued her lips, watching him eat. Waiting for him to take a break and give her an answer.

He kept his eyes cast downward, taking bite after bite, slowly chewing.

Fine, she'd eat, but he wouldn't escape for long. Patience was not on the top of the list of her attributes. She dug into her chicken sandwich and paused a moment to savor the flavors. The pesto and avocado mixed perfectly with the chicken. She took a couple more bites, then a sip of her lemonade. Again, she closed her eyes and relished the taste, the tang and sweetness a perfect combination.

When Clark didn't have anything left on his plate to occupy him, he surveyed the restaurant, a slight sheen of sweat popping out on his brow.

Nichelle asked, "What's going on? Why don't you want to answer my question? You look like you're having a panic attack."

"No, I'm not."

She waited.

"It's nothing really. We'll need to travel to Dallas to show the collector the ring."

Nichelle paused mid-bite. "Why? Can't we just send it to him?"

"I wouldn't recommend that. This is not the type of piece you send through the mail to someone."

The image of the special delivery of the ring popped into her head. She supposed he was right. Her grandmother took the precaution after all. "How much do you think it's worth?"

"I couldn't say. It would be a guess on my part, but at least a few thousand dollars."

That was significant for sure, and not unexpected. But going all the way to Texas seemed extreme. "Okay, but I can't ask you to drop everything you're doing and travel all the way to Dallas. That's like a four-hour flight one way."

Clark cleared his throat and shifted in his seat. "Actually, we'll need to drive."

"Drive?" Nichelle's eyes practically bugged out of her head. That was a two-day trip by car. She knew that well because her mother was from Austin, and they'd made the car trip many summers. "Why in the world would *we* need to drive?"

"I can't fly."

He didn't offer anything else. There was obviously a story there, but Nichelle wasn't in the habit of pushing someone to confess something they didn't want to share. "Okay. Well, even more reason I couldn't ask you to give up a week of your life to do me a favor." Oh, maybe it wasn't a favor. Did he want her to pay him? How much did something like that cost anyway?

"This isn't a favor."

Ah, she shouldn't have said that. "How much would I need to pay you?"

Clark's fair skin immediately flushed red, his eyes wild. "No, no, you misunderstand. I'm going because I need to. I'm not asking you for money."

Nichelle's face heated. She was beginning to feel some type a way about this conversation. It was like pulling teeth. "You need to?"

"Um, well yes. He's my contact so I would need to go.

We've been trying to meet for a while now. I don't mind, and I have some time. I have to testify in a case in two weeks, but otherwise my schedule is open. The auction isn't until next Monday, so that'll give us plenty of time to drive down there, meet him, then drive back."

No, this wasn't a favor. He was being a bit of a jerk actually. She could just fly down there next Monday morning since she wouldn't need to be back for the summer session until the following Monday, meet this collector, and return Monday night. Instead, he was turning this into a road trip. "I don't think that would be a good idea. We'll need to figure something else out." She'd go herself. How big could the auction house be anyway? She'd ask around and find Clark's contact herself.

"There's really nothing else I can do. I've done quite a bit of research so far and this is the only path forward."

Nichelle tapped her lip with one finger in thought. The most important item on her list was figuring out her birth family. She was happy she'd had the talk with Amanda and put her head back on straight. If Clark wanted to tag along, she was open to it in a professional way, but a road trip was a bridge too far. She'd figure it out. "I really appreciate everything you've done so far, but I'll take it from here. Do you have the ring?"

Clark's eyes widened, and he pressed a hand against the pocket of his jacket. "Er, I didn't bring it with me."

"Okey dokey. Well, I can follow you to the jewelry store.

I have some time before I need to get back to grading finals."

He fidgeted with his napkin, glancing around the restaurant but not focusing on anything. He finally looked at Nichelle and nodded. "I actually have somewhere to be, so I'll bring it to you tomorrow if that's okay."

Nichelle shrugged. She wasn't sure what Clark had going on and why he was extending his possession of the ring, but one more day wouldn't hurt. In the meantime, she'd book a flight for Dallas. "Sure."

CHAPTER SEVEN

Clark

C LARK ONLY HAD today to convince Nichelle to go on the road trip with him. He cycled to campus and locked up his bike at the closest rack next to the political science building. Hopefully she could be reasoned with. Since lunch the day before, he'd done some research on the ring's origins, trying to track down a family name Nichelle could use for her birth family search. So far, he hadn't come up with much other than general explanations of pink conch pearls in the Caribbean. He had such limited knowledge of rare gemstones, which is why they really needed to travel to Dallas for additional information. River rocks and sediment were more in his wheelhouse.

After crossing the lawn that separated the bike racks from the building's steps, Clark stopped in his tracks and frowned, then looked at his watch.

Nichelle descended the few stairs, not sparing Clark a glance, and walked toward the center of campus.

For a moment, Clark stood there dumbfounded, then

checked his watch one more time. He was five minutes early so certainly not enough time for Nichelle to venture off across campus and return in time. He sucked in a breath, rooted in uncertainty. Finally he took off at a trot to catch up to her. "Hi, um, Professor Sampson."

Nichelle rotated his way with wide eyes. "Oh my gosh. I totally forgot you were coming now." She grimaced then turned again. "Walk with me. I need to catch up with my undergrad sorors before they leave step practice." She took off without a backward glance.

Clark did the only thing he could and followed behind her.

"I'm so sorry. I forgot to put our appointment in my phone. I'm lost without a calendar entry." She shot Clark a smile. "And please call me Nichelle."

She was clearly frazzled, balancing a laptop case and an extra-large latte, but managing in comfortable jeans and flat shoes.

Clark frowned but easily kept up with her long strides. "Okay, I understand, but…we just made the appointment an hour ago." This probably wasn't the best tack to take considering he was here to convince her to take a trip with him. Unfortunately, charm wasn't high on his list of personality characteristics.

"What can I say, Clark? I'm not the most organized. Between a full load and teaching both summer sessions, keeping up with publishing academic papers, and being an advisor to my sorority sisters, it's a lot. Plus, add on family stuff and this whole ring business, I'm lucky I remember to wear matching socks." She glanced down at her feet then up to the sky. "Ugh, not matching."

"Oh well, I can try to be brief." It was difficult even conversing with her considering their quick clip. He wasn't sure how he would lay out his case under these circumstances; although with the strike, there was really no alternative now. Driving was the only option. "Or maybe I could return later when you're less busy."

Nichelle took a long swig of her coffee but kept up her pace. The campus was mostly deserted. There were no students milling about, and the windows to the buildings they passed were empty of life. "Now's fine. As soon as I run this errand, I'm all yours. The semester is done and the first summer term doesn't start for another couple weeks."

Clark blushed at the implication of her words then quickly recovered. "That's acceptable."

She glanced his way and grinned, then shook her head.

A chant sounded in the air of the otherwise mostly quiet campus. The rumble of a lawn mower near the next building greeted them along with the sweet smell of freshly cut grass. Clark sneezed and removed his sunglasses to dry his eyes.

When they turned into the quad, Clark saw where the chant was coming from. A group of women stood in three equal lines, clapping and stomping. *What in the world were they doing?* He spotted his sister, hands on her hips, standing off to the side with a couple other women.

Nichelle marched over to Franny and Clark hung back.

Clark noticed the moment Franny saw him because she cocked her head to the side and frowned, drawing her eyebrows together as if trying to figure out why he looked familiar. Then her eyebrows flew up her forehead. With wide eyes, she rotated to Nichelle who was in mid talk. Clark would imagine he appeared very much out of place to his sister, especially since he should be at the shop. He certainly never showed up to campus to surprise her.

Franny nodded and spoke to Nichelle, but although Clark wasn't terribly far away, the chanting and lawn mower drowned out any chance of discerning what the women were speaking about. When she was done, his sister shrugged and nodded again.

Nichelle headed his way, but his sight was still on Franny. He wanted to ensure she was okay.

Judging from her bright smile, all appeared well. She waved at Clark then turned her attention to the group. She called for them to stop and gave instructions in a loud, clear voice.

"Ready to head back?"

Clark dragged his gaze over to Nichelle, standing in front of him, waiting expectantly with raised brows. "Uh, yes. Is everything okay?"

Again, she didn't wait for Clark but took off in the direction of her office. This time at a much slower pace.

Again, Clark followed.

"Yes, everything's fine. Some last-minute adjustments before they head out on break. I just received the list of judges for the step show." She threw her empty cup into a recycling can. "I know a couple of them and how they judge. Franny's going to make some changes."

"Oh, I see." Clark did not see. He barely understood anything she was saying.

"You don't sound like you see. Have you never gone to a step show?"

Now she was speaking gibberish as far as Clark was concerned. Whatever her meaning, he was sure of the answer. "No."

"Not even to see Franny perform?"

"No, she's never mentioned it."

Nichelle was quiet a moment and they walked in silence a few steps.

His sister was well aware where Clark felt comfortable. Some sort of performance show would not be it. If it was important for him to be there, certainly he would go. Obviously it wasn't that important. They did other activities together, like cycling and tennis. Or they made dinner together and simply caught up with each other outside the store.

Nichelle glanced back over her shoulder at him. "So what's up? Did you bring the ring?"

Clark reached into his inner jacket pocket and pulled out

the ring. He'd replaced the plastic baggy with a more secure jewelry case. "I have it here. I wanted to speak with you more about what I proposed."

She turned forward again. She didn't reach for the case and Clark didn't offer it. "You mean the road trip all the way to Dallas?"

Texas wasn't that far away. He'd made the trip several times while attending undergraduate school in Austin. He reminded himself why he was here. And it wasn't to argue the distance to Dallas. "To meet my contact in Dallas, yes."

"I really feel like I can just fly out and back in a couple days. Driving would take us at least twice that long. I only have a couple weeks off then I'm right back in it."

"Did you have something else planned?"

She stopped and circled around to face him. He expected fury at his question that was clearly none of his business. He recognized that a little too late. Her expression was relaxed though, even slightly amused with a corner of her mouth somewhat upturned. "Just some relaxation. At least that was my plan before I found out about the adoption. Now I want to find my birth family."

"What better way than letting me accompany you to Dallas? I can continue research on the stone while we travel?"

She bit the side of her lip and glanced away. "I don't know, Clark. I barely know you and that seems like such a long trip with someone I don't know."

"Franny can vouch—"

Nichelle hurriedly placed a hand on Clark's forearm. "Oh my gosh, no. That's not what I meant at all." She grimaced and pulled her hand back. "I just meant… What would we talk about?"

Clark blinked. He didn't have an answer to that question. "Well, um." No, not even a small thought.

"Yeah, see what I mean? I should just fly out, meet your guy, then we can discuss his findings when I return."

This was his last card. "What about the air traffic controller strike?"

She waved a hand dismissively, then stepped toward her building. "I doubt that'll happen. They've been threatening for weeks."

Clark followed but removed his phone from his pants pocket, then pulled up the latest news. "You haven't heard." It wasn't a question. It was clear she hadn't. "Here, take a look."

Nichelle took the proffered phone and gasped. "No way." She stopped walking again and scrolled down the screen. "Wow." She swept her gaze over him. "Fine then."

He nodded. "We'll take my car."

She huffed. "No, we'll take mine."

CHAPTER EIGHT

Clark

THEY AGREED TO meet at the jewelry store. There was a small covered parking lot behind the store where Clark would leave his car. He still thought it would be better to drive his safer car, but Nichelle insisted. And since he'd had to convince her to drive to begin with, he gave in without argument.

Clark dropped the keys in his desk drawer in case Franny needed to move his car for some reason while he was away. If all went well, they'd make it to Dallas by Monday, then return home by Wednesday. He needed to testify early Friday morning so that should give them plenty of time.

It was still early on a Saturday morning, and Cathie wouldn't be in until much later to open the store, so he went back out the way he came, through the back door, reset the alarm, and circled the building to wait for Nichelle on the sidewalk. He had his suitcase packed and ready to go along with a backpack with his laptop. He brought a light jacket, but the weather was mild today and would only get hotter the farther south they drove.

According to his cell phone, Nichelle was already five minutes late, but when he looked up, she was pulling into the space in front of him. She leaned forward and gave him a little wave and a smile, then popped the trunk.

He rapped on the window, and she lowered it. "If it's all the same, I'd prefer to place my luggage in the back seat."

Her smile faltered, but she shrugged. "Um, maybe you haven't noticed, but I don't have a back seat."

"Yes, I've noticed. Whatever you call the compartment behind your seat. May I put it there?" It wasn't big enough for an adult to sit in, but probably had enough room for a small child—definitely for his bag. It was clear of any debris, and Clark's heart skipped a beat, thankful for the clean car. He wouldn't be able to function knowing his baggage had been compromised. When he rounded the car to close the trunk, the condition was nearly the opposite. Thankfully, he had the foresight to ask.

He slammed the trunk closed then slid into the passenger seat. "Are you okay to drive first shift?"

"First of all, good morning. How are you?"

Clark's face heated. "Good morning. I'm okay. I didn't sleep well. I never do the night before I travel."

"I understand. I'm fine to drive. I took a Benadryl for my allergies last night and slept like the dead."

She waited for Clark to fasten his seat belt then pulled out onto the street.

He was glad someone had a good night's rest and told her as much. They took the five-eighty out of the Bay Area and an hour later settled on the five. Clark's eyes were droopy despite the music blaring through the speakers. He could barely maintain open eyes.

"You can take a nap, you know. I can drive about eight hours, but you'll need to take over and from the way you look, I don't think you'll make it without a nap."

He nodded, and she lowered the volume on the music. "No, keep it up if that's helping you stay awake."

"Not at all. I have plenty to think about so I'm sure that'll occupy my time anyway."

"Okay." He was asleep almost before he finished the word.

When Clark awoke, he slowly opened his lids and glanced out the window. The highway was mostly empty, and there were fields as far as the eye could see on both sides. They were turning onto another highway; the deceleration must have been what woke him up. He rubbed the sleep out of his eyes. The sign read CA-58E. He slipped his phone from the pocket of his trousers and checked the time, and was surprised to see it was already nine a.m.

"Hi, sleepyhead."

Clark blinked and his cheeks heated with embarrassment. "I'm sorry. I didn't realize I was so tired." Even though he had realized it. He couldn't admit it though. "Do you want me to drive?"

"Not at all. I've only been behind the wheel three hours." The signal changed to green, and Nichelle pulled forward to make the right turn. "I have plenty of miles left in me."

He nodded although she wasn't looking his way. He cleared his throat before speaking. "Let me know when and we can switch."

"Sounds good. I think I'll be able to go another three or four hours. That should take us a good way into Arizona, then you can take over. You can go back to sleep if you want."

At this point, he couldn't possibly fall asleep again. Clark was surprised he had in the first place. He thought he'd be able to ride the adrenaline of anticipating the long road trip and finally meeting up with Charles in Dallas, but his body had other ideas. Which was a good turn of events because he'd rather have some rest under his belt before getting behind the wheel and risking both their lives. "I've had enough."

"Are you hungry?"

After monitoring his stomach, he decided he wasn't hungry. He'd consumed a full breakfast of two hard-boiled eggs, whole wheat toast with avocado, and honeydew melon mixed with blueberries and mint. "I'm not, but please stop if you are."

"I'm not. I ate some cereal before we left and limited myself to one cup of coffee since we were hitting the road. Although I'd give my right arm for another cup right about now."

"I can check on where the next coffee shop is located." He lifted his phone again and opened a navigational app. Once it pinpointed their location, he read through the list of nearby restaurants. "Are you particular about your coffee?"

"Absolutely, but I can be flexible considering where we are."

Outside the window was a tree-lined highway, but not a whole lot of anything else. It was clear they were almost outside of town and probably wouldn't have another opportunity for miles if he didn't hurry. Another look at his phone conjured up a local coffee shop. "Get off at the upcoming exit, and it'll be on the right about a quarter mile down, Kelley G's Coffee Shop. There's a drive-thru."

"Good work, Clark. Looks like you'll be of some use on this trip after all."

His eyes widened into circles as he whipped his head toward Nichelle.

She was grinning, then she laughed. "I'm just joking."

He relaxed into the seat and looked out the window as they exited, spotting the diner just up ahead.

The line was long. Considering it was nine in the morning, that made sense. "I hope it goes fast. Do you want anything?"

Coffee wasn't normally something he consumed, and from the looks of the place, they probably didn't serve gunpowder tea. "I'm fine. I have some water in my bag."

"Okay. Let me know if you change your mind." She glanced at him then the line of cars in front of them. "Looks like you'll have time."

"I brought enough for you."

She studied him and narrowed her eyebrows. This close, the burgundy in her eyes really shone through the brown.

"Water, I meant."

"Oh right. That was very thoughtful. Thanks."

His gaze darted around the inside of the car, finally landing on his lap. Nobody had ever called him thoughtful before. He brought enough water for them both with his mind on efficiency. Even though she said she had it covered, he'd mapped the trip out. If they minimized their stops, they could be in Phoenix by nightfall, and get a hotel there. He even made reservations for two rooms. Unfortunately, three hours in, they were already stopping. He ran a finger along the crease of his pants. And with this terribly long line, they probably wouldn't make it to the window for another five minutes. Maybe even ten. He wasn't sure how this detour would affect his careful planning.

The car inched forward ever so slowly, and Nichelle rolled down her window. "It feels great outside. Do you mind if I roll yours down too? We could even put the top down."

Clark's body tensed at the idea of flying down the California highway, through the desert, with no top on the car. "I'd rather not. If you don't mind."

She shrugged and faced forward again, her hand twirling around outside the car.

He took a couple of breaths to calm himself, then thought of conversation starters. He'd written several out on his phone but couldn't remember a single one. It would be too obvious if he were to open his notes app now.

"So, Clark. Where'd you go to school?"

He sighed in relief.

Nichelle narrowed her eyes. "Is that too personal?"

What did he do wrong now? She was obviously miffed about something, but he hadn't even spoken yet. "Not at all. I actually went to undergrad in Texas. UT. They have an excellent geochemist program."

"I thought maybe I'd offended you or was bothering you or something. That sigh was pretty deep."

"I'm not offended at all."

"Well, that's pretty neat. UT in Austin, right? That's my mom's hometown. It's really nice down there."

"It is. It reminds me of Northern California at times."

"I can see that."

Silence filled the car for a while. The sounds of freeway traffic floated in through Nichelle's open window. The closer they got to the drive-thru window, the stronger the smell of heavenly baked goods was. Clark didn't usually indulge but he could appreciate the smell.

"Did you drive home every time on holiday breaks and summers?"

"I drove my car there when I started, then home once I graduated. Otherwise I flew."

"But you don't fly now?"

"No." Clark figured she was curious as to why, but he didn't want to discuss it. He didn't like to be emotional around others, especially strangers. "Where did you go to school?"

"I teach at my alma mater. I did my master's in LA though, and then went back home for my PhD."

"I completed my master's degree in Los Angeles as well."

"What a coincidence. Did you like it down there?"

"Not really."

She snorted, then covered her mouth. "Oops. I didn't either. I've never met anyone from the Bay who has an appreciation for Southern California. The weather was great, and the beaches fun, but too overcrowded."

He nodded in agreement. "I go to Half Moon Bay sometimes and I rarely see another person."

She shivered and rubbed her arms. "Yeah, I bet. It's freezing out there. I don't care when you go. Surfers have a ball though. Are you a surfer?"

"No." Clark cringed. He wouldn't be caught dead surfing. "I cycle there."

"What? Like on a bike? That's gotta be fifty miles."

"About that, yes."

"Good Lord." She pulled the car up to the window, leaning halfway out to see the menu printed next to the cash register. Nichelle ordered an extra-large hazelnut latte.

Clark stifled the groan building in his throat. She'd probably need to stop at the bathroom several times more than he allotted. Who knew what time they'd make it to Phoenix at this rate. "Are you sure you want an extra-large?"

The withering glance Nichelle gave him certainly broadcasted her response, but obviously she felt the need to back it up verbally as well. "Clark." She pursed her lips before continuing. "We'll get along really well if you remember I'm a grown-ass woman, m'kay?"

His answering sigh was deep and long. "Yes, of course."

When the clerk passed Nichelle her cup of coffee, she settled it into a cup holder between their seats, and looked at Clark with a broad smile, no trace of the lingering irritation she'd just exhibited. "Ready?"

Was she looking for a response? Why wouldn't he be ready? "Yes."

She pulled the car into traffic then entered the freeway again. "I haven't forgotten what you said. Why in the world do you ride your bike fifty miles?"

"It's a hobby."

"Riding your bike a godforsaken amount of miles is a hobby? I can't imagine."

He tried not to sound indignant. "Long-distance cycling isn't for everyone."

"How long does it take to ride all the way out to Half Moon Bay?"

"About three and half hours."

Nichelle picked up her cup and held the opening to her mouth but didn't sip. "Still too hot." She put it back in the holder. "I can't imagine."

"You said that already."

"Yeah, because I can't. I'm not sure I could ride a mile, much less fifty."

Clark regarded her. She was wearing a sundress that hit just below her knees, sitting in the car like she was. Her legs were long, but strong and toned. "Do you have a hobby?"

"I suppose. I love genealogy, coincidentally enough."

"Coincidentally?"

"Oh, did Franny not tell you?"

He shook his head because he wasn't quite sure what she meant.

"The ring came from my grandmother."

"Right. You mentioned she was a grandmother you didn't realize you had."

"Ummm hmmm." She picked up the cup again and held it near her mouth. She clearly deemed it ready because she took a tentative sip, then held the cup in her lap.

Clark wanted to say something to her about his safety concerns with only one hand on the steering wheel, but she'd just given him such a stern warning.

"I found out I was adopted when I got this ring. My parents, who have been my parents for over thirty years, lied to me the entire time. I wouldn't have known if it weren't for that ring and the letter that came with it."

Clark wasn't sure what to say. His parents were mostly absent or ignored him when they were around, so he wasn't the expert on proper parental behavior. He'd be relieved to discover he wasn't actually related to them by blood. That probably wasn't the case for everyone.

"So anyway. That's why I'm trying to track down the origins of the ring. I'd like to discover who my birth family is. I'm hoping to trace them down through the line if we find out who originally owned the ring. Whoever my great-great-great however many times grandmother was."

"Have you thought about taking a DNA test? I hear those are easily accessible now."

"I've already spit in the tube. The results take a while to come back though, and I don't have that kind of patience. Plus, someone I'm related to would have to take it too or I still won't know anything."

As far as Clark was concerned, it seemed like the prudent path of DNA testing would be the more acceptable route. Also, checking with the agency the adoption went through. "Have you contacted the agency that handled your adoption?"

"I've written to the children's home and put the form on file so if my parent has a form on file, we can connect. I haven't heard anything yet. I've also asked for any non-identifying information. I love California, but they don't make it easy to find a parent who doesn't want to be found."

"Hopefully you'll hear back soon. Meanwhile, maybe we'll discover something in Dallas."

"I sure hope so."

His parents weren't the greatest, but there was no doubt they were his parents. How could you not know something like that? Curiosity tugged at him as he stared at her profile. "You really never had a clue you were adopted?"

"Nope, none. My parents were great to me. I had a brother, and they never treated me any differently. They loved…love me. I don't doubt that, but I'm not super happy with them right now."

"What happened to your brother? You said had?"

"He died from cancer six months ago."

He nodded because there was nothing to say to that. Nothing that he could think of at least.

Nichelle sipped her coffee and looked straight ahead.

Clark opened the notes app on his phone for something else to discuss.

CHAPTER NINE

Nichelle

N ICHELLE COULD ADMIT when she was wrong. Sometimes. She probably shouldn't have ordered such a large coffee because she needed to stop. Again. "Um, Clark?"

"Yes?"

She peered at him, zeroing in on his throat. He'd swallowed at least four times since responding. "I need to stop."

"There are no additional scheduled stops." As far as she could tell, he kept his gaze on the road. When he took over behind the wheel, he pulled out a pair of Ray-Ban Wayfarer sunglasses. They've been around forever, and Nichelle had seen them on plenty of men, but they just hit different on Clark. Sexy as hell.

He kept both hands on the steering wheel, but the tightening of his fingers told on him. He was tense.

After crossing and uncrossing her legs, she threw her hands in the air. "Look, I don't know who this mystery scheduler is, but if they don't want to get peed on, they might want to pencil in a stop. Know what I mean?"

Red rushed into Clark's cheeks, and he took off his sunglasses, sparing Nichelle a quick glare. He closed his eyes briefly, then glanced at the gas gauge. "The fuel level is at the halfway mark. I'll find a service station where you can, uh, use their facilities. Will that work?"

"Why yes, Clark. That will work just fine. Thank you."

After using *their facilities*, and filling up the gas tank, they got back on the road, and Nichelle promptly fell asleep.

Nichelle opened her tired eyes as Clark pulled the car into a parking lot. Seemed like she'd just fallen asleep. It was nearly dark so that couldn't be the case. "What time is it?"

"Just after eight."

"Where are we?" She looked up at the tall building in front of her.

"We're in Phoenix, Arizona."

Did he really think she didn't know where Phoenix was?

Clark pulled off his seatbelt and opened the driver's side door.

"I hope they have rooms available."

He didn't respond but pulled the seat forward and took his luggage out.

She'd gotten used to his minimal responses when they came at all. Seems like they should make sure there was room at the inn before unpacking, but whatever. She hoped for the best because besides being tired still, she needed to go to the bathroom. Getting Clark to stop was a major feat.

Before closing his door, Clark reached down to the floor

and pulled the lever triggering the trunk.

"Thanks." She picked up her purse and jumped out of the car, slamming the door closed.

Clark winced. "Are you upset with me?"

"What? Why?"

"I'm not certain, but you shut the door as if you were angry."

He seemed to internalize the slightest innocent actions as something she didn't mean. "Who hurt you?" She did her best to keep her eyes from rolling, but the strain was giving her a headache. "I was only making sure the door was closed all the way."

"Okay."

"No problem." She took her suitcase out of the trunk along with her messenger bag while Clark waited next to her. "Okay, ready."

He nodded and walked to the hotel front doors.

Nichelle followed. They stopped at the registration desk, and Nichelle held her breath when the clerk asked if he could help them.

Clark responded before she could release the breath. "Yes. Reservations for Lin-Lee and Sampson please."

What the hell? "How did you—"

The clerk said, "Yes, I see those reservations here in our system. I just need your IDs. Would you like to use the credit card you made the reservation with?"

Clark nodded.

Nichelle spoke up then. "I have a different credit card we'd like to use please." She dug in her purse and pulled out her driver's license and credit card, then slid both across the counter to the clerk. She narrowed her eyes and gave Clark a stern look. The nerve of this guy just making plans without her. How'd he even know they'd stop here? Before she could get too upset, the clerk handed her ID back to her along with a room key.

She stepped away from the counter to calm herself and took a look around while Clark checked in. This actually was a nice property. There was a relaxing waterfall in the lobby and gold accents enhancing the well-made furniture scattered throughout. On the opposite side of the room was the entrance to a full restaurant. She wasn't mad anymore. This was pretty perfect.

They rolled their luggage to the elevators, and Clark pressed the up button.

Nichelle's stomach snatched that opportunity to growl as loudly as possible. "Excuse me." She'd much rather take a shower and dive into bed, but she was hungry. She'd had to grab a gas-station burrito and chips to tide her over earlier. If Clark ate anything, she hadn't seen it. Maybe he had a protein bar or something hidden in that backpack of his and downed it while she slept. Along with his many bottles of water.

The elevator finally arrived, and they rode up to the seventh floor. Apparently, their rooms were adjacent. Nichelle stopped in front of her door and flashed the card key in front of the lock, releasing the latch. "Okay, see you in the morning." She'd sneak down to the restaurant by herself and get something to eat. The thought of exerting herself for another excruciating conversation with Clark was too tiring to imagine, no matter how pretty he was to look at.

He nodded and disappeared through the door to his room.

Nichelle barely made it into the bathroom before relieving her aching bladder. This trip had not been the fun time she hoped for. When Clark decided to engage in conversation, he was pleasant enough, even interesting depending on the subject, but it was all surface. She wasn't one to push, but she wanted to know more about him. Something a little deeper.

She decided to wash up and refresh herself. She'd only packed the right amount of clothes for the trip so she couldn't change or she'd run short. She had a workout outfit just in case, but it probably wasn't appropriate for the fancy restaurant downstairs. She hunted around for her pajamas which were nowhere to be found. How could she have forgotten to pack something to sleep in? She let out an exasperated sigh and unpacked what she was wearing the next day. They would need to get up super early to hit the road, because tomorrow would be even longer than today. They weren't even halfway to Dallas yet, but close.

Instead of putting back on the clothes she'd traveled in

all day, Nichelle decided to throw in the towel and order room service. It was probably for the best anyway. Just in case Clark was downstairs.

WHEN THEY CROSSED into Texas, Nichelle breathed a sigh of relief. They still had nine hours to go, but at least they'd covered some serious ground. Why in the hell did Texas have to be so big? Clark had just taken over, so Nichelle tried to get comfortable the best she could in her little two-seater. They'd left earlier today but since they'd gone to bed, separately of course, early the night before, it wasn't a problem for Nichelle to drive the first few hours, even without coffee. When they got to El Paso, she stopped to get gas and was able to get some then along with a breakfast sandwich. Again, Clark didn't buy anything. In a couple of hours, it would be lunch time, but there really wasn't a whole lot between where they were and Odessa. Not that Clark would allow them to stop anyway.

She glided her eyes to Clark's profile. He was ten and two-ing it. No surprise there. But he looked fresh, having slept most of the morning. They hadn't said more than a handful of words to each other so far, but he didn't seem upset. He just seemed...Clark.

A notification lit up his phone plugged into the charger between them.

"You're on Facebook?"

The tips of Clark's ear turned red. "What?"

"You didn't hear me?"

"Yes, I don't understand why you're asking."

"Sometimes people ask just to ask, Clark. There's no hidden meaning." She held up his phone, pointing at the now black screen. "You had a notification light up."

"Oh."

"I didn't peg you for a social media guy." She was awash in social media. Between keeping up with her vast family and the sorority, it was almost a full-time job. When she wanted to talk though, she texted.

"I'm not. There are groups I belong to on there. I never post. I don't even have a profile picture."

"What sort of groups?" Maybe that was too personal. "You don't have to answer if you don't want me to know."

The red from his ears climbed down to his cheeks. Was he in one of those fetish groups? Nichelle hadn't meant to make it sound dirty.

"Groups about rocks. That's all. That's how I connected with the man we're going to see." Clark reached his hand out.

When Nichelle passed his phone to him, her fingers lingered on his waiting palm.

That growing patch of red expanded to his neck.

Nichelle smiled to herself. "Okay, that makes sense. Does the store have social media?"

Clark cleared his throat. "Yes, but we have someone for that. Franny coordinates it."

Nichelle could understand. Francesca was busy with school and the sorority as chapter president so she wouldn't have a lot of extra time. The undergrad chapter elected an officer for that. "Your sister seems to have a real aptitude for business."

He nodded.

"Were you ever interested in the business side, or has it always been rocks?"

"I've never possessed an interest per se, but I took classes the summer after undergrad before I started my master's degree. Franny is the expert in that area, and the store probably wouldn't have thrived like it has if it hadn't been for her the past few years. I barely kept it afloat until she came of age."

"I'm sure you're selling yourself short."

Clark spared her a quick glance and swung his gaze right back to the road ahead of them. "I'm being completely truthful. I had a whole career in another field to launch. Those first few years after our grandparents died were challenging."

She hadn't thought of it that way. Only that Clark seemed so completely competent. It must have been a burden to keep the store open even though he didn't seem to have a lot of interest in it. He probably could have sold it. Nichelle fixed her mouth to inquire but closed it again. That was likely too much to ask at this point in their association.

The expanse of flat brown terrain spread before them and on both sides. There were plateaus in the distance, but not much else to look at. She should try to rest, but she wasn't sleepy yet. Probably shouldn't have drunk that coffee at the gas station. "It doesn't sound as though you have a lot of time for anything else. I'm really grateful you were able to take these few days to travel with me. Thank you."

He nodded.

She'd hoped they would make some headway in the conversation department, but riding across country with Clark was a whole mood. "What will we do when we get to Dallas?"

"We should be able to meet with Charles first thing tomorrow morning. When we stopped in El Paso, I left him a message in our group that we were on schedule."

"What about tonight?"

"It'll be late when we arrive, so it would be best to head straight to our rooms. Maybe get room service because the restaurant will be closed."

She'd already had room service last night and wasn't looking forward to it again. "Or—and just hear me out— maybe we could stop somewhere for dinner. It wouldn't have to be anywhere fancy."

Clark was silent so long, Nichelle gave up he was going to answer. "Okay."

Small victories. Nichelle's lips quirked in the corner, and

she settled against the door.

The lock made a small clicking noise against her side.

"Just ensuring your door is locked."

"That's very thoughtful of you."

He grumbled a word, but Nichelle couldn't hear what it was.

"I didn't catch that. What did you say?"

"Nothing." He was quiet, but his lips twitched. "I only wanted to ensure we keep our distractions to a minimum especially now that we're stopping for dinner."

Nichelle tapped her chin with one long finger. "So, let me get this straight. You locked my door because you were afraid I'd fall out of the car. Not because you're worried I may hurt myself, but because you don't want me falling out and delaying our trip. Do I understand that correctly?"

Clark's jaw tightened so much, Nichelle feared for his teeth. "Obviously I wouldn't want you to fall out of the car and injure yourself. That wasn't on my mind when I locked the door."

"So, you're not exactly thoughtful for thoughtful's sake. Not in a traditional way. More that you're ultra-responsible and that bleeds over into something resembling thoughtfulness."

She wondered about Clark. He was nice enough. Actually, he was kinder than he gave himself credit for. Clark shared he wasn't close to his parents so that relationship certainly shaped his outlook, just as hers with her parents formed her world-vision. Although in different ways more than likely. Nichelle's parents treated her with respect and love. They'd given their time too. Now that she discovered they weren't her biological parents, her life would be shaped by that too going forward. She would always love them—they were her parents—but she hoped to have a new set of parents in her life when she found them. They wouldn't be "Mom and Dad," but they'd be something. An enhancement she hoped. And maybe she had siblings. She'd grown up a de facto only child. She wouldn't even know how to have a real relationship with a sister. Honestly, not even a brother because she and Clifton had a very surface connection. She saw how her cousins were with each other so there was another way. Even Clark, with his frigid demeanor, and his sister were close. The tone of his voice was warmer whenever he talked about her. She wanted that.

"I hope Charles will be able to help us."

"I believe he will."

"I'm desperate to find my family."

"I hope you won't be disappointed."

Nichelle sat up and angled her body toward Clark. "Why would I be disappointed?"

He cleared his throat and took his time responding. "Parents aren't always perfect."

The snort escaped Nichelle's throat before she could catch it. "You don't have to tell me. Hello. Adopted here. Nobody told me...here."

"Right. I don't know your parents, and maybe they had their reasons, but that's one example. Otherwise, you've spoken highly of them. I know who your father is. He has a stellar reputation."

"He's great. I'm a cliché daddy's girl, but he still lied. I mostly blame my mother because..." She thought for a moment because that was a knee-jerk reaction. Her mother was a force of nature, so she assumed it was all her fault, but the reality is her dad went along with it. Maybe it was even his idea. "I guess I blame her because everyone blames the mother."

"In my case, I blame both parents. Admittedly, I was not an easy kid."

Nichelle would love to insert "No shit, Sherlock," but she was quiet because this was a rare moment, and she didn't want to scare him away. Not only was he carrying the conversation, but he was about to say something real about himself.

Clark sighed, then continued, "I was introverted, and advanced. I kept to myself—reading or studying, even before I went to kindergarten. They are artists and tried to bend me to be more like them, but I didn't have any interest." He shrugged and thinned his lips into a half-frown. "After a while, they figured out they didn't know what to do with me, so they mostly ignored me. My grandparents became more like my parents."

"I can't imagine. That's terrible."

"It was okay because my grandparents didn't mind me being around so much. When Franny came along, I was in middle school, and it got worse. Most of the time, they didn't remember I existed. I started spending weeks at a time with my grandparents." He let out a soft laugh. "They were from the Netherlands, so clothing was often optional. That was the only drawback. Seeing Oma coming out of the shower." He shuddered.

Nichelle hurt for younger Clark so much but imagining his older grandparents running around naked like it was nothing made her giggle. "Oh my gosh. Sounds like they were wonderful. We love to see it."

He shot her a quick glance, eyebrow raised. "Who is *we*?"

Jeesh. She forgot a minute who she was dealing with. "It's just a saying, Clark. So, what about your other grandparents?"

"They died before I was born. My father grew up in the West Indies. His father was Black and Chinese. That's where the last name comes from. One day, I plan to trace his grandfather back to China and visit."

In truth, Nichelle had wondered, although she never would have been an asshole and asked. When she met his father, he was obviously Black but had a hint of another ethnicity, although Nichelle wouldn't have guessed other than the clue of the last name. The first time she met Francesca, she introduced herself. And Nichelle said, "It's nice to meet you, Ms. Lindley." She probably pronounced that hard *d*. Francesca's response was to spell her last name, L. I. N. hyphen L. E. E. Obviously people were making that mistake all the time.

"I can help you with that if you want. I think I mentioned that my hobby is genealogy."

Clark sputtered, not forming actual words.

"Are you okay?"

"You want to see me when we return?"

What an odd thing to ask. "Sure, why not?" Nichelle enjoyed collecting friends. Clark was a tough nut to crack, but she had a small peek under the armor, and he was a decent guy. He had an interesting background, and she'd love to discover more about it. Plus, she'd never researched into China, and Clark's family sounded like a prime opportunity to stretch her skills. "I'd love to help you trace your family. You're helping me after all."

"Oh. Right. You want to help me."

She wasn't sure how to respond. There was a hurt lurking underneath.

"Sure. I hope we can be friends too."

Clark nodded, but his posture changed, more tucked into himself in his demeanor. He was closing off again, but Nichelle didn't know what to do about it.

Could he like her? She hated not being able to read these things. She studied his profile, noting his square jawline, his high cheekbones, and thick lashes.

He glanced at her, then turned his gaze right back to the

road.

Her face heated. Did he see her checking him out? She sunk into the door and calmed her spirit. "I'm going to take a nap. Don't forget to stop when it's dinnertime."

He didn't acknowledge her. She had enough experience with him the past day and night, and recognized he was deep into his thoughts. He closed back down so there would be no more deep conversation soon, and Nichelle had enough of the surface stuff. Hopefully he heard her because by the time she woke up, she wanted to see some Texas sites.

BRIGHT LIGHTS SHONE through the car, blinking red and blue.

Oh crap, did we get stopped by the police? Nichelle sprung up from her semi-prone position and hit her head on the low roof. She rubbed the new injury as well as the glitch in her neck.

Clark was staring at her with his eyebrows raised. "Are you okay?"

"Ouch. Where are we?" She looked out the front window where a building stood with strobe lights circling the roof. Now they'd changed to yellow and green. The parking lot was semi-full, and it was dark outside. Apparently, she'd slept the whole afternoon away. And of course Clark didn't get stopped by police. It's not like he would go even a mile over the speed limit.

"You wanted to stop for dinner. This is the only place I could find without veering from the route."

"But it's a bar."

"Well, actually, it's a bar and grill."

Her head snapped around, and she pointed a finger in Clark's chest. "You will never *well, actually* me as long as you live. Understand?"

The corner of Clark's mouth quirked up, offering her the smallest smile. It was glorious. "I didn't think grumpy was in your repertoire. I have to say, it doesn't suite you."

"What did you do with Clark? He's not this funny."

"Do you want to go in or not?"

She breathed in the air of the long-suffering. "Yes."

Once they walked through the door, Nichelle looked around to judge the safety of the space. She had great times visiting Austin while growing up, but she'd heard horror stories as well. As far as she knew, they could be near *The Texas Chainsaw Massacre* house. Was that a real house?

"Did you hear me?"

Nichelle swung her gaze Clark's way. "Did you ask me something?" That's when she noticed the tips of Clark's fingers touching her arm. And that light touch flew straight to her core. She already thought Clark attractive and with him loosening up and giving her a peek into his personality, she found herself wondering about him in more than a physical way.

He snatched his hand back and looked down at his shoes. "I asked if you want to stay."

There was no hostess stand, but there were tables scattered throughout with red and white checkered plastic table clothes. And lots of wood—wooden chairs, wooden bar, and wooden dance floor in the middle. The floor was packed with gyrating bodies. Waitresses with the same checkered aprons flitted here and there with stands of beer and shot glasses, and more importantly, food. "Yup."

"Looks like it's self-serve. Anywhere in particular?"

She spotted an empty table on the other side of the dance floor, near the edge, away from the speakers. A song was playing she'd never heard, but even if the music ended up being decent, she didn't want her eardrums blown out. "Follow me."

When they sat, a woman came up with a rag and wiped the table down. "Sorry about that. What can I get you?"

Clark looked at her and smiled. It was toothless, but a smile nonetheless. "What's good here?"

Again, Nichelle sat there glaring at Clark, wondering where this new, friendly personality came from. Was he being cordial? What gives?

"We make a mean chicken wing. Burgers are really good too."

"Any seafood?"

"Oh yeah. We've got a catfish and shrimp basket that will make you slap your momma."

He grinned and nodded. "I'll have that then. With lots of fries. And a Shiner Black." He turned to Nichelle. "Your turn to drive, right?"

Both the waitress and Clark stared at Nichelle, waiting for her to say something. Her lips were sewn together in shock. He was being so...bubbly.

Clark nudged her foot under the table.

"Eh, um. I guess I'll have a cheeseburger, please. And a Topo."

"Plain or flavored? We have lime and grapefruit."

"Grapefruit please."

The waitress left with their order and Nichelle stared at Clark, dumbfounded.

"What's wrong?"

"I feel like I'm in La La Land. Did we cross through another dimension while I slept and I'm with bizarro Clark now? Are bizarro Elaine and bizarro Jerry here?"

Clark drew his brows together, a very concerned look on his face. "How hard did you hit your head?"

"Not hard enough."

"I have no idea what any of those words mean."

"It's from *Seinfeld*. Do you never watch TV?"

He was thoughtful, really searching his brain if the biting of his lip and the lifting of his eyes were any indication. "Not much."

Shocker. Clark didn't seem like a *Netflix and chill* sorta fella. Not that Nichelle had enough time to watch too much either, but she loved a good romance reality TV show to get lost in. The ridiculousness always made her laugh and feel a little better about her own love life. Or lack thereof. "I didn't take you for a fish and shrimp kind of guy."

The waitress returned with their drinks.

Clark lifted the bottle to his lips. "When in Rome."

When in Rome indeed. Nichelle took a sip of her Topo, the citrusy taste barely noticeable. It was cold and refreshing considering the humidity ratcheted up since they arrived. The water was bubbly, but as smooth as she remembered.

Clark tipped his beer to her. "How's your water?"

"It slaps." She ignored the puzzled look on his face. "How's your beer?" Not words she ever thought she'd be asking Clark. A subtle reminder that she'd gotten to know him a bit over the last couple days, but there was plenty yet to uncover.

"It's really good. Shiner makes a great beer. It's a pity we can't get them at home."

"I'm more a Heineken kinda gal."

He nodded. "I like those too, especially the dark. I haven't had one since I was in Amsterdam though."

"I keep forgetting you're part Dutch." Nichelle took another sip and looked around the bar at the people. The music changed to a song she liked, and she tapped her foot along to the familiar beat. The crowd was fairly diverse. She hadn't thought to ask where they were exactly, but it was obviously within a couple hours of Dallas considering the level of darkness when they arrived. Just as she opened her mouth to ask, the bar exploded with a song only the most nonsocial person in the world wouldn't jump up and dance to. "Come on, Clark."

Looks like Nichelle was with that one person.

"I don't dance."

So much for the new, fun Clark who'd given her the smallest of glimpses. She grabbed his hand and dragged him to the middle of the throng of bodies, writhing and sweating, having a carefree time, the thrum beating strong within the tiny room.

Clark pulled away from her, red quickly spreading across his face, confusion in his eyes. "Did you not hear me?"

She leaned into him to hear better, and their bodies pressed together. "What?"

He didn't respond but swayed a bit with the music.

"That's it." That small movement was all the encouragement Nichelle needed. She smiled wide and put her hands on Clark's shoulders, shimmying up and down his body.

Clark slowed his movement even more, his eyes darting around.

Everyone let loose and nobody paid them any attention. Nichelle hoped this would be a turning point for her chemistry with Clark. She rotated and put her back against his front, moving her body against his. It could have been a visceral reaction, but now she was convinced he was at least physically attracted to her. There was no mistaking the hardness she was rubbing against.

When Nichelle turned back around, Clark had an unmistakable smolder in his hooded eyes. She licked her lips and put her hands back on his shoulders.

He placed his hands on her waist and never moved his eyes from hers. She still danced, and laughed, and teased him with her hips, but he was perfectly still, a small smile playing at the corner of his mouth.

The song ended, and everyone clapped, but Clark and Nichelle stood there staring at each other.

When the dance floor emptied, they moved with the crowd. Their food was waiting for them when they sat.

Nichelle sank into her thoughts a moment, contemplating her burger. The old familiar voice in the back of her head played on repeat. *He probably only wants to be friends but couldn't help getting hard with you rubbing against him like that.* She lifted her eyes to Clark.

He wasn't looking at her. He was slapping the bottom of the bottle of ketchup like he didn't just get a near rub-and-tug on the dance floor.

He obviously wasn't even thinking about their dirty dancing. Jeesh, why did she do this to herself every single time?

Clark glanced up. "How's your burger?"

She smiled, even though it was sad, and probably only noticeable to her. "I haven't tried it yet, but it looks great.

How's your seafood?"

He dipped a shrimp into the little paper carton of cocktail sauce, took a bite, then nodded. "Just like I remembered."

"That's great, Clark." She dug into her hamburger. Although he didn't actually have any feelings toward her, it would still be hard to forget the thrill of feeling Clark's erection against her butt. She'd try, but when she went to bed that night, no doubt that feeling would propel her into filthy dreams.

CHAPTER TEN

Clark

THE ALARM WENT off, but Clark woke at dawn. He dismissed the notification on his phone and opened the Facebook app to check for messages from Charles in their group.

There was nothing new, so he tapped out a message: *@charlesrocks, we made it late last night. What time can we meet you this morning?*

An immediate message wasn't forthcoming, so he swung his legs off the bed and sat there a moment. He hadn't been able to sleep during the remainder of the car ride into Dallas. The memory of Nichelle's butt against his dick kept him wired and awake. When they returned from the dance floor, try as he might, his erection would not deflate. He tried savoring his dinner, and drowning his salacious thoughts in a second beer, but if anything, that made it worse. Made him even hornier. He didn't want to be horny with Nichelle. Women were fine getting to know him on a physical level, but they never stuck around for anything deeper. He and

Nichelle had made a connection. At least until the dance floor incident. He liked her but didn't want to fall into the same sexual cycle. He was at the point in his life where he craved more.

By the time they checked in, it was after two in the morning. He barely slept, then woke up on his own before the alarm. He had an anxiousness coursing through his body since they'd left the bar and he wasn't sure why. Worry wasn't usually his thing. Control, over-analyzing, and planning were his things among many others. Not anxiety.

He checked his phone again, but no message, so he went into the bathroom and turned the shower on. While it was heating, he ambled over to the window. The light coming through the curtains was still weak, and downtown was bleak from his vantage point. They were on the twenty-eighth floor, so the view was vast, but the dreariness of the day didn't sit well with him.

Clark walked back to the bathroom and peered into the mirror. He slept nude, even when traveling unless he had to share with someone which was rare. His hair was mussed, sticking straight up, and his eyes were red. He reached into his traveling case and removed his toothbrush and tooth-paste, shampoo, and shower gel, then searched deeper for his eye relief drops. He packed everything from a list he'd formulated years ago and was never left wanting for anything on the road. But today, he wanted…something. He frowned, trying to tangle through the confusion in his mind. Something was off.

When he stepped under the hot water, his tense muscles slowly released the hold they had on his body. He took his time and savored the routine he used every morning. By the time he stepped out of the shower, he felt more like himself. The red was gone from his eyes, and his hair was back to its normal texture. He dried off and went for his phone again.

The return message that greeted him was not only an unwelcome surprise but threatened to throw a wrench in his carefully laid plans.

Charles: *Many apologies, Clark. I can't meet you until later this afternoon. I'll keep you posted if my schedule changes, but for now, it'll be at three.*

THIS WAS COMPLETELY unacceptable. Clark wanted to type out a reply, but he'd learned a long time ago to take a couple of cleansing breaths before he reacted. This may even be cause to open his meditation app, although he usually did that once he dressed. He tried the breaths but was still angry enough to reply with something he'd regret. Instead, he did push-ups, something else that calmed his spirit and helped him problem-solve. He counted them off as he rose and fell, using his arms to bear the brunt of his body weight. By the time he got to one hundred, his mood was considerably lighter.

He picked up the phone and tapped out a reply.

Clark: *Thank you for the update. We will meet you at your auction booth at three.*

NEXT, HE SENT a text to Nichelle.

Clark: *Our meeting has been postponed until three this afternoon. We'll need to stay an additional night. I'll update the arrangements.*

HE PUT THE phone down, then immediately picked it up again.

Clark: *If that's okay with you.*

SHE DIDN'T RESPOND right away so he went back into the bathroom to finish his morning routine and dress. The restaurant should be open, so he'd review the menu until Nichelle texted him back.

Fifteen minutes later, Clark's phone finally chimed.

Nichelle: *Was still sleeping. What happened? Never mind, you can tell me at breakfast. My schedule is open so if it's okay with you to stay an additional day, it's okay with me.*

HE RELAXED AGAINST the headboard and replied.

Clark: *I'll update our stay as well as the return hotels. What time can we meet?*

Nichelle: *Give me thirty minutes, okay?*

Clark: *I'll meet you in the restaurant.*

CLARK HAD NO intention of staying in his room another

thirty minutes. He opened his laptop and updated their reservation. Thankfully their rooms were available an additional night. He perused the nearby area for something to keep them occupied until their meeting. Besides playing basketball and dancing, he wasn't sure what other interests Nichelle possessed. She was a political science professor so maybe there was something engaging nearby on that front. He discovered an activity so obvious, the idea that he hadn't thought of it without looking really drove home how out-of-sorts he was. He closed his laptop and headed downstairs. He wouldn't order anything, but he'd at least stretch his legs while he waited.

THEY CIRCLED THE back of the building and queued in the line already forming. It was the first tour of the day, but a number of people were already outside waiting to get into The Sixth Floor Museum at Dealey Plaza. They'd already taken a turn around JFK Memorial Plaza, but the heavy Monday-morning traffic coming into downtown was nerve-wracking as they read through the monuments. The constant honking covered any conversation they attempted. Clark ended up taking a few pictures of Nichelle on his cell phone at her request, then crossed over to the souvenir shop across from the museum to buy the tickets for entrance. It was not an efficient setup, and Clark made his thoughts known to the manager there.

The line took up several minutes of time, then they were inside the cool building. "Do you want an audio guide?"

Nichelle pursed her lips, then shook her head. "No, there's plenty of audio buttons and I'd rather be able to discuss as we go through." Her smile lit up his mood considerably. This was the best idea he'd had in a while, and when he suggested it at breakfast, she nearly flew into his lap with excitement. Nearly. She remembered herself at the last moment and pulled back. Clark was grateful for that. He didn't want another sensitive situation akin to what transpired on the dance floor the evening before.

"Sounds good. Let's head to the elevators."

They rode up to the sixth floor with the other patrons eager to take in all the gory details of an American president's assassination. Clark's view was that painful past should stay in the past. As far as he was concerned, this type of museum was a bit macabre. He didn't mind a presidential library, although that wasn't his favorite. He'd only gone to the LBJ Library once the entire time he was on campus. His preference was a museum of natural history if he was forced to go to any museum. The one in Houston was especially fascinating.

A video played in a small room with benches. Clark's preference would have been to skip it since they already knew the history, but Nichelle pulled him by the hand into the room. The charge of that indiscriminate touch did not escape Clark's senses. He wanted to pull away, but he couldn't bear to hurt Nichelle's feelings. She seemed very much the sensitive sort.

When the video ended a few minutes later, the film started over from the beginning. They'd missed a big chunk of the movie, but thankfully Nichelle stood and headed out. The general ambiance of the place was hushed tones and emphatic reverence. This was not a place for anything other than intimate discussion. He and Nichelle huddled together in front of the corner window where the sniper laid in wait all those years ago, and Clark looked below to where they'd stood only an hour before. Nichelle walked over to one of the touch screens nearby and scrolled through the events of that day so long ago. Clark was mesmerized by this vantage point. Although this wasn't his thing, he could almost smell the discarded cartridges.

Before leaving, they watched one more video. This one illustrated JFK's legacy on civil rights, and Nichelle pursed her lips. "That's an interesting slant on what happened next."

"What do you mean?"

She shrugged. "We can talk about it when we're in the car on the way back to the Bay. Let's dip."

He furrowed his eyebrows, scanning through previous conversations with Nichelle to determine what she could possibly mean by *dip*, but came up empty.

"Come on, Clark. Let's get some lunch before our meeting. It's still on, right?"

He'd looked at his phone only five minutes before. There was no message from Charles then, but it couldn't hurt to check it again. "I don't see any updates so we're still a go for three. What do you feel like eating?"

She twisted her lips to the side and hummed. "Well, I wouldn't mind some great barbecue, but they probably wouldn't have options for you. What kind of food is Dallas known for?"

The question caught Clark by surprise. This wasn't something he knew because he'd never ventured over to Dallas the entire time he was in university. Rather than admit he didn't know, he said, "They're known for soul food." It was the South so his odds were good. He took the phone out of his pocket and thumbed through local eateries. "Looks like we're in luck. There's a four-and-a-half-star soul food restaurant a quarter of a mile away."

"Excellent. I'm getting hungry so I'll definitely be ready to eat by the time we walk over. Then we can walk it back off on the return." She grinned and shrugged.

Her carefree nature delighted Clark. She almost didn't seem to mind him. At least he hoped that was the case.

They strolled down North Houston at a comfortable pace, with a little time to kill before heading over to the auction.

"I hope you get what you need from Charles."

"Me too."

"What if you don't?"

She frowned, but he hurried on. "I know how important it is to track down your birth family. I'm just concerned you may not get what you need. You said you practice genealogy, correct?"

"Right. I've built a family tree with over one thousand members. Too bad they're not related to me."

They walked a few more steps, that reminder hanging in the air.

They passed a large parking structure, and Clark noted the sign: Dallas Holocaust and Human Rights Museum. He was grateful they didn't have enough time to stop at yet another museum. Her happiness spurred him on, but he had his limits. "Do you think you may try to create a new family tree?"

"Definitely. I'd like to find out any names I can from Charles, then build from there. I told you how I've taken one of those DNA tests and when I get the results, I'll build a tree from my matches. Unless my mother or father have taken the test too which would save me a lot of time." She laughed, but it was nervous. Not her usual joyous laugh.

"That's right. If you've taken a DNA test, why are we here?"

They crossed the street and turned right onto Ross Avenue. "The results could take up to a month or more."

A month? Patience wasn't Clark's primary quality, but he could have certainly waited a month rather than drive across country to obtain information that may or may not be helpful. He knew enough about Nichelle by now to keep his mouth closed on the subject. "Well, at least you have a backup."

"Yup. Plus, the children's society that handled my adoption. They won't give me names, but they will give me non-identifying information."

"Seems like your parents would have that from when they adopted you. Have you discussed any of this with them?"

They turned left and the smell of pizza bloomed in the air. Nichelle's stomach growled. "Oops." She giggled. "Yes, I finally confronted them. You'd think they would have something like that. My mother says they don't, and she doesn't remember if they ever did. More than likely, she either destroyed any paperwork, or it's hidden away in a safe deposit box somewhere." They dodged a truck backing into the service entrance of the building they were about to enter. "My vote is for the total destruction option. She never intended for me to find out."

That seemed diabolical to Clark. Why hide it forever, even after her parents' death? Surely Nichelle was mistaken in her estimation of her mother. Again, he came to the conclusion his opinion on the subject wasn't something she'd want voiced. Still, he was curious about her. "I know about your father, but what does your mother do for a living?"

"Until recently, she was the CFO for Eisinger Chemical's

North American division. Even though she's retired, they've pulled her into this huge case they're fighting. I'm not sure what it's about though."

Clark's lungs seized, and he struggled to inhale. He didn't believe in fate or providence, but how in the world could his luck be this bad? He thought about the work he'd been doing on the Eisinger Chemical case the last few months and frowned. Maybe it was a different chemical company. Eisinger wasn't a popular name so more than likely it was the same business. He was playing games with himself because of course it was the same company that hadn't cared a moment—other than their bottom line—about the pollution they tried to cover up. And to discover Nichelle's mother was knee-deep in the sludge was untenable. Now he needed to decide what to do about it.

They arrived at the door leading into the building that housed the restaurant and Nichelle pulled it open. "I'm starved."

Still dazed from the unexpected revelation, Clark followed her through the entrance.

CHAPTER ELEVEN

Nichelle

CHARLES HANDED THE ring back to Nichelle and nodded.

She and Clark sat across from the expert at his booth on the floor of the auction. They'd traveled the few short miles north of Dallas to the most affluent town in Texas, Highland Park. Nichelle had heard about it naturally—there were former governors and current NBA and NFL players and owners who lived there—but seeing it was a different story. At least what she could see of it before Clark drove them straight to the auction house, no detours. There were beautiful tree-lined streets and fountains galore. And the houses! It was true that everything was bigger in Texas.

The auction house was wedged between Christian Louboutin and Carolina Herrera stores. Not that Nichelle could afford such extravagance, but she wouldn't mind taking a little looky-look. Maybe she could even find a scarf for her mother. Wait. She was mad at her mother.

She focused back on Charles who was wiping down one

of his instruments. "What's the verdict?"

"It's definitely the ring I mentioned to Clark. Originated in Victorian Jamaica. Theft."

She blinked. "Theft? Who did it belong to?"

Charles pulled out his notebook and turned to the last entry he'd made. "Although the ring was reported stolen, it was widely believed to have been given to the man's mistress, a free Black woman named Henrietta Abernathy."

Nichelle's eyes widened, and she stood and reached for Clark's hand, squeezing his fingers as hard as she could. She needed the release of the excitement that was building, and this place was not somewhere you started hollering. Not if you didn't want to be escorted out with a quickness. "That fits. That was probably my great-great, however many times, grandmother."

Charles leaned forward and nodded. "Are you interested in selling the ring?"

She dropped Clark's hand and placed her hand on her hip. "Not at all."

"Don't you want to at least know its value before you decide?"

Of course she did. Not that she would ever sell it, but it couldn't hurt to at least know. She needed to get the ring insured anyway now that she knew it was valuable. "I've already decided, but I would like to know its value. Thank you."

He consulted his tablet and made some clicks before

turning back to her. "A one-of-a-kind rose-gold ring set with a 44.55-carat baroque pink conch pearl is approximately eighty-five thousand. US."

Nichelle plopped back down in her seat, dazed. She blinked a few times, her eyes suddenly becoming dry.

Clark rubbed her shoulders and tried to catch her gaze. "Are you okay?"

"Did he say what I think he said?" Her voice was breathy.

"It depends. Did you think he said that ring is worth nearly a hundred thousand dollars?"

She nodded. That was a lot of money, especially to receive from a stranger, grandmother or no. Wait. Did that mean her birth family was rich? And which side of the family was this? Mother or father? Would they be upset to discover Nichelle possessed this ring? A hundred other questions flew through her mind. But all she could mutter was, "Wow."

"Wow, indeed." Charles offered her a cold bottle of water. His demeanor was professional and even-keeled, but he had a small smile playing at the corner of his lips. Probably not every day something like this dropped into someone's lap.

"Thank you."

"Are you sure you don't want to sell?"

Nichelle took a deep breath and closed her eyes. She couldn't say she didn't need the money. Who didn't need eighty-five thousand dollars? That sort of money could help her buy a comfortable house and get her out of an apartment. Then again, she had more than enough room for herself. She wouldn't mind a flower garden though. "I'm sure but thank you for everything."

Clark stood and put his hand out, reaching for her. Somehow, he knew she'd have a tough time wobbling out of there of her own accord.

She took his hand and offered him a smile, raising her eyebrows, silently asking if he could believe this.

He squeezed her hand and offered the other hand to Charles. They shook and exchanged some words, but Nichelle couldn't concentrate on what they were. Her grandmother left her a priceless heirloom. Okay, it wasn't priceless, but damn. Still.

They walked silently to the car, hand-in-hand. He opened the passenger side for her, something he hadn't done the entire trip.

She slipped into the seat and tucked her purse in back of Clark's seat. The ring was still in her hand, but it felt heavier.

Clark slid behind the wheel and locked the doors. "How do you feel?"

"I feel like I've been carrying around a hugely expensive piece of jewelry like it was a Ring Pop. Why didn't you make me protect it more?"

Clark blinked.

Somehow that simple human gesture brought some logic back to her. "Gosh, I apologize, Clark. That wasn't nice.

Especially after everything you've done. Obviously it wasn't your responsibility to make sure I took more precautions. My grandmother literally said it was a rare ring. I should have known better."

"It's okay. I'm as surprised as you at the ring's value. I figured less than ten thousand. That shows you I need to stick to river rocks." He shook his head and blew out a hard breath. "I didn't want you to ship it without knowing its worth, but there's no way I expected the pearl to appraise with that huge market price."

"Well now that we know, I need to get it insured."

"You're right. By the time we get back to the hotel, you should have the appraisal in your email inbox. You can reach out to your agent and get it insured."

Nichelle turned the ring over in her hand, really studying the gem. The smooth surface of the pearl gave way to the rough grooves of the claw setting. "I don't think this is something I can call my car insurance agent about."

"No, of course not. Text Franny and she'll send you a list of companies we recommend. I can pull it up when we get back to the hotel, but I'd feel better contacting someone sooner than later. It's still early on the West Coast, but I don't want to chance it."

"Okay, I'll do that. I don't want to chance it either." Nichelle fired off a text to Francesca and waited for her response.

Meanwhile, Clark started the car and headed back to the

highway.

This time, Nichelle didn't see any of the big houses, fountains, or tree-lined streets. They were still there, but her gaze was fixated on the ring in her hands. This whole situation was becoming too much to wrap her head around. She was adopted. That was shock enough. Now this. Should she continue to look for her birth parents? She would be heartbroken if they not only gave her away, but now came after her for a material possession. She didn't know the circumstances around her adoption, but with a ring like this in her grandmother's possession, it couldn't have been money. That drove a lot of people to give their babies up. Hers was about something else obviously, but what?

She sighed, having come to a conclusion. At the end of the day, it was the only decision she could live with. She needed to know where she came from.

CHAPTER TWELVE

Nichelle

THEY LEFT THE hotel right after breakfast. Clark was being a tiny bit more patient with Nichelle, and she appreciated it. She'd been a bit of a mess since the afternoon before when she discovered she'd inherited more than a new mystery family. It was still beyond her to have something like the conch pearl ring. Her parents were upper middle class, but nothing too extravagant. Sure, she'd inherit a whole house from them and insurance and stocks and whatever. But her mother didn't have eighty-thousand-dollar rings laying around the house. At least Nichelle assumed she didn't. With all the lying, she really didn't know what was what anymore.

Clark mostly left her to her thoughts the first couple of hours and listened to his podcasts through his earbuds. He'd helped her pick an insurance agent and even talked to the woman on the phone, and aided Nichelle with filling out the online forms. That was a relief, because the ring had been burning a hole in her pocket since they arrived at the hotel.

She thought about calling the front desk and maybe getting it stored in a safe or something, but in the end, she reasoned that might draw attention to it. Maybe it wouldn't, but she'd never had something so expensive in her possession before. She didn't have a clue how to act.

The sun rose pretty high in the sky, and the air conditioning was on full blast. Which was fine, but the fresh air just hit different. She still wanted to take the top down, but Clark would probably get out on the side of the road. Something about the wind blowing through her hair excited her while it mortified Clark. They were so different, but she couldn't help the attraction building. It was the little things: the way he comforted her after the ring surprise, the care he used when planning the trip to the museum, and the way he tried to be a better person when she called him out on his shit. There were some other things too—like his beautiful face and rock-hard body.

She glanced at him before focusing on the road again.

Clark took his earbuds out. "Did you need something?"

"No, was just checking on you. Good podcast?"

"It's okay. The world is falling apart around us, etc., etc., etc." He grinned and the slightest dimple creased the side of his mouth.

Nichelle added that dimple to her pro Clark list.

He turned down the radio and rotated his body in the seat and faced her. "You want to talk about anything?"

"Tell me more about your childhood."

The breath that escaped him could be called shaky at best. "I don't want to be a downer. Why don't you tell me more about yours."

"What do you want to know?"

"You said you had a brother, but he died."

Speaking of downer. "Yeah, Clifton. He died of prostate cancer a few months ago. He was eighteen when I was born, or adopted or whatever, so we were never especially close. And goodness, we were so different."

"Physically, or…"

"Definitely physically. But more than that, we didn't have anything in common. The thing is, he didn't really have anything in common with any of us. Academia was the last thing on his mind. He was more of a hands-on person and became an electrician. That required training and an apprenticeship, so he was super responsible and driven in that way, but the rest of us could never understand, I guess. He was so smart, but he wanted to use his hands as well as his mind. I guess that's admirable now that I think about it."

Clark nodded, and Nichelle caught the movement out of the corner of her eye. She really didn't do too much of a deep dive with her relationship with her brother because it made her mother upset. Her mom had wanted Nichelle and Clifton to have a much closer relationship, but they weren't compatible. Nichelle tried—she called him sometimes—but they didn't have much to talk about. He was quiet and although she wasn't, there was only so much of a one-sided conversation someone could expect to carry. It frustrated her. Actually, that reminded her of Clark, especially the first day of the trip. She thought about those terrible hours when he was awake and she worried she wouldn't be able to make it the whole week. Who knew she'd look forward to being with him now? Funny how things like that worked.

"Anyway, we had a relationship, and it wasn't strained. It was just regular. We didn't joke around or hang out. We'd see each other at our parent's house and that was about it. We spent all our holidays together, but..." She shrugged, unsure what else was left to say about that. "I envy you and Francesca. You're quiet like my brother, and Francesca is definitely talkative like me. But it's different for the two of you. At least the small amount of time I've seen you together. I guess you could've been faking it."

The bark of laughter that left Clark's throat was unexpected to say the least. Nichelle hadn't heard that kind of abandonment since the bar a couple of nights before. "I don't think either of us would know how to fake anything. Believe me."

"Yeah, I can see that. I've worked with the undergrad chapter for a couple of years, and Francesca's definitely one of the more genuine sorors. She's well-liked too. That's why she's president I guess." Nichelle thought about her mother being president of the grad chapter. She was well-liked too, just not by Nichelle at the moment. Although that wasn't usually the case.

She thought back to those scrapes she would get playing with her neighbors, and she'd run for her mom to get patched up, bypassing her dad altogether. And another time when she was a little girl and they'd gone fishing. Her dad had his pole in the water, and Nichelle kept running up and down the bank. It was near a boat launch, so the incline was paved over. Her mom went up the bank to the car to take out the sandwiches they'd packed when Nichelle finally tumbled into the water. She could remember being underneath so clearly, hanging on to a weed, seeing her father through the clear water…laughing his ass off. She managed to pull herself out of the river, and screamed her way up the hill, calling to her mom all the way. Her dad behind her still laughing, the words, "I told you" floating behind her. Her mom pulled her into her loving embrace and comforted the tears away. Years later when they spoke of it, of course the water was shallow near the bank, and there was no current, but at the time, Nichelle could only think of getting to the safety of her mother's bosom.

"Our dad's sister was in the sorority. At Howard. She filled Franny's head with sisterhood and service since she was small."

Nichelle blinked rapidly.

"Not that there's anything wrong with that. Not at all. I just wonder if she would have been interested if it weren't for our aunt."

"Is this on the same side of your family as the grandparents you mostly stayed with?"

"No, those were my Dutch grandparents. My mother's parents."

Nichelle mentally kicked herself. Why couldn't she remember that? "Oh, that's right."

"Yeah, Aunt Corrine is my father's sister. She's a journalist and still lives near D.C. In Maryland though."

"Do you ever visit her?"

"No. She and Franny are close. I don't really see her unless she comes to the Bay. And then it's mostly when she's visiting with Franny. I don't go over to my parents much."

"Ah, and now we're back to your childhood where we began." Nichelle shot him a grin.

Clark didn't look put-out though. His face was relaxed as though he was remembering happier times instead of the loneliness he'd mentioned before. "My grandparents were the biggest nature lovers. We'd drive down to Monterey and Carmel-by-the-Sea. Sometimes we'd stay in a cabin in the forest and hike out to the beach."

"Oh my gosh. We did that in science camp."

"Science camp?"

"Clark, you grew up in California and didn't go to science camp? Everyone in sixth grade went to science camp."

He adjusted in his seat and faced forward again. "It sounds vaguely familiar."

"What's wrong? I didn't mean to trigger a bad memory. It's just when you mentioned hiking out of the woods to the beach, it reminded me of doing that and ending up on Pebble Beach."

"It's okay. Yeah, Pebble Beach was one of the places we'd hike to as well. I wonder if my grandparents took me as some sort of make-up trip. Because I didn't go to science camp."

Nichelle didn't say anything, letting him sit in his memories for a bit.

"I think I mentioned I really didn't hang out with other kids. It was a bit similar to your story about your brother. Only instead of not having anything in common with one person, it was a whole class. Around that time, I was already in the gifted program at school, and we were very much segregated from the rest of the school. Three girls and one other boy shared a classroom with me, but even in that environment, I didn't have the social skills to interact with them." He huffed and slouched in his seat. "What does that say when a twelve-year-old would much rather camp in the woods with his elderly grandparents than kids his own age?"

"I'm not sure, but I don't think it says loser if that's what you're thinking."

His head snapped around to Nichelle and she immediately saw her mistake. "I didn't mean that you were a loser. Not at all. You sounded like an amazing kid who persevered even without the support of his parents. And look at you now. You're oozing with social skills."

"Now you're being patronizing."

"Okay, maybe I overdid it a little. But I really like spending time with you, so I guess my point is, you've come a long way."

Clark shifted again and cleared his throat. He reached behind Nichelle's seat into his bag, and pulled out the reusable water bottle he'd filled up at the hotel. After taking a deep drink, he closed the top and set it between his legs. He cleared his throat once more. "Thanks. I like spending time with you too."

Nichelle grabbed Clark's hand and squeezed.

AFTER AN UNEVENTFUL night at another hotel very much like the first one where they'd stopped, Nichelle and Clark hit the road again. Clark volunteered to drive the first shift, which Nichelle gladly let him do because she hadn't slept more than an hour or two. Nichelle laid awake in her bed thinking about Clark almost all night. At some point, her thoughts took a turn, and she wished she'd brought her pulsating friend along with her. Even though she didn't have a lot of practice, turns out her own two fingers got the job done just as well. She even considered that maybe the next time her batteries ran out, she wouldn't replace them. She'd heard about the handless ones that sort of clipped onto a woman's clit and sat there. It could be used with or without a partner. Exploring that option may be in her near future, especially if a relationship with Clark progressed at all.

She couldn't believe she'd been up thinking about relationships and sex with Clark when all they'd agreed on was that they liked each other. When they returned home, would this budding romance last? Or would they go back to the corners of their lives and pick up where they left off? Maybe Clark would realize she was more friend than girlfriend material.

The sun was directly overheard so Nichelle estimated it must be close to noon. They hadn't been on the road that long, maybe two hours at the most. Even though they were a day behind, they'd gotten a late start that morning because Nichelle didn't feel like rushing. Her natural inclination was to sleep in even though Clark said he was usually an early riser. They'd agreed to meet at eight for breakfast then check out. When Nichelle's alarm finally went off at seven, she realized she'd only been asleep about an hour, so she fired off a quick text to Clark that she needed more sleep and reset her alarm for nine. Checkout was at eleven, so they had time to eat even after the delay. For once, Clark hadn't seemed annoyed in the least.

Nichelle flopped her head from one side of the seat to the other, taking in Clark's profile. She'd gotten in another few winks so she could be alert enough to drive when he got tired. She lowered the volume on the podcast Clark paired with her Bluetooth speakers. "You alright?"

The side she was facing of Clark's mouth went up a bit. "I'm great. How about you?"

"I'm miserably tired, but I can't sleep anymore."

"I still don't understand why you weren't able to sleep last night. I slept like a baby."

"Technically, I slept like a baby. Babies don't sleep all that well. They wake up every couple of hours and drive their parents to the brink. Although I wasn't in there with you, I'd say you slept like the dead given your sunny disposition this morning." Nichelle's face immediately heated, realizing what she'd implied. No, she wasn't in there with him, but she sorely wanted to be.

"Okay. Technically you still haven't answered my question."

Ugh, more heat to her face. Now her neck joined in on the party. It's not like she could tell him she was up all night thinking about him. Or could she? "I was…uh." Could she? Would he pull back again like at the bar? "We talked about liking each other so I think it was weighing heavily on my mind. Where this 'like' might take us."

As she suspected, Clark's posture stiffened.

"Forget I said anything. I was mostly just thinking."

"No, I don't want to forget it. I'm only a bit concerned."

She sat up in her seat then, matching her posture to his. "Concerned about what, Clark?"

He bent his neck to the side, and a small cracking sound emanated from it. "I mentioned to you I haven't had a great track record with girlfriends. I love that we get along so well. I've connected with you better than anyone I've ever known other than Franny. I'm looking long term and would hate it if we didn't continue."

Motherfuck. Friend-zoned again. She would never have a serious relationship. She thought she'd mostly accepted it, but here came Clark, all beautiful and kind, and maybe a little quirky, but still a good person even after his parents screwed him over. Now she was right back to where she started. "Yeah, you're right. I would hate to lose what we have too. It's been a great few days." She sank back down in her seat and turned away from him. "I'm going to try and get a little more rest before it's my turn to drive. Wake me up when you get tired."

Clark didn't say anything else, nor did he turn his podcast back up. He sat on his side of the car, quietly driving down the stretch of Arizona highway.

Nichelle pretended to sleep, taking in deeper and deeper breaths. Of course, she wasn't sleepy at all. She didn't think she'd be able to sleep around Clark anymore. She'd fooled herself again.

NICHELLE ENDED UP falling asleep after all. She had a serious crook in her neck when she sat up and looked out her car window. They were stopped near a park. "Where are we?"

"Flagstaff, Arizona."

She was back to being irritated when he felt the need to

say the state. He clearly felt superior, intelligence-wise. Typical. She had a Ph-fucking-D, but he thought he was smarter than her. "Why are we at a park?" She was also still salty about him friend-zoning her. Clark was supposed to be different.

"I pulled off the road when I got too tired to keep going. You were sleeping well, so I thought I'd find somewhere to relax for a few minutes. I apologize if stopping the car woke you up."

A quick glance at her phone revealed the time to be a little after three in the afternoon. Nichelle opened her car door and stepped out onto the concrete parking area to stretch. She looked across the park to the distance where Mount Elden stood just outside the city. There wasn't snow on the peaks, but it was still majestic and beautiful. Then she looked in the near distance. The park was large with a play area for kids, a soccer field, and... She brought her hand up to her brow to shield the sun. Was that a basketball court? Oh hells to the yeah.

The suitcase she brought on the trip was in the trunk, so she spun around and headed that way. "Pop the trunk, Clark."

He moved halfway out of the car and spoke to her over the roof. "Sorry, what?"

"Pop. The. Trunk."

The frown on his face would have been comical, but Nichelle wasn't in a laughing mood. She was about to let off some steam, and if Clark knew what was good for him, he'd pop the damn trunk. He reached back in the car, and the trunk clicked open.

Nichelle didn't bother taking the luggage out but turned it around in the trunk and opened it. She had several other items back there, including her basketball and shoes. She was already wearing a T-shirt, but her jeans wouldn't cut it, so she dropped them right there in the parking lot and slid on the shorts she'd removed from her case.

The inquisitive frown on Clark's face turned to a surprised one. His eyes widened and he glanced around. "What are you doing?"

"What does it look like I'm doing?" Of course, Nichelle had already scoped out the situation and wasn't worried about anyone seeing her. It's not like she wanted to be put in an Arizona jail. She wasn't completely stupid. At least not about this.

After dropping to the hot cement to lace up her high-tops, she rose, dusted off her butt, and grabbed her basketball from the trunk, giving it a couple of quick bounces. Even if it was flat, she kept an air pump in the trunk too.

Clark didn't follow as Nichelle headed toward the court.

She spun around and glared at him. "You staying there?"

"Nichelle, what's happening right now?"

"I'm going to shoot a few hoops. You can come along and watch, or even join in if you want."

He ran his hand across his face and let loose the deepest

sigh yet. "We are in the middle of a road trip. I need to be in court bright and early Friday morning which means I need to be back by tomorrow night. We have a reservation in Bakersfield that I'd like to keep. I've already changed it once when we spent an extra night in Dallas."

"You, Clark Lin-Lee, need to relax and have some fun sometimes." She didn't care if he had fun or not, really. That was just something to cut him a little. She hadn't planned to have fun either. "We'll make it to Bakersfield in plenty of time, I'm sure."

This time when she rotated toward the court, he followed. He didn't bother changing from his gray pants. They were lightweight, and if he really wanted to play, the pants would be fine. More than likely, he wasn't planning on participating. She didn't know him that well, especially not as well as she'd thought, but he'd probably sit on the bench and pout the entire time.

When they got to the court, it was empty. There weren't a lot of people in the park which made sense considering the sweltering heat. Shit, Nichelle forgot to bring water. She probably wouldn't be able to stay out there too long without replenishing fluids.

She bounced the basketball a couple of times, then took off toward the opposite basket, laying the ball against the backboard, but it bounced off instead of swishing through. When she grabbed the rebound, she glanced at Clark. True to form, he was seated on the bench bordering the court.

"How about some twenty-one? Or a game of horse?"

He raised his voice to match hers considering she was still a ways away. "I don't know what any of those words mean."

What a loser. Okay, that was unkind. Plus, he rode his bike fifty miles at a time while she couldn't ride down the block if someone paid her. She wanted to harbor mean thoughts, but it wasn't in her. It wasn't his fault if he wasn't into her. Although he did lead her on a little. Then again, maybe when he said he liked her, it didn't mean what she meant when she said it. "Just come out here and I'll show you."

Clark ambled over, no happiness on his stern face.

She opened her mouth to ask him how he didn't know about horse, then thought better of it. Of course she'd learned on the elementary school playground. Clark wouldn't have had that same experience given the way he grew up. "So, to play horse, I'll shoot. If I make it, you have to try the same shot. If I miss, it's your turn to set the shot. Got it?"

He chewed on his bottom lip and looked from the basketball to the basket, and back again. "In theory."

She dribbled, then pulled up for a jumper. This time the ball hit the rim but fell through the net. She ran to get the ball and passed it to Clark from under the basket.

He didn't even try to catch it.

"Ummm, what gives?"

"Oh, were you throwing that to me?" His face was completely bland and serious, but there was a small twinkle in his eyes.

Okay, now he was messing with her. She rolled her eyes and ran after the ball. "It's your turn. I'm going to throw you the rock."

"The rock?"

She blew out a quick sigh. "It's just a slang name for the basketball, Clark." This time, she waited for him to acknowledge her before passing him the ball.

He caught it with ease, then bounced it once with both hands.

"Have you really never even held a basketball?"

"I can't say I've had the pleasure." He bounced it a few more times until he was able to control it with one hand. Then he shot it. Flat-footed. No arc. The ball flew straight up in the air and fell back down not too far from Nichelle's feet.

She grabbed it and dribbled to the basket, laying it in that time. "Okay, so maybe this wasn't as great an idea as I thought." The basketball bounced into the grass, but Nichelle was already tired and didn't run after it. She wiped sweat from her face using the bottom of her T-shirt. The heat was not playing around.

Clark jogged back to the bench and picked up his reusable water bottle along with a second bottle.

Nichelle hadn't seen him bring the water, but not for the

first time, she was grateful he planned ahead.

When he handed her a bottle, she closed her eyes and took a deep swallow. "Thanks. I really needed that." She finished off the bottle and tossed it back to Clark who was taking small sips from his own. "How are you not thirsty? It's a hundred degrees out here."

"I find the more training I manage, the less fluids I need to replenish."

The hard stare Nichelle gave him made her eyes hurt. He'd just told her she was out of shape. She knew that already, but he didn't need to slap it in her face. "Yeah, okay. Whatever."

"I wasn't passing judgment on you, honestly. Stating facts, that's it."

"Ummm hmmm." She picked up the basketball and dribbled around while he threw away her bottle and placed his back on the bench. She was definitely ready to do a little damage now that she'd given herself a water boost. A group of kids approached the court with their own ball. There were five of them, both boys and girls, maybe tweens or a little older, and they headed to the other basket. Nichelle didn't want to miss her chance to get some real balling in before they hit the road. She rolled her ball over to Clark at the bench and strolled over to the kids.

They all turned to her with varying degrees of smiles.

"Looks to me like you need one more for a little three-on-three."

One of the girls laughed. She was almost as tall as Nichelle but was rail thin. "You sure, lady? We don't want you to hurt yourself out here in this heat."

"Oh, I'm sure." The girl was right though. She'd definitely need more water if she wanted to spend an extended amount of time out there running around. She glanced over to Clark and made the universal sign for needing a drink, holding her curved hand up to her mouth.

Before she could lower her hand, Clark nodded and jumped off the bench, heading to the car.

The girl checked her, and she threw the ball back. Yeah, this was going to be fun and would hopefully get her mind off Clark for at least a little while.

CHAPTER THIRTEEN

Clark

I T WAS GOOD to be back on the road, at least moving toward their destination. With Nichelle driving, they made good headway, but the sky had already darkened, and the delay would mean they wouldn't make it to Bakersfield that night as Clark hoped. Normally, he was against breaking the law and speeding, but he didn't mention anything to her because he needed to get back, and she'd wasted enough of their time at the park. By his estimation, at least two hours.

As soon as they returned to the car after Nichelle's impromptu basketball game, and Clark realized what the time was, he'd canceled their reservation. Because he wasn't sure where they'd end up, he couldn't make another one, but at least they'd crossed back into California. The urgency he felt in his stomach made his unease skyrocket. On top of the lie by omission about Nichelle's mother he was fostering, he couldn't miss court. That would be disastrous. If he did, the whole problem of testifying against the company his girlfriend's mother worked at would easily vanish. He sighed.

That's absolutely what he wanted from Nichelle, but how could he ask for it knowing his deceit?

At first, Clark couldn't understand why Nichelle felt the need to play a "pickup game" of basketball as she called it. The longer he sat there watching her have fun with those kids, the more he realized she was expelling some built-up fury. Fury he'd probably caused. Not that he meant to. He was sure his behavior was confusing at best. More than likely, Nichelle believed the worst—he was toying with her. He understood why she would be convinced of that, but his actions were purely based on his inner turmoil with wanting her desperately weighed against his integrity as a consulting geochemist. Sure, he could converse honestly with her, but he couldn't trust she wouldn't call her mother and give away the state's offense. It was her mother, and she shouldn't even be put into such a position. Most likely, if Clark were put in the same position, he would not give his own mother inside information. But he'd come to understand that although Nichelle was upset with her parents for their dishonesty around the circumstances of her birth, she loved them dearly. Absolutely she would tell her mother.

"What's your case about anyway?"

Clark blinked. Was what he'd been thinking broadcasted on his face? "Sorry?"

"Seriously? All you've been talking about is getting back in time for your case. Now you don't know what I'm talking about?"

Had that been all he talked about? Of course he mentioned they shouldn't dally in the park—which she'd patently ignored. But he'd barely broached the subject. Or so he thought. "Oh, I, um." What could he say without compromising the case and cluing her in? "I'm not at liberty to discuss the case to any extent, but it concerns environmental cleanup. Protecting local fish and game which are in danger from, at least, neglect. Maybe even maliciousness."

"That's awful. I hope you get the bastards."

The heat creeping up his neck was on its way to smothering him. Just a few more inches, and shame would close his windpipe. He cleared his throat, struggling to take a tolerable breath. "Yes, we'll see."

"If a company is willfully polluting the environment for profit, they should be put under the jail. My mother always says that. She should know. She's been in the chemical business since before I was born."

Clark found that interesting. He hadn't thought her mother was involved directly but wondered how she could be so convicted yet clueless to her own company's mistreatment. Especially as an executive. It wasn't up to him to wonder though. His job was to analyze and present the facts. The court would figure out the rest. "I agree with your mother." He glanced out the window at the mileage sign on the side of the road. "Barstow is only twenty miles away, so we should probably stop there for the night. There's still over two hours to Bakersfield and it's already close to midnight."

Clark opened the app on his phone and looked for a suitable hotel.

"That's fine." Nichelle yawned and rubbed her eyes. "I'm ready to hit the hay anyway. That sun took it out of me today."

The need was strong to remind Nichelle she wouldn't be so tired if she'd listened to him and skipped the physical exertion in nearly one-hundred-degree weather. He quelled that particular desire because speaking that out loud would not be appreciated in the least. Instead, he continued to check availability. So far, he'd blown through several hotels who had none. Next, he checked on why that could be possible in Barstow, population downward of twenty-four thousand. What in the world was the Eternal Devotion Conference? He didn't have the desire to investigate further. Whatever the conference was, the event was keeping him and Nichelle from having somewhere to lay their heads for the night. "I'm having difficulties finding a place for us to stay. Apparently, there's a convention in town, and they've booked most of the hotels."

"Most? Or all?"

"I'm still looking."

"Okay, because we need to stop, Clark." She yawned again. "Unless you're prepared to drive two more hours in the middle of the night."

He was not prepared. Since they'd left Flagstaff over five hours before, he hadn't slept at all. A mistake on his part, but he'd been too worried about the whole court matter. "I'll find something." After a few more futile minutes, he finally found a room. One room. His stomach dropped a little in apprehension. He glanced sidelong at her. "I may have found something, but there's only one room available."

The hushed silence in the car roared loudly. Nichelle shifted in her seat and huffed, briefly closing her eyes. "Book it."

Clark booked it. Then he laid back in his seat, releasing some of the tension that straightened his spine. There was a new unease building in his stomach, but he'd deal with that when the time came. More-than-likely, there'd be a sofa in the room, and he'd only have to endure her proximity from ten feet away instead of ten inches.

CLARK GLANCED AROUND the small room with one queen-sized bed; at least that's what was advertised, although this one didn't look bigger than a full-sized. There was an end table, a cramped dresser, and…nothing else. No sofa. Not even a desk with a chair. He turned his attention to Nichelle who was glaring his way. His face heated with shame. Did she think he planned this? "I'm sorry. I thought there would at least be a loveseat." Ugh. Why didn't he just say sofa? Or couch?

"Sure. Was there not a description of the room?"

"Well, yes. It listed a queen-sized bed but didn't really mention amenities. We were desperate, and I didn't want to lose the room by taking my time." She was the one who told him to book after all.

Her posture loosened maybe a centimeter. Enough to give Clark hope that she believed him. He didn't want to be in this situation either. At least not under these circumstances, with so much unsettled between them. The court case and his testimony needed to be behind him before he could even think about a physical relationship with Nichelle. Plus, he wanted so much more from her. Physical relationships were never a problem for him in the past. They'd been building something deeper before he pulled away and upset her. How could he explain his inner agitation with this entire situation? He couldn't. Not without revealing the company he'd be testifying against.

She opened the closet door and looked inside. "There's barely enough room for one suitcase."

"That's fine. I'll prop mine in the corner."

Next, she peeked in the bathroom. "Clean, at least."

"This is a small hotel. Or inn as they call it, but at least it's a trusted chain."

"Hmmm."

Clark set his suitcase on its side in the corner as he promised. His bones ached with fatigue, and he wanted nothing more than to take a shower and slide under the covers. His hand froze over the zipper to his bag. What was he thinking not bringing pajamas? Well, he wasn't thinking he'd have to share a room. He had a clean T-shirt left, but only his last pair of chinos for the next day. They'd spent an unexpected extra day in Dallas, and while he always planned ahead with an extra set of clothes, he hadn't planned for a night spent with someone else. At least not like this. His anxiety ratcheted up exponentially, and he couldn't think. Plus, he only ate a fast-food salad in the car because they were so far behind schedule. His tank was empty. *Think, Clark.* But he couldn't think. Instead, he did the only thing that would calm him enough to rein his thoughts in. He got into the push-up position.

"What in the holy hell are you doing?"

He dropped to his knees and peered at Nichelle. Her hands were spread in front of her, palms up. She was clearly waiting for an answer. "Push-ups."

"I can see that."

"Then why did you ask?"

"*Why* are you doing push-ups, Clark?"

He took a couple of deep breaths. "I can't think straight, and I'm hungry. Push-ups will help me gather my thoughts."

Her hand flew to her parted lips, but she didn't say anything.

Clark regained the position and counted off the repetition of pumping up and down. When he reached fifty, the door to the bathroom slammed shut. He kept going until he reached a hundred, then hopped up and looked in his suitcase again. Nothing changed, but he did remember packing several extra pairs of underwear so he would match boxers with the T-shirt and call it a night. There was no help for it. He'd just have to wear the T-shirt all night and the next day too.

Minutes passed before the water from the shower turned on. Clark gathered his improvised sleepwear, shower shoes, and toiletries bag. He sat on the side of the bed and removed his shoes and socks. This would be fine. Obviously she was angry enough with him that he needn't worry about any accidental touching. Or more. Thankfully she was that angry because it would take everything within to resist her. He was unsure he possessed that amount of strength, especially when he'd been dreaming about touching her for days.

He scrubbed his hand across his face and let out a thunderous sigh. How would he make it through this night? There's no way he'd be able to fall asleep next to her no matter how much fatigue plagued him. The push-ups increased his blood-flow sufficiently to figure out his clothing predicament, but also enough to wake up other parts of him. Anything physical between them was morally wrong. Not with his knowledge of testifying against her mother.

The water turned off, and there was a small amount of shuffling in the bathroom. Clark slipped his feet into the shower shoes and readied the remaining items for the shower, only Nichelle didn't come out. He listened for any movement, but it was a good five minutes before the door cracked.

"Can you turn your head, please."

"Sure." He rotated and faced the far wall, away from the entrance to the bathroom.

The sound of the door opened, and a rush of warmth hit the back of his neck. The smell of flowers came next. "Everything okay?"

A sigh floated over to him. Sighing wasn't something he'd heard from Nichelle before. "I forgot to pack my pajamas. It wasn't a problem until tonight."

He huffed a strong breath from his nose, stifling the sigh he himself wanted to release. Before Nichelle, he hadn't noticed how much he sighed. Now he was hyper-conscious of the coping mechanism. "I didn't bring any either. I never sleep in pajamas at home."

"What's that in your hand then?"

He started to turn, but she verbally stopped him. "Wait."

"Sorry. It's a habit of mine to look people in the eye when I speak to them."

"Okay, but I only have a towel wrapped around me and I'd rather figure this out before you turn around."

"I understand. I have the T-shirt I'm going to wear tomorrow and some underwear." He shrugged. "It's all I could come up with."

"Yeah. At least all the vital bits will be covered. I need to cover my important bits too, but I don't have anything."

Clark thought for a moment. "Can you sleep in your

clothes you're wearing tomorrow?"

"I used my extra workout stuff at the park, so I don't have anything clean left. I only brought enough clothes for the trip."

Of course she did. At this point, he wouldn't expect anything more of her. How did someone keep themselves alive into their thirties, acquire a PhD, and remain gainfully employed with no planning or organizational skills whatsoever? "Not even underwear?" The tips of his ears heated considerably. Why did he ask that?

"Do you happen to have an extra T-shirt in your bag?"

He stood, keeping his back to her, and shuffled sideways over to his suitcase. He knew exactly what he'd packed, but somehow thought that maybe looking again might conjure an extra T-shirt he didn't know was inside. Good thing he did look because as flustered as he was, he forgot the extra underwear he'd packed. Also, clean undershirts still in the package so he extracted one along with the boxers. He could use one of the undershirts instead of his T-shirt too. "I don't have a T-shirt, but maybe these will do." He held the garments above his head so she could see them since he was still facing away from her.

"That would be perfect. Thanks, Clark." Relief was evident in both her words and tone of her voice.

He made his way back to the bed and set the clothes on the corner for her. When the bathroom door closed again, he let out a breath. The lighthearted way she thanked him relieved some of the pressure lodged in his sternum. They would endure this night. He was confident of it now.

The bathroom door opened again, then the bed dipped. "All yours. Thanks again for the clothes."

"You're welcome." Clark entered the bathroom considerably lighter. He switched on the water in the shower and set his bag on the counter, placing his clothes next to it on the tiny sink. The mirror was completely fogged, but Clark didn't need it anyway. If it were clear, he'd see a man considerably more relaxed than he'd been a half an hour before. He quickly undressed and stepped under the scalding water. He needed the heat to further loosen the remaining tightness in his muscles from his impromptu workout. The water was soothing and relaxed him to the point of causing his eyes to close on their own. He was bone tired.

After completing his nightly routine, he pulled on the undershirt and boxers, ensuring the front slit was properly closed. The last thing he wanted was to accidentally flash Nichelle. She would definitely believe it purposeful.

The bedroom was dark when he emerged from the bathroom, but finding his suitcase in the compact room wasn't a problem. After replacing his smaller kit and the dirty clothes he'd pulled off, he made his way over to the bed. His eyes adjusted to the dimness, but he still couldn't make out which side of the bed was left for him.

"I'm here." Nichelle raised her arm and waved.

The room held enough light to illuminate the movement, so Clark pulled the covers back on his side of the bed and sat down. "Do we need some rules? I want you to be comfortable."

"Just get in the bed, Clark. I'm sleepy."

He grinned to himself. He overthought everything while she gave nothing but the smallest notion to anything. With anyone else, the idea of someone flying by the seat of their pants would be maddening. Somehow on Nichelle, it was exceedingly charming. Maybe it was because it was tiring being so ultra-responsible all the time. She was successful despite her lack of rumination. Then again, it was entirely possible she was effective because of it. Different strokes and all. He slipped under the covers, careful to stay on his side.

"Try to relax, Clark. I can feel your stiffness through the invisible barrier you've drawn down the middle of the bed. If we accidentally touch, it won't kill either of us. I promise. I also promise not to purposefully touch you and make you more uncomfortable." She chuckled, and added under her breath, "If that's at all possible."

"I think you have the wrong impression of my feelings."

"I think you've been quite clear about your feelings. You like me as a friend, but that's it. I get it." She let out another laugh, this time humorless. "Believe me, nobody gets it more than I do."

Clark turned to face her. He could just make out the curve of her jaw. He was so close to her. How often he'd imagined just this scenario the past couple of days. "Friendship isn't on my mind when I look at you. At least, not only friendship. I like you, but my life is a bit complicated right now." Complicated was an understatement. His testimony could cause her mother quite a bit of problems.

Her breath caught, and then she released it a moment later and turned to face him. "How is it complicated?"

"The court case. I can't really say more than that."

"The court case is keeping you from something with me?"

Now it was Clark's turn for his breathing to be interrupted. Did she really want a relationship with him? "Yes, but it won't always be like that."

Nichelle nodded and reached across Clark's invisible barrier that he indeed constructed. She didn't touch him but rested her hand on top of the blanket very near him. "I wish you could tell me more, but I understand and trust you."

"You trust me?"

"Clark, I've never met a more trustworthy person in my life. That includes my parents."

"Thank you. That means a lot." And it did, but he couldn't repress the notion that he didn't deserve her trust. He was keeping important information from her that could affect her mother. If it were up to him, he'd tell her. But it wasn't up to him. His integrity meant everything to him. Although his character was in question concerning Nichelle. He couldn't both be true to his commitment to his profession and tell her the truth.

"Do you want to have kids?"

Where did that come from. "Now? Or ever?"

She chuckled again, but it was mirthless. "I meant ever, Clark."

"Yes." Where was this going? Clark shifted the position of his legs and checked the flap of his boxers again.

"I'm not sure I do. I wanted you to know."

Clark's stomach twisted in knots. He'd finally found someone who took him seriously, but maybe had no desire for children, something he'd been wishing for since his grandparents died. "Have you ever wanted children?"

"Yes. In theory, I've always wished for kids someday. I wasn't sure I'd ever meet someone who wanted them with me, but I held out hope that maybe someday."

"What changed your mind?"

"It's not that I don't want them. It's more that I'm afraid to have them. I have no idea about my own medical history anymore so I wouldn't want to saddle my kids with some unknown life-threatening genetic traits."

Clark bit the corner of his lip. He wasn't sure how to respond. To him, this wasn't a valid reason to not have children. Unless genetic testing was explored, nobody knew for sure they weren't passing along a troublesome condition. He couldn't trust his parents to give him vital medical information. They'd have to care enough first. Even though he didn't agree with Nichelle, he understood why she struggled with the notion of having kids considering her recent parentage revelations. More than likely, she'd change her mind once she worked through the adoption fiasco. "I understand. Maybe you'll feel different once you've discovered your birth parents."

"Do you really think I'll find them?"

He smiled then, a genuine smile that he couldn't help. He'd only known Nichelle a short time, but she was tenacious. That much was evident. "I believe with all certainty you will."

This time, she extended her hand farther and did touch him. She stroked his forearm which was lying on top of the covers. The feel of her skin on his, even a finger, raised goose bumps on his arm. He sucked in a breath.

"Is this okay, Clark."

He exhaled a soft, "Yes."

She scooted closer and ran her hand up his arm, and down again.

He needed to make a decision, and for the life of him, he couldn't. His body wanted to sway him one way—that was evident as blood rushed south and what little bit was left, pulsated in his ears. His mind pulled against his body though. He desired this more than anything—his dreams were the evidence—but he also wanted more from Nichelle. He couldn't have more until he told her about her mother's company though. But if he rejected her once more, she may never be open to him again.

By the time her hand reached his neck, he'd made a decision.

CHAPTER FOURTEEN

Nichelle

WHAT WAS NICHELLE doing? She'd been angry and a little embarrassed because she thought Clark rejected her. Then he did those push-ups, and she nearly lost all her senses. Watching him pump up and down, his strong arms flexing with each motion... She'd rushed into the bathroom to get herself together. She wanted nothing more than to rub one out right there, but knowing Clark, he'd figure out what she was doing. As it was, she took her time undressing, caressing her own body as she went. The shower helped, but when she came out and remembered she didn't have pajamas, angry embarrassment flushed through her all over again. He'd think she wasn't a planner and forgot to pack her pajamas. He'd be right, of course, but she still didn't want his thoughts to be confirmed.

But then he figured it out for her and didn't seem upset about it in the least. She'd slipped his boxers on, and her skin flushed with lust. Imagining his beautiful body in the same underwear she'd slid on was almost too much. The under-

149

shirt he handed her was loose when she eased it over her head, except where it hugged her breasts. There it was extremely tight, and her nipples shone through easily. She would have loved to put her bra on, but it was currently pressed between a towel along with a pair of her panties that she'd washed out. Next time, she would plan. She chuckled to herself. Of course she wouldn't plan.

With only a couple inches of mattress, and even less fabric between them, Nichelle only had touching Clark on her mind. She literally couldn't think of anything else, so when he gave consent, and she ran her hand up his arm, and finally settled into that silky hair of his, her soul felt joy for the first time in weeks. Her family problems momentarily taking a back seat in her thoughts. He was perfectly still, a total Clark thing to do, or not do. Although he didn't withdraw from her, there was a sudden stiffness replacing the stillness. She wouldn't embarrass herself by making a move on him only to be rejected again. He'd have to initiate anything between them.

The audible breath leaving Clark's lungs gave Nichelle her answer. She was well-versed in his *sigh-language* by now, but he followed it up with words. "I want nothing more than to explore this further, but we must maintain level heads."

"What does that even mean, Clark? Sex is not that big of a deal."

"It is to me."

Nichelle withdrew her hand, but Clark reached across

their invisible barrier and rested his hand on her waist. She closed her eyes to concentrate on keeping herself from getting turned on. The heaviness of his fingers pressing through the thin undershirt she was wearing pulsated in her mind. Thoughts of scooting to him, wedging herself under him traipsed through her brain. She popped her eyes open to get her bearings. "Maybe we should just get some sleep."

He moved his hand to her face and stroked the heated skin of her cheek. "I do want you. Very much so. Just give me some time."

She leaned into his touch, internally scolding herself for so easily believing him when that line of thinking never served her well before. But hope bloomed in her chest and anchored there. Too late to do anything about it. "Okay."

THE CALIFORNIA SUN peeked through the cheap inn curtains earlier than Nichelle anticipated. A quick look at her cell phone notified her that it wasn't quite as early as she thought. Her back was against Clark, so she shifted to get a look at him before he woke up.

Clark stared back at her and smiled. "Good morning, beautiful."

She grinned, then ducked her head. She wasn't beautiful on her best day. No way was she close to beautiful after forgetting to find her bonnet before jumping into bed. Plus, she'd stayed up way too late quelling her desire. Instead, she'd played big spoon to Clark's little spoon against his nearly naked back, and finally drifted off to sleep, soaking in his warmth. Sometime during the night, they'd switched positions. She covered her mouthful of morning breath. "Morning."

He laughed and sat up on the side of the bed. "Checkout's in an hour, and I'm starved. We better get ourselves together."

"Okay, but can we find a coffee shop at least? I can't imagine what passes for breakfast around here."

The look on his face spoke to the argument brewing in his brain, but finally he said, "Okay." He stood, completely without reservation or modesty in the morning light, and strode over to his suitcase.

Nichelle crept out of the bed while Clark's back was turned—with reluctance and bashfulness—and trudged into the bathroom to retrieve her thankfully dry underwear. She slipped out of Clark's boxers and undershirt and slid on her bra and panties, then wrapped a towel around herself, and brushed her teeth.

Clark squeezed in behind her dressed in a T-shirt and a light-gray pair of pants.

She spit in the sink. "Do you only own shades of gray clothes?"

He looked down, then reached around her to retrieve his own toothbrush. "My shirt is white."

"Technically, sure. But I've only seen you in white, black, or gray. To me, black and white are subsets of gray."

He shrugged, then chuckled. "Sure. If you say so. I guess I've never really paid attention."

Nichelle picked up a washcloth and scrubbed her face, then looked in the mirror.

Clark was watching her as he brushed his teeth, a sexy smolder shading his big, nearly obsidian eyes.

"I better get dressed." She pulled on her jeans, stiffened from wear, and the cleanest blouse from her suitcase, then went back to the bathroom to tackle her hair, bumping into Clark on his way out. "You got ready fast."

His loose curls were perfectly styled as usual. "Not a whole lot to do. Just wash my face and rub a little gel into my hair."

"I wish I could just rub a little gel into my hair. It's a hot mess."

He ran a hand through her strands, catching on tangles for his trouble.

"Told ya."

"Still beautiful."

The bald-faced lie was appreciated, and she couldn't help but smile. She was never the prettiest girl in the room, but he didn't seem to care. "Get out of here so I can finish."

When they finally made it on the road after a sizable breakfast of French toast, sausage, and hash browns for Nichelle, and oatmeal with blueberries and whole grain toast for Clark, the lack of a full night's sleep combined with a hefty breakfast was catching up to Nichelle. "Will you be okay by yourself?"

He squeezed her hand. "For now. You get some sleep, and I'll catch up on the news of the day. I'm good at least until Kettleman City."

Nichelle relaxed into the seat and closed her eyes. As tired as she was, she didn't fall asleep right away. Instead, she thought about her budding relationship with Clark. She was feeling okay about where they were. They'd talked, even though somewhat briefly, and she believed him when he said he liked her and wanted more than friendship from her. They hadn't discussed what that more was, but she wasn't worried about it. She wasn't really concerned about their lack of intimacy. If Clark said he needed time, she'd give him time. That wouldn't stop her from fantasizing though. She smiled to herself, filthy images floating through her brain as she finally drifted off.

When Nichelle woke, she rubbed her eyes and glanced at Clark. He seemed alert. "Hi, where are we?"

Clark reached for the radio knob and lowered the volume. "Hi, yourself. We just passed the exit for Spicer City so about another half hour to Kettleman City. How'd you sleep?"

"Like the dead. It's good to see you're still spry."

He grinned and reached across the middle console. "Okay for me to rub your thigh?"

Nichelle giggled and grabbed his hand, pulling it the rest of the way, and settling it on her leg. "More than okay. You're not tired?"

"Not really. I thought I would be, but I've settled into a rhythm. Plus, we're only a little over three hours from home, and I'm no longer stressed about making it back in time."

"I'm glad. I never did apologize for being a brat and holding us up in Flagstaff. Forgive me?"

"Forgiven."

"You're not going to ask me why I was being a brat?"

He pressed his hand into her thigh with a little added pressure and sent a zing to Nichelle's core. "No. I think I have an idea why. It was my fault, and I shouldn't have sent mixed messages."

"You're forgiven too."

"What's your plan when you get home? I mean your next step in finding your birth family?"

"Now that I have a name, I'll build a family tree. Or at least try to. Maybe do some research on the original owner who reported it stolen."

"I can do the research if you want."

"Will you have time?"

"Not until after I testify in the morning, but after that I should. I have a ride early Saturday morning so definitely in the afternoon if I don't get to it tomorrow. Franny says everything's fine at the store, so I'll verify after court." Clark removed his hand to steer while he turned the blinker on with his other hand. A car was driving so slowly in the middle lane that they both turned to look who was behind the wheel. "Someone texting. Figures."

Clark was the ultimate rule follower, but even Nichelle could agree with his assessment. "Texting and driving is almost as bad as driving under the influence." She turned her body to face him, missing the warmth of his hand. "That would be great if you could research him. Thanks."

"No problem at all. I want to help anyway I can."

"You've already done a ton, Clark. I know I haven't always shown it, but I appreciate this entire trip. I'm still stunned by the information we found from Charles." When he settled back into the middle lane, Nichelle reached over and placed his hand back on her thigh.

A grin split Clark's face, as he rubbed her thigh again. "It was a very productive trip. All the way around."

"Agreed. While I'm building the tree, hopefully at least my birth report comes in. Bonus points if my DNA results come back. That way, even if I don't have a close match, I can still use whatever matches I do get to help build the tree."

"All of that sounds fascinating. It will all come together. I'm confident."

"But then I'll have to deal with my mother."

"Deal with her?"

"Yeah, I just mean that I'm convinced she didn't tell me or anyone else in the family because she wanted to pretend I was their natural child. Whether she was embarrassed or just being shady, I don't know, but I do know that finding my birth family is going to be a problem. Because when I find them, I'll want to meet them if they're open to it. That will not go over well with Betty Sampson."

"Because she won't want to share." Clark didn't phrase that as a question.

It was suddenly obvious why her mother kept it a secret. "Hundred percent. That's exactly why. But she doesn't realize that me finding out like this, after thirty years of lies... It almost feels like I'm less than a full member of the family now."

Clark increased the pressure on her leg, rubbing circles instead of the inside thigh-grab he was doing before. "I know what that feels like."

She hadn't meant to make him feel bad or remind him of his own terrible family dynamic. It was bad enough that her adopted parents lied to her all these years, but at least she'd always felt loved by both of them. "You're absolutely right. I shouldn't have said that. They've never made me feel less than."

"You're allowed your feelings. My parents are terrible people. Don't compare your family with mine."

"Yeah. Okay. I guess what I mean is that all this time, I've been proud to be a Sampson. I talked about how much I looked like my dad. How much like him I was. I identified so much with that side of the family, and now I feel so stupid. Like everyone was making fun of me when I said such idiotic things. I feel humiliated." A tear leaked out of her eye, completely unexpected.

Clark moved his hand again, but this time turned on his blinker to get off at the upcoming exit.

"What's going on?"

"I just want to pull off for a minute. You deserve my full attention."

"You don't have to." With his act of kindness, the dam broke. She hadn't given herself time to cry before. She hadn't wanted to upset her parents. She'd tried to ignore her feelings, but now they were laid open raw, and she couldn't disregard them any longer. Suppressing her feelings had been eating her up inside, and she hadn't even paid attention.

Clark opened her door and held out his hand.

She hadn't even noticed they stopped. She closed her hand around his and let him pull her up into his arms. She pressed so hard against his chest, she thought she might cut off his breathing. But he wrapped his strong arms around her and held her even closer while she cried and cried. "I've been so foolish."

"I'm sorry you're hurting. What can I do?"

She sniffed and shook her head. "You're already doing it. I needed to get it out. I hadn't realized how much I'd stuffed down. I tried to accept the reasons my parents gave me, but they rang untrue. I don't know what to think." She calmed enough to stand on her own and looked at Clark's shirt. It was soaked, but otherwise no worse for wear. At least she wasn't wearing mascara. "I'm okay. Let's get back on the road."

Clark nodded.

"And thank you." She settled back in her seat. She really needed that cry. Nothing about this situation was fair, but it wasn't the worst thing in the world that could happen to her. She didn't know why she was put up for adoption, but she did know there were two people who wanted her. Two people who never let her go without love and attention a day in her life. Yes, they'd lied to her, and it would take her a while to get over that, but they'd also given her a good life. For that, she was grateful.

CHAPTER FIFTEEN

Nichelle

NICHELLE'S STOMACH SANK as she drove off, leaving Clark on the sidewalk. It was silly, really. They'd see each other and build on what they'd started on their road trip. It was only the beginning for them. He had stuff to do, and Lord knows she did too with summer school starting next week plus research on her birth family.

She drove home on autopilot, but even after nearly a week away, she didn't want to be there. It wasn't so much being alone, she didn't mind that, but her empty apartment reminded her of her real life. The one where her parents told her lies. She rolled her suitcase inside her place and left it in the laundry room. She'd unpack and wash her clothes later. When she strolled into her living room, it was the same as she'd left it. Two half bottles of water left on the coffee table, an open Poli-Sci book on the couch, and some jewelry left on the bar separating that room from the kitchen. Oh, she hadn't done her hourly check of her purse to make sure the pearl ring was still there. She found it right where it always was and laughed to herself. She would be glad when she could secure it and not worry about the ring anymore.

Clark promised to send her a link to a home safe company he recommended but never got around to it. Would texting him seem too needy? She could just ask Francesca. Or look up one herself and order something. She'd insured the ring, and even though that gave her some peace of mind from a financial perspective, it was an heirloom she didn't want to part with. That was more important to her than anything. It was too late to do anything about the safe, so she'd handle it the next day. She really just wanted to get out of there, so she walked to her bedroom and pulled off the clothes she'd worn at least twice and slipped on a clean pair of shorts and a lightweight blouse from her closet. She put the ring in a shoebox way in the back.

When Nichelle got back in her car, she called Amanda through the Bluetooth.

Amanda answered on the first ring. "Hey, girl. I got your text you'd be a day late, but dang, I didn't think this late."

Nichelle frowned and noted the time on her stereo screen. "It's only six. And hello to you too."

"Uh oh. I don't like that tone. What happened? I thought you and Jewelry Boy were getting along well. At least after the first day."

"We are. Are you busy?"

"Never too busy for you, love."

"I'll be there in five. I hope you have something to eat."

"Girl, bye."

On the way to Amanda's, Nichelle thought about how she'd broach the Clark subject with her friend. Amanda had warned her off pursuing anything with him, and of course, she'd flung herself headfirst into...not a relationship, it was too early for that. But something.

Amanda had witnessed too many false-start relationships with Nichelle in the past. She'd like a guy, think he liked her too, and it turned out he liked playing basketball with her, or wanted a job at the university, or any number of things. She didn't think Clark wanted anything like those other men, but she'd never been a good judge either. Best to talk it out with her bestie to give herself some peace of mind. If she got it wrong this time... She sighed. She really liked him. This time, she didn't know how she'd recover from such a rebuff.

Nichelle settled herself on Amanda's couch and finally relaxed. She should be bone-tired, and she supposed she was, but being near her sister-friend gave her the boost she needed. Amanda's three-bedroom house sat just off campus in an expensive section of town. She'd come from money, quite a bit of it, but somehow developed a strong work ethic. First came her PhD and then a nice university job, strictly on merit. She could have used her talent, and considerable trust fund, in a studio somewhere, wiling the days away on her craft, but she'd chosen to teach and share her skills with others.

The smell of pasta and tomato sauce drifted out of the

kitchen, and Nichelle's stomach rumbled. "Smells good, A."

"You're lucky I made spaghetti, instead of a steak for one."

"At least someone, somewhere is looking out for me."

Amanda came into the room with a sympathetic look on her face, her bottom lip jutting out. "That bad, huh?" She wiped her hands on the towel she'd placed across one shoulder. "Come on. Let's eat and you can tell me all about it."

The table in the breakfast nook was set for two. It was called a nook, but the room was large enough to hold a wooden block table for six people. There was a dining room, but Amanda saved that for big dinners like Thanksgiving or other times when her family visited from Louisiana. Special occasions were when she broke out the good plates and flatware from the china closet. Tonight, they used the unadorned plates from the kitchen cabinet. Nichelle definitely wasn't in a fancy mood and was grateful her friend offered her dinner. After the long, emotional day on the road with Clark—who although lovely, was new to her drama—it was a comfort to be back in the company of a long-time friend who knew her.

They sat down and helped themselves from the platter of pasta, a bowl of goat cheese and walnut salad, and garlic bread. Nichelle stared at her plate.

"What's wrong? You need some cracked black pepper or cheese?" She pushed both Nichelle's way.

A soft laugh escaped Nichelle's lips. "Wrong? Nothing's wrong. This is restaurant quality, you know that, right? And not normal spaghetti. What kind of noodles are these?"

"Girl, you know me. It's actually Bucatini all'Amatriciana. Same difference."

"Definitely not the same." Nichelle lifted a forkful of the thick noodles to her mouth, and savored the smell, before shoveling the mound in. "Oh my—"

"Didn't you momma teach you not to speak with your mouth full?" Amanda laughed, then her eyes widened. "Oh, sorry."

Nichelle shook her head, chewing and swallowing the too-big portion she'd stuffed into her mouth. "Don't be sorry. I'm still upset with Mom, but I'm happy she and Dad rescued me from an orphanage, basically. They both taught me a lot, including how to chew with my mouth closed. This is delicious by the way."

"Thanks. Well, if you aren't upset about your parents, what's going on?"

She *was* upset about her parents, but the whole story about Clark came rushing out even though she hadn't intended to talk about it first.

Amanda placed another helping of salad on her plate but didn't look Nichelle's way.

"We have that big step show coming up too. So I have to work a lot with Franny. I'm not sure if Clark said anything to her...about us."

The look on Amanda's face sunk Nichelle's heart. Of course her friend warned her of just this possibility. Amanda wouldn't rub her face in it though.

"Okay, I know that I have to put my big-girl panties on and just get this over with. You were right and I was wrong, but now I have to honor our charter. It's about service, not about me."

Amanda threw her hands in the air, palms out, and dipped her head to the side. "Hey, I didn't say anything."

"And I appreciate that. Do you remember Andre?"

"Whew, chile, fine ass Andre, the basketball player? The one you were crushin' on so hard, I thought you were going to break a tooth? That Andre?"

Nichelle rolled her eyes. "Yeah, that one."

"What about him?"

"I just knew we were going to get married, have two point five kids, and grow old together."

Amanda tilted her head and scratched the back of ear, avoiding Nichelle's gaze. "Really?"

"Yeah, really. We studied together, ate together, hooped." She shrugged and shook her head. "And sex. Hooboy, the sex was otherworldly. I thought I'd found my soul mate."

"But—"

"I know, Amanda. I wasn't the only one he was doing all that with. He was shocked when I got in my feelings after I saw him hugged up with Stephanie in the student center."

They both took sips of their wine.

Nichelle looked down at her plate. Thankfully her memories hadn't affected her appetite. "Anyway, I was so sure about him. He wasn't the first either. What if I'm wrong about Clark?"

"There's only one way to find out."

Amanda had a point. She'd assumed one time too many. But they'd only started hanging out. Would she run him off for sure with such a heavy conversation? She picked her glass up again, swallowing a sizable gulp. "What's for dessert?"

IT WAS DIFFICULT to concentrate with the breezy warmth blowing through Nichelle's hair. Not for the first time, she looked up at the cloudless sky and momentarily closed her eyes. Perhaps meeting Franny outside on the grass wasn't her best idea. Nichelle had a list of tasks a mile long but found doing anything other than soaking up vitamin D right now a waste of time. She probably should have scheduled the time in her office.

The political science department was nearly empty, not unusual for a Friday afternoon. Especially in the summer. Jamie was teaching for the second summer term, but not the first so the office was all Nichelle's for the next four weeks. She didn't normally conduct sorority business there though so chose to meet Francesca outside.

Thankfully, the other Professor Sampson wasn't around either. He must have headed home for the weekend. Although she'd texted her mother since being back, she hadn't talked to either of her parents. The rawness of finding out she was adopted the way she had was still rubbing against her nerves. The shock of discovering the ring's worth hadn't subsided either. She wanted to tell them, but she wasn't ready. Plus, there was plenty of work to do in putting all the pieces together first. She wanted her whole birth family stuff lined up before laying anything at the feet of her parents.

Her phone beeped, broadcasting five minutes before the hour, so Nichelle opened her laptop in preparation for her and Francesca to discuss the step show changes including one soror who hadn't kept her grades up so now couldn't participate. As president, it was Francesca's responsibility to stay on top of any offenders, but as graduate advisor, it was up to Nichelle to offer advice on how to enforce the rules.

Francesca plopped down on the grass across from Nichelle right on time. "Hi, Soror Nichelle." She looked around quickly. "Sorry, I mean Professor Sampson."

It was a blurry line between sorority activities and academic ones, and since Nichelle didn't have any of her younger sorors in class, she allowed them the sisterly moniker. If she were to have one of her sorors in class, that would be different. So far, it hadn't been an issue. "It's okay. We're alone out here mostly." The closest person was walking down the path leading to one of the dining halls.

Francesca sat her backpack behind her and leaned back.

Nichelle took a deep breath. "As I mentioned in my text, there is a soror who has not met the minimum grade requirements. I've emailed her and asked she request her transcript and have it sent to you and Soror Trina. As membership chair, she'll need to be involved in this as well. She went back home to Boston for the summer, so you'll have to coordinate long-distance. By all rights, we should all be off from the usual sorority duties for the summer, but if we don't jump on this right away, you'll lose your vice president in the Fall. Not a great start to your senior year."

The way Francesca angled her lips to the side beamed everything Nichelle needed to know about Francesca's feeling on the subject. "I understand. I just wish she said something. We could have helped. What's the point of being in a sisterhood if you don't rely on your sisters?"

She had a great point, but sometimes it took time to develop that instinct. There wasn't anywhere Nichelle could go where a soror wouldn't lend a hand if she were in need. Matter-of-fact, she should have thought of that when they were traveling through Barstow. But then the closeness with Clark may have never happened. She admonished herself for thinking of Clark while his sister sat right across from her. Nichelle promised herself she wouldn't let Clark-laced thoughts occupy space in her head while conducting sorority business with his sister. She didn't want to blur those lines. "She should have, but hopefully this will be a lesson. We'll help her every way we can. So, here's what I've come up with."

Nichelle spun her laptop around so Francesca could see the screen and showed her soror how they'd get their sister back on track. "She'll utilize the tutoring services and need to bring you weekly progress reports. That's for first summer term and second."

Francesca checked her watch. "Thank you, Soror Nichelle. I'll email her when I get home. Can we reschedule to talk about the step show? I need to meet my counselor."

"Of course. Matter-of-fact, I'll type up my notes and email them to you."

She picked up her backpack and stood but didn't leave. "Clark's been MIA since he's been back. How'd everything go on your trip?"

Nichelle froze, unsure how to respond. It wasn't her place to say anything. "Um. Yeah, it was fine. We discovered the origins of the ring and now I just need to do some research."

Francesca stared at Nichelle, her brows drawn together with a deep crease separating them. "What did he do?"

Talking about something like this was not a good idea. Nichelle hoped to look neutral when she told Francesca about the trip. She kept it to the ring because that was the whole purpose of going. Falling for Clark was not part of the plan. Judging from the look on Francesca's face, and the question she asked, Nichelle hadn't done a great job at being objective. "Nothing. He didn't do anything. And it's inappropriate for me to discuss what happened with you."

"OMG, what happened?" She tucked a wisp of hair behind her ear and bit the inside of her lip. The gesture reminded Nichelle so much of Clark, a spark dug into her chest. "You understand he's a total introvert, right? He's literally never around people. Okay, maybe not literally, but hardly ever around people. Sometimes he comes across a little cold, and maybe a bit of a know-it-all, but he has a very good heart. I was hoping you two would hit it off."

Mortification grabbed Nichelle's throat, choking her. Was Francesca really trying to set her up with Clark? Is that why she introduced them? "I-I thought you said he could help me. That's why you wanted me to meet him."

"Well, yeah. At first. But when you two met at the store, and you had heart-eyes, I was thinking…or at least hoping, that you'd get along. Maybe be a thing."

"I did not have heart-eyes. I don't ever have heart-eyes."

Francesca snorted, then slapped her hand across her mouth. "Sorry."

"He was helping me find the origins of my ring."

She shrugged. "Yeah, okay. If you say so. You don't have to tell me. Clark doesn't keep anything from me, so I'll know how he screwed everything up soon enough. It's a shame because you two would have been great together." She pointed one delicate, polish-covered fingernail at her nose. "I have a nose for these things. Anyway, I'll get on this other stuff. Thanks, Soror."

Nichelle stood as Francesca walked off down the trail. To say she was stunned into silence would have been an understatement. She sunk back onto the grass and blinked. The girl saw right through her. She wanted Clark desperately, probably since she'd laid eyes on him, and she hadn't been able to hide it.

CHAPTER SIXTEEN

Nichelle

*W*HERE THE HELL *are you?* Nichelle blew out a frustrated breath, and created another box with a last name, but no first name. She estimated the year of birth as twenty years younger than his possible father. Completing a family tree with so little information was maddening. It was difficult enough when she knew where to start as she did with the Sampson family tree. Creating one from scratch with a possible however-many-times great-grandmother was proving impossible.

It was still early Saturday morning, but she couldn't sleep in with thoughts of unknown ancestors running through her mind. Between that and thoughts of Clark, she hadn't slept well all night actually, so she finally gave up and tried to occupy her brain with some family tree research until a decent enough time to call Clark. Since he was an early riser, she called him instead of texting. He answered on the first ring. "Hi." His voice was scratchy with sleep.

Maybe early was all about perspective. "Good morning.

You're still asleep?"

There was shuffling on his end, and he cleared his throat. "No, I'm awake. I haven't used my voice yet."

"What time do you have to leave to meet your bike club?"

He blew a small breath into the phone. "Cycling group. I have two hours yet. Are you busy later?"

"Busy like…you want to come over?"

"Or you could come here. Either way. Or we could go out. Besides playing basketball, what else would you want to do?"

His rambling was cute, and Nichelle grinned. "I'm not busy. Just trying to build a family tree from a single name. It's not going well."

"Can I help with anything? Other than researching the man who originally owned the ring. Which I haven't had time to do yet." He let out a whisper of a laugh. "I suppose I should start there."

"Take your time. I know you have other stuff to do." As much as she wanted to be his priority, it wasn't fair to expect that after only knowing her a couple weeks. "In the meantime, I paid extra to access international documents since we know the ring originated in Jamaica, but there isn't a whole lot to go on even with the additional permissions. Birth and marriage records are scarce, especially for recently released slaves."

"I'm sorry, Nichelle. And you can't be certain your ancestor was even married. She'd been the original owner's mistress according to Charles, but what does that mean exactly? Had he been her master?"

She closed her laptop and put the phone on speaker, then rubbed her temples. "Who knows. Without my DNA matches, this is getting me nowhere." She plodded over to an open window and shut it. There was some unseasonably cold air blowing in off the Bay, and it was downright cold in her apartment. She was used to that at night, but in the daytime, it was normally milder. "So later...do you just want to go somewhere? I wouldn't mind relaxing here."

"That's my preference as well. Should I bring dinner with me?"

"That would be excellent. Seven okay?"

"See you then."

"I'm really looking forward to it." She pulled the throw blanket around her shoulders as she plopped back down on the couch, then picked up her cell phone from the table and checked the time. Still too early to call, but she shot off a text. Her father would be up in the next half hour, in his office with his first cup of coffee of the day. Her mother, despite the recent dust-up of the court case, had already learned the beauty of sleeping in. She had really never wanted to get up early but did it out of necessity for her job. Nichelle would go over and talk to her father and finish before her mother woke up. Nichelle knew it was wrong, but she somehow blamed her mother more than her father. She just did.

The shower was just hot enough to knock the chill off her body, and by the time she dressed, a reply text came.

Dad: *Come on over. Your mother spent the night at Aunt Blink's.*

AUNT BLINK WAS her mother's widowed sister. Blink was a nickname, but Nichelle was an adult before she realized her aunt's actual name was Gwendolyn. Her husband died over a year before, but sometimes the sisters engaged in weekend sleepovers comforting each other over their shared grief. They had two other sisters, but both lived back in Texas. Aunt Blink birthed five children as well, but Nichelle guessed there was nothing like a sister's love and comfort. Nichelle could only guess though because even though she always wished for a sister, she didn't have one. Amanda was the closest she would get.

Of course her dad knew why she was hesitant to visit. It was like that with them. He enjoyed a special intuitive nature with his daughter, and Nichelle always thought it was biological. Turns out, maybe that's just the kind of guy her father was.

This time when Nichelle arrived at the house she grew

up in, she used her key to the front door. As expected, her father was sitting behind his desk in the study, a steaming mug nearby. "Hey, darling."

"Hi, Dad." Nichelle gave him a peck on the forehead and made her way back to the kitchen for coffee. He'd made a full carafe, so she poured herself a cup from the French press. She glanced around the kitchen. There was a framed picture on the wall next to the refrigerator—Nichelle's first fingerpainting attempt in kindergarten. If she walked through the house, there would be other reminders of her childhood. Although there were plenty of reminders of her brother—mostly photos and awards from work—there weren't the trinkets of childhood. It's almost like he plopped into her parents lives full grown. Nichelle wasn't sure if there was anything questionable going on, and it could just be that he grew up before widespread camera usage, but with her own parentage under question, she didn't trust her parents from keeping something from her.

She shook the feeling and headed back to the study. She'd specifically chosen this time to stay away from too much family drama. She wanted to pick her father's brain about her adoption. Surely her father knew something of her birth parents. Without her mother around, maybe he'd be willing to share.

The soft leather of the couch always reminded Nichelle of happy times. The last instance of her sitting there, she'd been upset with both her mother and father. There'd been a soft confrontation, but Nichelle held most of her fury inside. This time when she sunk into the couch's leathery depths, she wasn't angry, only confused. And curious. There was a whole other family out there in the world, and she wanted to know about them. "How are you, Dad?"

"I'm fine. How about you? I hear you were out of town."

"I'm okay. Yeah, I went down to Texas to a rare jewel collector. He moves around the world, from auction to auction, and was in Dallas for their big one." She wasn't ready to tell him the full extent of what she found out about the ring, especially that it was worth a grip, but this was a good entry into one of the conversations she wanted to have. "He told me the ring originated in Jamaica sometime around the middle of the nineteenth century."

Robert's eyebrows crawled up his forehead. "Really? That's fascinating." Although her father was a political science professor, he loved history too. This was catnip for him, as Nichelle knew it would be. He put his glasses on and peered at her. "Do you have the ring with you? I'd love to take a look."

"No, but I'll bring it next time. The story is that a man reported it stolen because he'd given it to his Black mistress behind his wife's back. I'm not sure where it went from there, but according to the note that came with it, it passed down through the family." Nichelle still struggled saying words like *grandmother* or *her family* in front of her adoptive parents. Wanting to embrace her birth family felt like a betrayal. Her father would understand that.

"Interesting indeed."

"What do you know, Dad?"

He took a sip of his coffee and sat back in his chair, then took the glasses off. "It's been so long, but we received a birth report with your adoption. Your mother says she doesn't know where it is, so I can only give you whatever details I remember. Even those can't be a hundred percent trusted because like I said, it's been so long."

"Yeah, I know. Thirty-two years ago." Her entire life ago.

"Right. From what I can remember, your birth mother was eighteen when she gave birth to you, short-ish, blond, and blue-eyed. And your fa—"

"Hold up a minute. What do you mean, blond and blue-eyed?"

He shifted in his seat and set the cup of coffee back on his desk. "Yes, I believe she was white, and your birth father was Black, and tall. About six-two if memory serves. There were some details about how they met, but I can't remember, maybe through a mutual friend. Also, references to your grandparents, aunts and uncles, and such, but I only remember your grandfather was blind. There was an accident with an arrow as a child."

"I, uh." Nichelle shivered with shock. She went from being Black to...well, she was still Black as far as she was concerned, but all of a sudden had a white parent. What a mind-fuck. Tears pricked the back of her eyes, but she blinked them down. "Wow. That's a lot to take in."

"I know, honey, but you're still our daughter, no matter what, and we love you."

She knew he meant well, and that it was true, but declarations of love didn't erase the pain of their lying for thirty years. Her entire identity was at question now. She thought about Clark and how he had a white mother too, grew up with her and his Dutch grandparents. What did he think about his identity? Francesca too. Other than they both wanted to discover more about their Chinese heritage. Thinking about the Lin-Lees probably wasn't the most productive right now. She could go down a Clark-shaped rabbit hole for hours.

"Thanks, Dad. I know, but it doesn't hurt less."

Neither of them looked at the other, but sat there silently, both absorbing her painful words.

She took a sip of her cold coffee. "Ugh, I'll be back. I need to nuke my coffee. Do you want some more or anything from the kitchen?"

He shook his head but still didn't meet her gaze.

When she returned, she was still shook but ready for a subject change. She'd get all the details whenever her birth report came in the mail. "So, what's been going on in the department while I was gone?"

They spoke for an hour about office politics and upcoming class loads. Nichelle got lost in the ease of conversation with her father, birth parents temporarily forgotten.

CHAPTER SEVENTEEN

Clark

"SHE SEEMS DEPRESSED. You should call her."

Clark glared at his sister and set down the sample he was about to analyze, reworking and reviewing his report. He'd been ready to testify the day before, but by the time Nichelle dropped him off at the store, the prosecutor informed him there was a continuance in the case and he wouldn't be needed to testify for another month. This threw a considerably large wrench in his consideration concerning Nichelle and their possible relationship. It would be unprofessional enough to give Nichelle confidential information the eve before he was set to testify. Giving it to her a month before was unconscionable. He wouldn't ask her to keep something like that from her mother either. It wouldn't be fair to her, considering everything else she was going through with her parents.

There was no easy way out of his predicament. He couldn't tell her. But he couldn't stay away from her either.

"I assume you're referring to Nichelle. Why would she be

depressed? She seemed fine when I spoke with her earlier this morning."

Franny's eyes widened to the size of basketballs.

Clark withheld a smile. Nichelle's lexicon was seeping into his consciousness.

"You talked to her? Spill."

"You first. Answer my question."

She bit the inside corner of her lip, reminding him of their mother.

His chest tightened a bit.

"When I met with her yesterday, she wasn't her normal, cheerful self."

"Maybe the nature of your meeting was at fault. She wasn't pleased your sorority sister wasn't forthcoming about her grades."

"You know about that?"

Clark thought for a moment. Nichelle hadn't mentioned she was revealing confidential information. "Yes."

She tapped a finger on her chin and grinned. "Then I asked about the trip, and she sputtered. I thought you'd done something because…" She shrugged, a mixture of guilt and delight alighting her features. "You normally do something. But I see where I went wrong. She was nervous that you'd done something really right." She clapped her hands and grinned like a possum.

Leaning against the counter, Clark fortified himself for the onslaught.

"I knew it! You like each other. I was totally right. When are you seeing her again? Is she your girlfriend now? Do you think you'll get married? Oh, did you—" She scrunched her nose. "Do it?"

The bright room tilted and dimmed. Clark grabbed hold of the counter and blinked away the vertigo. Did his baby sister just ask him if he had relations with her graduate advisor? "That is extremely inappropriate, Franny."

"That's not a no."

"She's not my girlfriend. We're still getting to know each other." The familiar stone that set up residence in Clark's chest made itself known. He was deceitful, and desiring everything from Nichelle before his duplicity became known was wrong. Yet, he couldn't seem to stop himself from wanting her.

Franny tilted her head, studying her brother. "You want her, but there's something wrong."

"Yes."

"What, Clark?"

Keeping information from Franny wasn't something Clark made a habit of doing. "I wish I could tell you, but it's work-related. I have a severe conflict of interest. That's all I can say." Franny wouldn't push him. She understood more than anyone else how important Clark's integrity in his chosen profession was to him.

She nodded but sighed. "Okay. I trust you know what you're doing. If it helps, I've never seen her hold a grudge against anyone. She'll understand once you're able to explain it to her."

Was that hope blooming in Clark's chest, squeezing that stone out? "Thanks."

Franny kissed his temple and walked from his lab toward the main showroom.

Clark gathered everything he'd been working on and secured the samples in their respective specimen trays. When his work area was back to normal, meaning totally cleared of anything other than the equipment that was usually housed there, he washed his hands in one of the two sinks. He allowed the water to warm his hands that somehow had become like a block of ice. Closing his eyes allowed him to listen to the running water, which calmed him. If only it was as easy to wash his troubles down the sink.

CLARK DID SOME research on Nichelle's ring as he promised and was in possession of the man's name who reported it stolen, but he wasn't sure how that would help her. He set the box of Chinese food on the ground and pulled the sticky note with the man's name written on it out of his pocket and knocked on Nichelle's second-floor apartment door. From what he could tell, it was a small complex with just the one building. There were shady trees and flowers still in bloom decorating the grounds, the stairwell leading up to her apartment nearly hidden. She lived only a quick fifteen-minute bike ride away, but since he needed to pick up the food, he drove. She was so close; next time he would take his bike.

Nichelle greeted him with a bright smile and open arms. "Hi there, handsome."

The trepidation of her referencing his physicality was quickly replaced with the undiluted joy of seeing her again. It had only been a couple days but felt more like a week. He stepped into her waiting arms and circled her body with his own. Her soft body curved into his. Clark closed his eyes and breathed in her potent burnt vanilla fragrance. "I missed you."

She stepped back, much too soon for Clark's preference, and looked him in the eyes, her voice a soft murmur. "I missed you too." She grinned and stood aside, sweeping her hand toward the living room. "Come on in. Food smells good, and I'm starving."

Her apartment was small, but neat and homey. Her touches were all over it, from her navy blue and silver sorority colors accenting the living space to the jumbled papers and books lining the dining room table. This would drive Clark to drink, but Nichelle thrived in the chaos. He set the box of food in her kitchen which appeared much neater. "Nice place."

"Thanks." Nichelle opened cabinets, rummaging around. She was barefoot, wearing a thin sleeveless sundress. "You can wash your hands in the powder room, down the hall to the right."

Clark did as instructed, and when he returned, Nichelle cleared the clutter from the dining room table and replaced it with two plates of piping hot pan-seared Sichuan shrimp with mung bean noodles, and crab soup dumplings. Next to the plates were two Heinekens. "No Shiner Bock I'm afraid."

"That would have been quite a feat. Heineken is a good substitute though."

She sat and motioned for him to do the same.

While Nichelle's head was bent in prayer, he checked her out. He wasn't sure he agreed with his sister's initial assessment, but there was definitely a difference in Nichelle's demeanor. Her normally vibrant personality was dimmed, but not muted. She looked up in time to catch him staring and raised her brows. "What?"

"How are you?"

"I'm good. This looks fantastic. Let's enjoy our meal."

Clearly there was something on Nichelle's mind, but Clark wouldn't push. She'd share when she was ready, and honestly, he wanted to enjoy this time together back in the real world. He ate his food, stealing glances between forkfuls. Then he remembered the sticky note. "I almost forgot. I found the name of the man who originally owned the ring. I must have left it in the box I brought in."

"That's fantastic, Clark. I saw it. I wondered whose name it was."

"I hope it'll help you."

She frowned and slow-blinked.

Was she about to cry? "Nichelle?"

"I just feel…" She took a deep breath, then a gulp of her beer. "I'm frustrated, I guess." She lifted her shoulders somewhere around her ears, then let them drop.

Clark wasn't sure what to say so he nodded and continued eating. When they finished, he reached for their plates and placed them in the kitchen sink.

Nichelle called from the other room. "I'll get those later. Come sit with me." She moved over to the sofa in the living room and patted the seat next to her.

He sat and looked her in the eye, searching for clues to what was really bothering her. Had she changed her mind about him, and was having trouble telling him? Or found out about his deception? "I really like you."

She smiled, the softness in her eyes giving him some relief. Then she rested her head on his shoulder. "I really like you too."

He nodded. "I'm glad." If their relationship status wasn't bothering her, then it must be her family. "How is everything else? No luck on your birth family yet?"

"Nah. I'd hoped when I started on the new family tree, I'd have better luck now that I have my ancestor's name. Maybe adding the ring owner's name will help, although I have no idea if he is in my lineage. Oh, and my DNA matches came back after I spoke with you this morning, but the closest matches are a second cousin and a third cousin. Loads of fourth cousins, but those don't help at all. I've been building trees for those close matches, but so far I haven't been able to connect the two sides."

"How can you tell they're on two different sides?"

"Oh, that's right, I haven't talked to you. My father gave me some birth info that was confirmed by my DNA. Turns out my birth father is Black, but my birth mother is half European Jewish and…drum roll, please. Half Dutch." She shrugged.

"Wow, really? Wouldn't that be funny if we were actually related?"

She bugged her eyes at him, and deadpanned, "Sure. Hilarious."

"No, you're right. I saw the error of that question too late. That would definitely not be funny."

"Nope, not even a little bit."

"How do you feel? I mean, about your birth mother."

She pulled a throw blanket from the arm of the sofa into her lap, and picked at the fringe edges, tears welling in her eyes again. "It's strange, I guess. My identity already took a huge hit with the whole adoption thing. Now, I just don't know who I am anymore."

"Totally understandable. Do you think finding your birth family will help?"

The huff that exploded from her throat ghosted across Clark's face. "I feel like that's a moot question. I'm not getting anywhere. I even received my birth report, but without knowing who these people are, it's just meaningless words on a page. Sure, I have their medical history from thirty years ago. They were eighteen and twenty-one when I was born. Of course, it's not a surprise they were healthy then."

Clark nodded. He was riddled with his own family issues, but he'd always known who he was even if his parents didn't necessarily like him.

A tear slipped from Nichelle's eye, and her gaze bore into Clark's. "What should I do next? Do you have any ideas?"

Clark gazed at the teary-eyed Nichelle and shuddered. He always procured the answers, but for once in his life he didn't have a clue what to do. Should he comfort her? Did she even need comfort? This is exactly why he stayed in his lab or hidden in the back of the jewelry store. Rocks and gems were always the same. But he'd come to care too much for Nichelle to ignore her, even if emotions made him uncomfortable. He opened his arms and she slid right into them. He wanted so much more from her, but in this instance, until she figured her family out, he was happy to at least give her this.

CHAPTER EIGHTEEN

Nichelle

N ICHELLE WAS SAD about her sudden lot in life, but that went right out the window as soon as Clark wrapped his arms around her. Now it was all about Clark and her growing feelings for him. She turned in his arms and slid her fingers into his glossy hair. "Do you want to kiss me?"

He nodded and dipped his head, covering her mouth with his. His lips were as silken as his hair, but firm as they pressed against hers. He sighed against her mouth, and she understood completely. Over the past couple weeks, she'd come to realize what his different sighs meant. Although she hadn't heard this one before, there was no doubt in her mind it represented contentment. She parted her lips to let him inside. Kissing Clark was calm, and tender, and everything she thought it would be. It was sexy too, and heat spread across her skin as they deepened the kiss.

He pulled back and looked at her. The heat in his eyes conveyed his intentions. "Is this still okay?"

"It's more than okay. I never want you to stop kissing

me."

He smiled against her mouth before parting her lips with his tongue.

Nichelle stroked his firm chest, then ran her hands around his neck and down his shoulders. He was so strong, and she could imagine how many push-ups he did in his life considering how tightly he was strung. She didn't want to think about that though.

Clark matched her movements, rubbing her shoulders and back, then cupping her waist in sure hands. "Still okay?"

"Yes. You can grab my ass if you want." She let out a soft laugh, but he caught the sound in his mouth.

Then he grabbed her ass. He really grabbed it, squeezing and spreading her cheeks through her panties. Okay, so this was happening. Their actions didn't seem calm anymore. If he felt anything like the urgency of the blood rushing through her veins, then he would be inside her in five point two seconds.

He wasn't though, and she wasn't sure she could stand it any longer. She moved closer to him, pressing her breasts against his solid chest. The move put her in direct contact with his firm dick through his trousers. It pressed against her stomach, and she moved into his lap, grinding against his hardness. Her breath came quicker as they rocked against each other.

"Clark."

He kissed down her neck, moving to her breasts through

the thin sundress. "Yes? Are you okay? Do you want to stop?"

"No, but do you want to move to my bedroom?"

He stilled, and the groan that escaped his lips against her chest was unmistakable. "I can't. Not yet."

She pulled back, placing the palm of her hand against his chest, staring into his eyes. "Not yet?" His hesitation was a gut punch to her fragile self-esteem.

"I mean intercourse."

"Yes, Clark, I'm getting the gist of what you're saying. What I'm wondering is why are you saying it?" She scooted off him, and back onto the couch, but he didn't move his hands from her.

His eyes were tight, his expression pained. "I need to figure out some things first. I told you how complicated work is for me right now."

"Right, and for some unknown reason, you can't share it with me."

He sighed, long and deep. "There are issues about my work I want more than anything to share with you, but it's morally impossible at the moment. Until I can be completely open, it would be unethical for me to have intercourse with you."

Nichelle shuddered at Clark's words. It all sounded so clinical, not to mention mysterious. Why would his work have anything to do with them having sex? Something in the back of her mind niggled her, but she couldn't quite grasp it.

"So, for the next month, we can't have any physical contact?"

Clark was quiet, his skin hot where it touched hers. He bit the side of his lip and looked at her under hooded eyes. "I didn't say that exactly." He grabbed her waist again, pulling her on top of him.

She went gladly, forgetting completely about his reluctance, positioning her panty-covered slit against the hardness of his covered dick. She bent down to kiss him again and rode him with a slow pace. Sparks flew where they connected through their clothed bodies. Nichelle broke the kiss, gasping for breath. Clark kissed down her neck and across her shoulders. She pulled her sleeveless dress down to give him access, and he kissed the tops of her breasts. He laved one nipple at a time while he guided her movements with his hands on her hips, speeding the pace. She reached between them and touched her clit through her underwear, and that was all she wrote. Her orgasm tugged at her stomach then tore through her. He held onto her hips with great strength while she pressed into him hard, prolonging her pleasure.

After collapsing on his chest, she reached down between them again, placing her hand inside his pants and tugging his hard length from his boxers.

He breathed hard against her ear. "You don't have to."

"I know. I want to." She stroked him slowly at first, then with more urgency as he pumped into her hand.

"Oh my—Nichelle, it's—" He gasped, and his head lifted from the couch, burrowing into Nichelle's breasts as he came.

She rolled off him but stayed pressed into his side. "Oops, I'm not sure if that was inbounds."

Clark chuckled and sighed. "I'm not sure, but completely worth it."

"Yeah, it was." Nichelle's breathing returned to normal, but her skin was still flushed with pleasure. And contentment. She didn't want this night to end, but she didn't want to push Clark either. He'd set up clear boundaries.

He adjusted himself back into his trousers but held his shirt up. "I think I need to clean up."

There was an immediate coolness when Clark moved, and Nichelle's insecurities came rushing back. But then Clark turned to her and held his hand out. "Shall we?"

She grinned and eased herself off the couch, holding onto Clark's hand. She needed to get over herself. They were going to work fine. Clark was a sweet guy and straightforward, completely trustworthy. They definitely could build from there.

THE FIRST GOLDEN streaks shredded the gunmetal sky as Nichelle sat on the wooden bench on her balcony, sipping the latte she made herself. She hadn't intended to wake up so early, but she'd been having trouble sleeping in the past couple of mornings. She was only teaching one class for the summer and wanted to take advantage of not having to wake early. The class didn't start until noon and lasted all afternoon. She and Clark had cuddled on the couch until late into the night, talking about her family stuff. He'd left when she began to nod off.

She kept a set of tray tables in the storage closet on the porch, so she removed one and set her laptop on it. There'd been no movement on the whole finding-her-birth-family front. She clicked over to the genealogy site on the off chance there'd be a closer match than the second cousin she'd already matched up with. The thought of digging back into her genealogy had Nichelle setting her laptop aside and making another cup of coffee.

Maybe a madeleine would help her through her morning. She shrugged and took one out of the package she'd picked up the day before from the bakery just on the other side of the border in Oakland. Then again, two would be even better. She placed them on a saucer and balanced it on top of her refreshed latte while sliding the door open with her hip. She savored the rich lemony petite cakes and sipped her coffee, looking over the surrounding area. She was on the second floor but couldn't see as much of the city as she'd like because of the thick trees covering the property. The air was cool, but comfortable which she also relished along with her pastries. She preferred fresh air to air conditioning any day of the week. That reminded her of the drive down to Texas. She'd hoped to let the wind flow through her hair, but Clark and his many hang-ups couldn't bear it. She smiled to herself. Why did all her thoughts circle back to Clark, even when he was being ridiculous?

She made another run at the genealogy page. To her utter surprise, there was a new match. Another second-cousin male, twenty years older than her, but he appeared in the list above the first match. That meant he was a closer match.

Her workspace became too cluttered, so she cleared it of the half-drunk coffee and the fully empty saucer and got down to business. Working with the new information would take a little time, and currently, time was not a surplus. She still had a couple of hours before needing to ready herself for class though.

An interesting tidbit about this match was that he was mostly Dutch and English. Her other second-cousin match was a hundred percent European Jewish. That meant this was truly a brand-new clue in the grand scheme of things. Where these two cousins met would be her grandparents. She was so excited, she picked up her phone and texted Clark without thinking about how early it was.

Her cell phone lit up with an incoming call. There was no need to look to figure out who was calling. But she was on a roll and didn't want to stop her research. He was probably only calling to share her excitement of finding the new match. She could talk with him about it later. She ignored the call and kept reviewing hints and connecting family boxes. A cloud passed in front of the steadily rising sun and temporarily darkened the sky. The light from her cell beamed up into her face, pulsing as if broadcasting *answer me, answer me.* Fine, she'd answer. "Hi, Clark."

"Hi. You're up really early."

Thanks, Captain Obvious. "Yup."

"I'm excited for you. Do you mind if I come around before my ride to see what you're doing? I only have a few minutes."

A grin split her face. Even though she didn't want to break her research, she wouldn't give up a chance to spend a little time with Clark before he set off on his cycling journey. "Sure, I'll unlock the front door. I'm out on the balcony."

This was becoming a problem. She woke up with Clark on her mind, and he never strayed far from her thoughts until she laid her head on the pillow at night. She needed to remember to keep balance in her life. She put everything into her career and could be single-minded. Now wasn't the time to trade one obsession for another.

After she unlocked the front door, she went into her bathroom to check out her appearance. She wasn't completely happy with who stared back, so she jerked a brush through her curls and tied them up in a high ponytail. Then she ran into her closet and threw off her ratty sweats and tank top and slid on a green sundress. She slipped on a pair of thongs and ran back out to the patio.

She'd barely caught her breath when Clark opened the sliding-glass door. "Hi."

"Hi, yourself." She moved the cup and saucer to the concrete floor beneath her bench. "Have a seat."

He stood next to her, bent at the waist, and stared at the open laptop. "So that's the new cousin?"

"Ummm hmmm." She couldn't put a coherent sentence together with his biking shorts hugging his taut ass practically in her face. She'd had her hands on that butt just the night before and planned to again very soon. After giving herself a bit of a shake, she tried again. "Yeah, that's him. You can sit."

He turned and looked down at her. "Sure. Just for a minute though. I'm meeting the club in…" He checked the watch on his wrist—one he'd never worn before as far as she knew—and squinted. "About twenty minutes. I have a little more time than I thought. I got to your place fast."

She knew they didn't live very far from each other. He'd mentioned last night. "How far are you going today?"

"Not sure. I'll find out when we meet up."

"Seriously? There's no way I could start out exercising without knowing the what's what."

Clark grunted. "We've somehow switched places."

Nichelle groaned. "You're right. What's happening?"

He sat down and pressed a loving kiss on Nichelle's lips before turning his attention back to her laptop screen. "How long before you crack the code?"

She clicked a couple more hints and added another link, then stared at the tree laid out before her. Something wasn't right. "I should be able to link the two families together on my mother's side, but something's missing."

Clark studied the tree, and after a few minutes, pointed at a box with a woman's name. "Why is her surname the same as her husband's? Didn't you say maiden names were needed?"

"I did say that." He was right, of course. Nichelle opened the box and read through the life events attached to the woman's profile. For some reason, Nichelle kept Perkins as the woman's surname when it should have been Berger. "Oh my God. How could I make such a huge mistake? I coulda been figuring this out." Berger was the original last name of the first match she'd received. At some point down the family line, his father or grandfather changed their name to be more anglicized. That was the original wrench in Nichelle's research.

A couple more clicks and she was staring at her grandparents. She moved down to their children—two sons and one daughter. That daughter was no doubt her mother. "My birth mother's name is Anika Perkins." Why did that name sound familiar?

Clark stood up, eyes wide. "Nichelle! You found your birth mother."

She was numb. Her feet sunk through the concrete and settled there. Her sundress billowed around her legs with the breeze that slowly turned warmer. And still she stared at her computer.

Clark cupped her cheek. "Nichelle? Are you okay?"

The tear that slipped down her face surprised her.

With a light touch, Clark wiped it away.

It was only a name on the screen. There were hundreds of people on this tree. Many weren't related to her, just rabbit holes she'd gone down, but many were, and most had pictures attached to their profile. Little thumbnail faces taunting her. Her mother didn't have a face though. One of her uncles did, and so did her grandparents. Her uncle was blond with a friendly smile. Her grandparents' picture was one where they'd posed together. She clicked on the picture and stared at it. Her grandfather was so much taller than her grandmother, his arm circled her shoulders. Both of her arms wrapped around his waist, a huge smile on her face. He was blond, but her hair was dark. He offered a small smile to the camera and was staring right into the lens. He was blind so maybe that was a key to his disposition. "I'm...okay-ish, I guess. It's very surreal."

He sat back next to her and placed his arm around her shoulder. "I bet. This is great though, right? You finally have a name."

She nodded and leaned into him. Yeah, it was great, but also complicated. And even though she only had a third cousin match on her father's side, she'd narrowed it down considerably after getting her birth report. She needed to do a little social media stalking when her class was over, and she'd probably have him too by the end of the day. She always knew she was close on her father, but for some reason, she wanted to identify her mother first. It was unreasonable, and she couldn't put a voice to why, but that's how she'd felt. Now that she knew, what was she going to do about it?

CHAPTER NINETEEN

Nichelle

W HEN NICHELLE FINALLY placed the letters in the mailbox, her skin numb and her senses dazed, she stepped back, scanning her surroundings with wild eyes. Other patrons were milling around handling their postage needs, not paying an ounce of attention to her. She'd made up her mind she wanted to pursue relationships with her birth parents, but the cold reality of actually initiating contact with no way of taking it back was chilling.

"Are you okay?" Clark put a comforting arm around her shoulder, pulling her into his chest.

Her birth father was named Henry Maddox. She'd traced him back to her three times great-grandmother, Henrietta Abernathy. Henry's mother, Florence Bottoms, was the one who recently died and left her the extremely expensive ring. She wondered if Henry would ask her for it back. And if he did, what would Nichelle say? How would she feel?

"Yeah. I mean, I'll be okay when those things get delivered." She wrapped an arm around his waist as they exited the post office. "Thanks for coming with me. I definitely needed the moral support."

He kissed her temple quickly before opening the door to her car. He biked over when Nichelle called him, shivering in the parking lot. "I've got to get to the store, but I'll see you later after your class, right?"

Nichelle grinned. "Sure will. Do you want me to pick you up?"

His shoulders rose as if starting a sigh, but he caught himself and let out an unhappy chuckle. "Looks like I'll be riding with Franny directly from the store."

She laughed, but before getting in her car, she reached for Clark's hand, and pulled him near. "Kiss me."

He gave her a peck and looked around.

"Are you embarrassed to kiss me, Clark?" She reddened as her old insecurities came rushing back.

He frowned, then bent down, circling his hand around the nape of her neck. He was close enough his breath ghosted against her lips. "I'm honored to kiss you." Then he did just that, full on the mouth, tracing the seam of her lips with his tongue until she parted them reflexively. She lost herself in that kiss, in Clark, for just a moment. Birth parents faded from her consciousness. There was only Clark, tasting of cinnamon gum, and feeling like home.

She broke the kiss and inhaled deeply. "That was nice."

The corner of his mouth may or may not have angled up just slightly. "I'll see you later."

The car door was already open, so she slid behind the wheel and fastened her seatbelt, all the while watching Clark while he put his helmet and pads on, taut muscles in his butt and thighs on full display underneath his pants.

When Clark mounted his bike, he turned back to Nichelle and waved before pedaling off.

She sat in her car a few minutes and thought about those letters she'd just dropped in the box. Both were addressed locally. She put her return address on them after some serious thought. When her birth parents received her letter with apartment number two-one-four in the return address, would that scream loser? She was still single, and never had a serious boyfriend. She hoped that would change with Clark, but they hadn't made any declarations. They'd only just met. Plus, she still lived in a one-bedroom apartment because… Well, where else would she live by herself? Buying a house wasn't impossible, but it hadn't been on the top of her list.

She was still the youngest to achieve what she had in their department, advanced degree included. No, she was accomplished on the career front. It was the rest of her life that had her rethinking.

The only thing left to do was wait. That was truly going to be the hardest part.

She drove to her building's parking lot and walked to her office, taking the flight of stairs up to the office she shared with Jamie, and put her purse in the bottom drawer of her desk. She had some time before class started.

A rustle at the door caught her attention as Jamie struggled inside, hands full of books.

Nichelle jumped up to help. "Goodness, what's all this?"

"It was supposed to be assigned reading, but my class was canceled. Someone discovered mold in my classroom, and they have to move us somewhere else. That's two precious hours of a summer school day down the drain. Plus, I lugged all these books back."

"That's a shame." Nichelle stacked the rest of the books on the bureau behind Jamie's already full desk. "Mold is scary though. I hope they get it all."

"Same." When Jamie's hands were finally free, she gave Nichelle a quick hug. "You're here early."

"Yeah. I just dropped the letters in the mail."

"Eek. I can't believe you finally found them. This is so exciting. How do you feel? What's next? How many siblings did you say you have now?"

Nichelle laughed at her friend's barrage of questions. "Girl. I guess the next step is to wait and see if they contact me. As far as I could tell, I have two sisters on my father's side and two brothers on my mother's side." Her sisters were easy to figure out, but she couldn't find anything about her brothers based on their birth certificates of record. One was four years younger than Nichelle, and the other six. They had a common last name of Harris which made the search more difficult.

"I'm still going to work on figuring out my brothers, but

so far I've been flummoxed at every turn. Harris is such a common name." All she could hope for now was for her mother to contact her so she could meet them. Because that was the real thing for Nichelle—she had siblings and wanted to know them. How alike would they be? Would they get along and have stuff in common? She wanted to meet her birth parents, sure, but she really wanted to finally have the close family relationship with a brother or sister she didn't have with Clifton.

"Oh interesting."

"What?"

Jamie stacked the books on the desk into a box by her feet. "That's my husband's last name. Or it was."

"I thought his last name was Perkins, like yours."

"It is, but he changed his name when he was in college back to his mother's last name. Neither he nor Noah get along with their father, so they had enough of him by then."

The air in the room stilled suddenly and warmed considerably. It didn't matter though because Nichelle's arms sprouted goose bumps all over. She stared at Jamie with wide eyes.

Jamie stopped packing her box and sat up. "What?"

During Nichelle's research, she'd discovered her brothers' names on their birth certificates, but nothing else. They were Asaf and Noah Harris. Nichelle never met Jamie's husband, but of course she'd talked about him and her kids often. She called him Asa, but could that be a nickname?

Nichelle blew out a strained breath. "So, Noah's name was Noah Harris before he changed it to Noah Perkins, right?"

"Yeah."

"And your husband is Asa Perkins, formerly Asa Harris? Not Asaf Harris, right?"

"Nichelle." Jamie's hand flew to her open mouth.

"Oh my God. Are you saying his name is actually Asaf?"

She nodded, eyes so wide, Nichelle hoped she wouldn't burst a vessel.

"Your husband is my brother. Noah, the IT guy, is my brother?"

"Holy shit."

"Yeah, tell me about it."

"Wait, wait, wait." She stood up and placed a hand on her hip, waving the other one. "Anika is your actual mother? My mother-in-law, Anika? Holiest of shittest."

Nichelle couldn't do anything but nod her head. She thought back to the times she'd interacted with Noah. There weren't many, but she did feel like there was something familiar about him. Now, she knew what it was. "This is wild."

"Yeah, it is." She placed her hand back over her mouth and rubbed. "I have to call him."

"Wait."

"Why? Are kidding me? You're his sister. He has no idea he has a sister."

"Exactly. In those letters, I told both my parents I wouldn't interrupt their lives if they didn't want me invading their privacy. The fact that Asaf doesn't know he has a sister tells you something, right?"

"Maybe." She bit her lip, thinking. "Or maybe not. Maybe Asaf does know, but never mentioned it to me."

"How freakin' likely is that?"

"Not likely. You're right." She spun around, looking at the photos on her desk. "Now that I pay attention, you do have the same face structure."

Nichelle took a closer look at the photos of her possible brother. He was the opposite of Noah in every way, but they still looked very much alike. Noah was blond and blue-eyed, as their mother was listed on Nichelle's birth report. Asaf had black hair and dark brown eyes. He was taller than Jamie by a solid five or six inches so maybe about six feet, but Noah was only about five-ten, closer to Nichelle's height. She could see the similarities in face structure, just as Jamie mentioned, but little else. And that could only be wishful thinking.

Jamie barked a loud laugh.

"Jeesh, J. You scared me. What in the world is so funny?"

"I'm just thinking about my mother-in-law." She slapped her hand across her mouth again. "Oh my goodness, your mother. I'm not sure I'll ever get used to that. She is such an ostrich. This should be fun."

"Fun, sure. That's exactly what I was thinking. And by

ostrich, meaning she keeps her head in the…"

"Sand. Exactly. I bet Asaf has no idea about you."

"You know, technically that's a myth. About the ostriches." She remembered Clark mentioned that to her during their road trip.

Jamie walked over to Nichelle and put her arms around her. "I'm sorry, luv. I know this has got to be a shock for you. And here I am, joking about it."

"It's okay." Jamie was right though. Nichelle shook with adrenaline. This was not what she was expecting when she came on campus today. "I'm really nervous about this now."

"Yeah, I get it. But you know I can't keep this from my husband, right? A lie by omission is still a lie, and Asaf and I don't lie to each other."

Nichelle sat down hard, thinking back to the letter she'd just put in the mailbox. It hadn't even left the post office yet. She wanted to start off on the right foot with her mother, but telling her one thing, then doing the exact opposite was not that foot. "I understand, but do you think you could at least give the letter time to get there? Give her a chance to say something first?"

Jamie bit her lip, then smiled. It was an open smile, her dimples freed. "I'll make a deal with you. I won't tell Asaf until the letter arrives. It shouldn't be over four days, right?"

Nichelle nodded. "Right. A deal implies an exchange of some sort, huh?"

"We need to walk over and introduce you to your other

brother, Noah. Right now."

"How is that any better, J?"

"Because when Asaf finds out, he won't think I was going to permanently keep it from him. As soon as I found out, I told Noah. Get it?"

"Not really. Won't Noah call his mother?"

Jamie laughed and plopped down in her chair. "Whew, there's so much I need to tell you about your new family's dynamics. I don't even know where to start. I guess, first of all, Noah wouldn't say anything to Anika. There's a lot of stuff that's gone down through the years. I'll let your brothers tell you, but Noah only comes around for Shabbat, and that's only when we beg him. He usually finds an excuse to miss it."

"He doesn't like his mother?"

"He loves his mother. He just likes to maintain a healthy distance for his own mental health."

"But Asaf doesn't have that problem?"

"My husband is an ostrich like his mother. They ostrich all over the place together. Believe me."

"I'm not sure."

"Trust me, Nichelle. I know this family."

Nichelle did trust Jamie. They'd been work friends for a couple of years. They lunched together, shared an office, and bounced ideas off each other. All of this new information though, was too much. Would this make Jamie her sister-in-law now? That was just too weird to imagine. All of it was too much, but she needed to make a decision. And there was really only one thing she could do.

NICHELLE FOUND HERSELF standing at the long counter in the IT department, staring at a different student assistant than the last time they were there getting her laptop fixed. The young woman watched Nichelle as Jamie explained they needed to go upstairs to see Noah, but didn't want to be announced. For some reason, Jamie thought that was the better way to handle it rather than letting him know they were there. Apparently, Noah could be a bit high-strung and worried easily.

"I can't really do that. It's against the rules, and I could get in trouble."

"But I'm his sister." She glanced at Nichelle, a small smile playing at the corners of her mouth. "Well, sister-in-law. I have some news, but if you call him, he'll be worried."

The woman eyed Jamie, a lack of confidence creasing her brow, her lips pursed. "Do you promise I won't get in trouble?"

Jamie shoved a thumb Nichelle's way. "Her father is a department head. If Mr. Perkins gives you any problems, you can always come over to the political science department to work."

Nichelle and the student assistant shared a wide-eyed

stare.

Jamie laughed. "I'm just kidding. You'll be fine. I pinky-swear."

There was a half door attached to the end of the counter, and the student went over and unlatched it. As Jamie and Nichelle passed through, she said under her breath, "I hope this doesn't come back to bite me in the ass."

Jamie chuckled.

Nichelle was too nervous. Any laugh she attempted would surely rival a hyena's. As it was, she only eked out, "Thanks."

A staff elevator led up to Noah's office. Although Nichelle had been on a higher floor in this building before, it was in the common area accessible by a different elevator. Protecting the campus servers was taken seriously around here, especially with student grades and other personal information on-site. Jamie hit the button for the tenth floor and settled in for the ride. The building was older and the elevator slower than a lot of other places on campus, and for that, Nichelle was grateful. It gave her time to pull her nerves together and think about what she would say to Noah.

By the time the doors opened on the tenth floor, Nichelle was no closer to having her speech ready. All she could think about on the way up was if Noah rejected her. How would that make her feel? About herself but also about her new brother?

Jamie remained quiet on the way up, giving Nichelle her

space. She smiled and shrugged, stopping outside Noah's door, poised to knock. "Ready?"

"Not really, but we did come all this way." Nichelle took a deep breath and held it as Jamie knocked.

"Come in." Noah's voice was muted through the door, but friendly, if not a bit hurried.

When Jamie and Nichelle stepped into his office, Noah looked up and frowned. He glanced at Nichelle but stared at Jamie. "What's wrong?"

"Nothing is wrong. Goodness." She sat in one of the chairs in front of his desk. "Sit down, Nichelle."

Noah looked at Nichelle then, his gaze remaining on her a few seconds longer, scanning her face. His brow furrowed at whatever he saw there. He turned back to Jamie. "I think something's wrong."

"Not at all. We have something to tell you. Personally, I think it's fantastic news."

"Okay." He turned back to Nichelle. "Would you like to sit?"

Nichelle jumped a bit, then took a nervous glance at the chair. "Oh yes. Thank you." She sat and crossed her legs, then uncrossed them again, placing her purse on her lap.

The three of them gaped at each other expectantly. Finally, Jamie cleared her throat. "I think Nichelle has a story to tell you. It won't take long." She turned to Nichelle, eyes big, and tilted her head toward Noah.

Nichelle's hands gripped the arms of the chair until her

fingers protested. She took a couple of deep breaths, then finally looked at Noah. "Okay, here's the thing. A few weeks ago, I received a family heirloom from my grandmother." She looked at him to make sure he was paying attention, like they hadn't just barged into his workspace acting all cagey.

"Okay. Mazel tov?"

She cleared her throat and picked up the thread of her story. "Thanks. In reality, it was from a grandmother I didn't know I had. She died and left the ring to me along with a note that informed me I'd been adopted."

She looked at him again, hoping that maybe he had a clue, and she wouldn't have to spell it out. No luck though. His brows were drawn together in thorough confusion.

"So, my parents confirmed that I indeed had been adopted, but they didn't have any information on my birth parents. I took one of those genealogy DNA tests that are everywhere these days, got some matches, and have been doing research. I finally figured out my birth parents, and I sent them both a letter today to make contact." She took more breaths, shaky at best.

Noah stood and opened the mini fridge in the corner of his office. He handed Nichelle a cold bottle of water and removed another one, raising his eyebrows to Jamie. She shook her head, so he put the second bottle back, and sat down behind his desk.

Nichelle took a deep drink of water until her throat stung. "Wow, that's really cold."

Noah nodded.

She took one more swig and recapped the bottle, setting it on the carpeted floor. "Turns out I have two sisters on my father's side, and two brothers on my mother's side. I identified my sisters easily but had a bit of trouble with my other siblings. I could view their birth certificates but then it was like they disappeared. I was talking with Jamie about it, and she suggested they may have changed their surname." Nichelle picked the water up again but didn't open the bottle. Her gaze was pointed somewhere over Noah's shoulder. "To make a long story short." She laughed. "Too late, right? Anyway, looks like we're related."

Noah blinked. "Really? Oh wow. How?"

Nichelle let out a loud huff, rivaling any sigh Clark ever had. "Siblings?"

The size of Noah's eyes widened to an unbelievable level. He didn't appear angry, just wholly surprised. "What?"

"Yup, it would seem that we have the same mother." She shrugged, but the vulnerability she felt stiffened her shoulders and made the gesture awkward.

"This is definitely a shock. But I can't really say I'm surprised."

"Oh, you knew? Or suspected?"

"Not in the least. I'm not surprised Mom would have kept a secret like this. She can really compartmentalize. Although, this is a hell of a compartment."

Jamie chuckled. "Isn't that the truth? So now you know,

but you can't say anything yet. Nichelle wants to give her letter time to reach Anika."

"Okaaaaay."

"And we haven't told Asa yet. So you can't mention it to him either."

"Jeesh. Are you sure?"

Jamie nodded. "Yes. You know what will happen if we tell Asa."

Noah wrapped his knuckles on his desk, startling Nichelle. "Oh, sorry." He turned to Jamie. "Yes, I do know. He won't last an hour without having to ask her about it."

Nichelle asked, "How do you think she'll handle it?"

Jamie and Noah exchanged a meaningful look. Finally, Noah said, "I'm not sure, but more than likely she'll try to pretend it didn't happen. That's pretty much her modus operandi with anything. Asa's sick and they all pretend he isn't."

The quickness Jamie snapped her head up gave Nichelle pause. In the middle of Asaf's illness was not where she wanted to be. Jamie made it clear it wasn't a topic of discussion, but Noah didn't seem to be on the same page. "We don't pretend, Noah. We're only honoring his wishes. Plus, he's fine."

Nichelle unraveled the label on her water bottle. Everything was quiet except for the noise of the plastic crinkling as she worked. Finally, she stood. "We should go. I've taken up enough of your time considering you're at work. And I apologize for just springing it on you."

Noah stood too and put his hands in the pockets of his jeans. "You're fine. And I'm glad you told me. I've always wanted to have a sister." He looked at Jamie and grinned. "No offense."

"None taken."

"Nichelle, if you're open to it, would you like to come around to dinner this weekend? I'd love for you to meet your niece."

"That would be…" Nichelle took in a couple of breaths, holding at bay the tears stinging the backs of her eyes. "Yes, I would love to. I'm looking forward to getting to know you better."

"Me too."

Noah said to Jamie, "I won't tell Asaf, and you know I probably won't talk to Mom before the letter arrives. But can you let me know when it does?"

Jamie snorted. "Yeah, if I find out."

"That's a good point. We'll give her until Shabbat to come clean. Nichelle, please don't be disappointed if she doesn't. There's so much I can tell you about our mother, and then you'll understand to not take it personally."

Nichelle appreciated the sentiment, but it was a little hard to not take personally a parent's absolute rejection. She wasn't holding a grudge about being given up for adoption—she understood that unplanned pregnancies happened and sometimes they were difficult for the parents, especially teens—but she wasn't sure how she'd feel if her mother continued to ignore her. It was definitely a possibility. Her birth report hinted at the type of person her birth mother was, and it had been confirmed by the cryptic messages both Jamie and Noah had been sending her way. She only hoped that her mother had gotten over herself by now. It had been more than thirty years for goodness' sake. In a few days she would know. At least now she'd gained a brother out of the bargain. And he'd been so gracious, especially the way they sprung it on him. He couldn't have been nicer about it. That thought gave Nichelle hope for the future. Now she only needed to see what came of these letters.

CHAPTER TWENTY

Clark

CLARK RODE TO Nichelle's apartment after she texted him that she'd made an important discovery. They planned to meet later in the evening, but she said it couldn't wait. He pulled off his helmet and knocked.

"Hey."

"Hey?"

"Okay, Clark, I get it. You want to know why I wanted you to rush over here." She yanked him by the hand into the apartment.

Sometimes Nichelle really perplexed him. He hadn't made that big a deal. "Is everything okay? Don't you have class?"

"Oh yeah. Everything's fine. I let them go early." She pulled him to the couch and straddled his lap.

"Uh." Since he'd last saw her, she'd changed into yet another sundress with the thinnest straps securing it from falling and revealing her breasts. How many of these did she own? The thought of her panties flush against his zipper again was rather distracting. This was not how he wanted to be distracted though. He needed to ensure they were on the same relationship page before being physical, and that couldn't happen with any integrity until after he testified and came clean. He'd barely made it out the last time. Intercourse with Nichelle would be a disaster. She'd hate him once she found out about his deception.

He took in a cleansing breath, calming the hope in his dick.

"I was talking to my officemate, Jamie, about the research I've been doing, and how I hit a roadblock with my brothers."

Interesting conversation to have with coworkers, but Clark supposed work relationships were different for everyone. He couldn't imagine sharing something so personal with Cathie. "Your officemate, got it."

"She's a friend too. We've been working together awhile."

"Okay. Your officemate, coworker, friend. Named Jamie. Continue."

"Ugh." She adjusted herself ever so slightly, and Clark entered into another calming conversation with his crotch. "Anyway, so I was telling her about the roadblock, and it turns out her husband and his brother are my brothers. Can you freaking believe that?"

Shock coursed down Clark's spine. "Are you sure? How can that be?"

"Her husband, Asaf, changed his name from Harris to Perkins when he came of age. It's a long story, but something about hating his dad. His brother, Noah, did too. So now instead of Asaf and Noah Harris, who I was looking for, they're Asaf and Noah Perkins. That's why I couldn't find anything. Can you believe that?"

It was indeed difficult to believe. "That's...a lot."

"I know, right? So anyway, we went over and saw Noah. Did I mention he works on campus?"

"You did not. What a coincidence."

She slapped his chest, grinning. "Man, this is incredible. Anyway, he was really cool about it and even invited me over for dinner to meet his daughter Saturday. Gah. My niece! Isn't that awesome?"

"I'm very happy for you." And he was happy for her, even though a little disappointed for himself. He'd hoped to spend Saturday evening with her. "What about your birth mother then? Can you just call her now?"

Nichelle quieted for a moment and averted her gaze. "So, about my birth mother. I honestly don't know. I didn't mention it before, but I got the impression from my birth report that she's a little selfish."

Clark huffed. He knew all about selfish parents. "I don't think we needed your birth report for that."

She slid off his lap and tucked herself under his arm. "It's more than just giving me away. The tone of the report was telling. Whoever interviewed her and wrote up the report was clearly throwing shade."

"I'm sorry, what?" He could maybe tell from context clues about half of what Nichelle ever said to him, but throwing shade was outside his deductive skills.

"You're the worst." She tempered that insult by rubbing his cheek with a soft touch. "They were passing judgment. Anyhoo, they wrote when she came back for her follow-up appointment two weeks later, she didn't ask anything about her baby, only complained she hadn't lost weight yet. Also, when I was first born, she looked at me through a window. I guess they still had nurseries back then instead of having the kid in the same room like they do now." Her voice caught.

"Oh, sweetheart." He pulled her even closer and kissed her temple.

She sucked in a shaky breath. "I'll be okay. It's just so heartbreaking to read something like that. My heart breaks for baby me. She left me in a children's home and never turned back. I could have grown up in the system and she didn't care. I'm not a mother, but I can't imagine leaving my child out in the world to fend for herself." She shrugged and pursed her lips. "I sure hope she lost her baby weight though."

Now he got it. Nichelle was "throwing shade."

"Are you sure you want to meet her?"

"I'm not sure, but I want to at least have the opportunity. Adult me doesn't hold this against her, but reading that report has me all emotional."

"I understand." Clark understood parental failures more than most. He hated that Nichelle was going through this, but at least she possessed two parents, although flawed, who loved her. "If you need me to do anything, you only have to tell me."

"I know, Clark. I appreciate that about you. I'm so happy I met you."

And there it was. Maybe he finally found someone who liked him for more than what he could offer physically, who saw past his social restrictions. Would she still feel the same way once she discovered he was trying to sink her mother's company and couldn't tell her? *Wouldn't* tell her because of his deep sense of integrity. Maybe his ethics were skewed. He lived in a bubble, so he only relied on his own counsel. Perhaps speaking to Franny would help, but he couldn't put her in that situation. She and Nichelle were sorority sisters. From what he'd learned the past few weeks, that was a serious bond. Not deeper than siblings, but he would never set her up to choose.

"Are you still with me?"

He looked at her and blinked. "Yes, sorry. There's a lot to consider."

Nichelle kissed his lips.

He abruptly stood, slithering out of her grasp. "I should get back to the store."

Nichelle stood too and wrapped her arms around his waist. "Are you sure you want to leave?"

He strode to the door, and grabbed his helmet, barely throwing the words over his shoulder. "I'll meet you there." He rushed out the door and down the stairs to where he'd locked his bike. Looking up at the sky, he let out a deep sigh. That was the most inelegant departure he'd ever executed. He had about two hours before he saw Nichelle again and had to explain to her what happened. First, he needed to figure it out himself.

CHAPTER TWENTY-ONE

Nichelle

WHIPLASH. THAT'S THE only way Nichelle could explain Clark's visit. One minute he was saying all the right things and comforting her and whatnot. The next moment, he was practically dumping her on the floor, and rushing out the door. Her neck was sore from all those sudden movements. Did he like her or not? He said he did, but as soon as they were in a position of intimacy again, he jetted. She knew sex was off the table for the time being, but after they made each other come, she thought he was comfortable with at least that much.

The knock on the door was unexpected. Nichelle narrowed her eyes and peered into the peephole. "Can I help you?"

"May I come in?"

She twisted her lips to the side. He'd only been gone about two minutes, and she wasn't ready for round two of having her head on a swivel. "It depends. What do you want?"

"To explain."

Nichelle eased the door open just enough for Clark to slip through. She stood in the entryway instead of inviting him in.

"Can we sit?"

"How about we stand here a minute; you say what you came back to say, and then we'll see about sitting. Sound like a plan?" She stiffened her back, reminding herself to listen first before easily forgiving. They clearly weren't on the same page, and she was tired of guessing.

The gray helmet balanced in his hands was the only thing separating them. Clark set it on the floor and reached for her hand.

Ever so slowly, she slipped her hand into his. The connection reminded her how much she'd fallen for this guy. And she really didn't know if he felt the same way. Maybe he was about to tell her he only thought of her as a friend.

Maybe with benefits.

"I really like you." He chewed at the corner of his lip and stared at her.

Was he expecting a reply? Nichelle lifted her brows in question. He'd said he liked her before, but that didn't mean anything.

"I'm not sure what you're thinking." His hand went clammy in hers.

"Obviously we need to clear the air because I'm not sure what you mean by 'like.' Do you friend-like me or more?"

"I. Uh. I romantically like you, but..." He ran his free hand through his hair.

Clark was always calm. Cool. Definitely collected. She'd never seen him muss his hair like that. "But what, Clark?"

"Is there any way we can sit down."

She rolled her eyes but dropped his hand and plodded over to the sofa.

Clark followed and eased onto the seat next to her. Close, but not as close as they were before. "Thanks." He swallowed.

Nichelle could visually track the movement. Again, that struck her as unusual.

He shifted on the sofa so his body was turned to hers. "We've talked before about past girlfriends. Not particulars, but that I've had them."

"Yes, I believe that was after you spit your water all over the table at one of our hotel stops when I asked if you were a virgin."

The tips of his ears turned pink. "Right. I've had girl-friends, but they were superficial relationships. Either they were embarrassed of me because of my..." He swept his hand up and down his head and chest area.

"Embarrassed because you're so ridiculously good-looking?" Nichelle hoped to bring a smile to his serious face, but he only scowled harder.

"I understand people find me attractive. The problem is what comes with the outward package. The awkwardness.

The control issues. The—"

"Need to always be right." Nichelle let her voice trail off at the end. She could probably name a few more items, but now wasn't the time. And it didn't matter anyway. She liked those things about him. They complemented each other.

"Yes, there's that. Inevitably, those qualities became an issue. Normally within a few weeks."

Nichelle leaned back against the sofa and moved her head side-to-side, closing her eyes. "I'm not tracking, Clark."

"I want more than a physical relationship with you. I want to try for something more…" He cleared his throat. "Permanent."

She popped her eyes open at that revelation. "You do? I want that too, Clark." She sat up again, scooting closer to him.

He nodded. "That's good. So you understand?"

She nodded, then shook her head. "Understand what?"

"Concerning the physical aspect of our relationship."

"Um, not sure. You want more than physical. Right? But no intercourse yet because of the work thing you can't tell me about." She blinked as understanding hit her smack on top of the head. "Oh, you mean zero sexual contact. Not even what we did last time that didn't involve 'intercourse.' Wait, are you saying you don't trust me when I say I want the same thing?"

"You do understand then."

She jumped up, placing an indignant hand on her hip.

"You have no reason not to trust me."

Clark put his hands up, palms forward. "I only met you a few weeks ago. It would be nonsensical to trust someone you've known such a minuscule amount of time."

"Well, I trust you."

His eyes widened in disbelief. Then again, there was something else there in his face Nichelle couldn't quite put her finger on.

"Are you untrustworthy?"

He blinked. "No. Not usually."

"What the hell does that mean?" There went her neck again. It went from sore to aching in a matter of minutes. Without another word, Nichelle left Clark in the living room and went in search of an Advil. She pulled open bathroom drawers, rummaging through hair ties, palettes of eye shadow she rarely used, and nail polish bottles she used even less. *I know I have pills in here somewhere.*

The light touch on her back was the first indication Clark followed her. "You don't want physical contact, remember?"

"That's not what I meant, Nichelle. Of course I do. It's like I said the other night, I only want to wait a bit before intercourse."

"Because you don't trust me. Right."

He rubbed her back. "I don't mean to be hurtful. I'm trying to be as honest I can. It appears our feelings aren't aligned."

The bottle of Advil fell to the floor. Finally, she'd found it. Nichelle stood and turned, facing Clark. "You did hurt my feelings. And I get that wasn't your intention, but I get to be hurt if that's how I feel."

Clark nodded. "I didn't mean to imply otherwise."

"You didn't. Listen, I may be overreacting. I know you're not trying to hurt me on purpose, but I'm still hurt. Let's go back to the living room. I need some water."

While Nichelle poured water from her filtered pitcher, Clark perched himself back on the couch. She swallowed the pill with the water and sat next to him again. "Thank you for telling me about your past. I, of all people, should comprehend how our past shapes us. I haven't had a great track record with men, and maybe I should have mentioned it before. I get it wrong all the time, and when you said, yanno, what you said, it felt familiar. Like maybe you were really saying you only want a friendship. Without benefits even."

"I'll only ever say what I mean."

"Yeah, I get that. You're not a 'read between the lines' kinda guy. So, what now?"

"It's up to you. I want to be with you. That hasn't changed."

She curled herself up into his lap, and grinned, headache abated. "Exactly how long does it normally take you to trust?"

He laid back, resting his head on the couch.

Nichelle didn't have to guess what might be going

through his mind. If the hardness pushing against her thigh was any indication, he was warring with himself.

She was no temptress, but if Clark would just relax and let loose for once in his life, they could really get this relationship off the ground. It was his decision though.

He turned to her with a small, sexy smile, and eyes filled with desire. Cupping her cheek, he said, "Being close to you does strange things to my reasoning skills." He leaned in for a kiss, and she met him halfway, tongues colliding, urgency finally rising.

Nichelle's lips tingled from the kiss. He tasted of cinnamon gum and something uniquely Clark. "I think your reasoning skills are just fine. You want this as much as I do."

He put his hands in Nichelle's hair, scraping her scalp, and kissed her again, swirling his tongue with hers. He broke the kiss and stared into her eyes. "I do want you so much. But we shouldn't."

Nichelle straddled him and rubbed against his erection.

Clark groaned and reached between them, rubbing her clit through her panties, then slipped a finger inside.

"Let's move this off the couch, shall we?" She stood, and pulled him up with her, leading him to her bedroom.

This time, he willingly followed, trailing kisses down the back of her neck as they walked.

She pulled out the drawer of her nightstand and removed a box. "Condoms."

Clark nodded. "Good. I won't have to dig in my wallet."

They were on the same page, and Nichelle wouldn't have to worry that she'd seduced him against his will. "Can you stay until the practice?"

He sat on the bed and circled her waist with his hands. "Yes."

That was Clark, always short and to the point. Nichelle didn't mind though. "Good." She leaned down as he looked up, and offered her lips again which he greedily took, pulling her into his lap.

She turned to straddle him, rubbing with vigor against his stiff erection, the friction causing an overwhelming sensation between her legs. She hadn't waited this long just to come in her underwear again, so ever so reluctantly, she slowed her movements and broke the kiss. "Let's get naked."

Clark didn't waste any time with words and shucked his black pants before she could stand all the way up.

She pulled her sundress over her head and stood there, looking down at him while he kissed her stomach, his hands on her butt, securing her in place. He was tender and unhurried, and Nichelle fell in love with him right then. When he looked up, his feelings were evident in his eyes.

This time, she was sure. She smiled down at him, hands on his shoulders.

After a deep sigh, Clark hooked a finger in the band of her panties and looked up at her. "Okay?"

"Yes, more than okay."

He tugged at her underwear, and they finally joined her

dress on the floor. He stood and shed his own boxers, and simply looked at Nichelle.

She didn't feel self-conscious, although she hadn't been fully undressed in front of a man in quite a while. Clark conveyed nothing but love and admiration, and she was ready for them to finally seal this particular deal. She took him in her hand and stroked.

Clark's eyes closed for a moment, then reopened, lust-filled. He cupped her breasts and gently caressed, but pinched a nipple when Nichelle's grasp tightened. "Is that okay?"

"It's perfect. Let's get in the bed." Nichelle pulled back the covers and laid down on her back, pulling Clark down on top of her.

He kissed her with greater urgency, swirling his tongue with hers, and nipping her lips. His hands traveled her body, massaging and stroking, before breaking their kiss, and moving to her breasts.

Nichelle felt affection in every touch of Clark's hands, every breathy kiss, and every brush of his lips across her tender skin. She was buzzing with her growing arousal, teeming with the velvety sensation of Clark's skin against hers, and in awe of how their spirits fit together.

Clark inched down her body, kiss by breathless kiss, until he reached her core, and kissed the inside of her thighs, breathing against her heightened nub. "Still okay?"

She wanted to yell at him to get on with it, but she also

appreciated him checking in with her. She had no intention of changing her mind, but it was great to know that if she did, he would stop. "Very okay."

The first glide of his tongue through her folds pulled the breath out of Nichelle's lungs. She grabbed the sheets and steadied herself, but he intensified the intimate kiss, and she rocked against him. Clark grasped her hips to hold her steady, and plunged his tongued inside her, dragging it over her clit as he exited, over and over again. At first rhythmic and slow until Nichelle's quivering became more intense, pushing harder against Clark's mouth. He increased the pressure and pace, digging his fingertips into the flesh of her hips, and Nichelle rode the momentum until she orgasmed, calling his name.

"I'm here." He kissed back up her body and pulled a hard nipple into his mouth.

Nichelle's boneless body responded to Clark's loving touch, as he coaxed her arousal forward again. She spoke to the top of his head while he licked and sucked. "You're incredible." She wanted to tell him she loved him, but she'd wait so he would be certain it wasn't a passion-fueled endearment. She reached over to the nightstand for the foil packet and pushed it into Clark's hand. "I really want you inside me now."

He grinned against her breast and sat back on his haunches, rolling the condom on. "I'm happy to accommodate."

When Clark pushed inside her, inch by slow inch, she reached around and grabbed his fabulous ass, urging him deeper, kissing his neck, then chest. When he seated himself all the way in, he stared into her eyes. "You feel amazing." He pulled back and thrust again, and soon they moved against each other in flawless rhythm. Clark nuzzled her neck, breathing really hard. "Yes."

Nichelle could relate to the sentiment. Clark felt unbelievable inside her, his dick the ideal fit. His soft skin was incredible under her palms, and the sweet scent of jasmine and vanilla that often clung to him from the store filled her nose. She wanted this forever.

Clark rolled to his back and pulled her on top of him, never breaking their connection. "I want to see you."

She grinned down at him, happy to be seen because that meant she could see him too. She controlled their pace, sliding against him, and holding onto his shoulders for balance, her hair falling onto his firm chest. Clark met her thrusts, and in this new position, she wouldn't last too much longer. The orgasm began slowly this time, creeping through her stomach and building down into her pelvis. "I'm coming." She threw her head back and let her climax carry her.

Clark grabbed her ass and pushed upward, harder and faster, finding his own release.

Nichelle collapsed on Clark's chest, fighting to get her breathing under control.

His chest was moving up and down quickly, and

Nichelle took comfort in the melodic tempo as it eased to a slower pace. In that moment, she saw her future, and she was happy and untroubled.

CHAPTER TWENTY-TWO

Clark

I T WAS TOO soon. That's all Clark could think as he rode with Franny to the practice at the university. He had a joint meeting with his mind, his heart, and his dick, and the latter two came out on top even though the former knew nothing, but disaster could come from getting in deeper with Nichelle. He hadn't meant to let it go that far, and yet he couldn't stop. She was quickly becoming everything to him.

"Why the sour mood, Clark?" His sister turned to him at a stoplight. "I mean, more sour than usual."

The light turned green, and Clark sunk lower in the passenger seat. He couldn't even look at Franny, instead focusing his gaze on the passing lush landscape and houses. "I've made a serious error in judgment, and I fear the consequences."

Franny let out a small laugh. "Oh, brother. You're such an alarmist. I'm sure it's not as bad as all that. It never is."

"This time it is indeed that bad."

"Do you want to tell me about it?"

"I can't."

She pulled into the parking lot near the student center and searched for a spot. "You, more than anyone I know, always make thoughtful decisions. I can't imagine this situation is any different."

Clark couldn't tell her about the case, but he could tell her about his feelings. "I, um, have been spending a lot of time with Nichelle since we've been back."

"Eep. I knew you'd be perfect together." She finally found a spot at the farthest end of the parking lot and killed the engine.

"It's not that simple."

She turned to him and grabbed his hand. "Oh, Clark. When is it ever that simple for you? Nichelle is the most easygoing, free person I've ever met. She forgives easily and doesn't sweat the small stuff. And all your hang-ups are the small stuff. You have no idea how truly amazing you are."

He huffed a huge breath and rotated toward his sister. Betraying Nichelle by testifying against her mother's company and not warning her was definitely not the small stuff. Quite the opposite. "I'm keeping something from her that will likely make her hate me. And instead of keeping my distance, I've hardly been able to leave her side. She's my first thought when I wake. All of my attention is focused on her. I—"

"Oh my gosh, you love her."

Clark's stomach flipped, and he shook his head. "It's too

soon."

"I don't think there's a time stamp on that kind of thing, Clark. I know you, and I know what this is. Do you think she feels the same way?" Franny dragged her hands through her hair. "Why am I asking you? Of course you don't know."

"It doesn't matter because once she discovers my deception, that will be the end of it."

Franny's expression softened, her frustration rushing away. She squeezed Clark's hand. "Give her a chance, Clark. Whatever the situation, she'll forgive you. That's the kind of person she is." She looked at her phone. "Shit, we better hurry."

Clark would never get accustomed to Franny swearing. Intellectually, he knew she was an adult. She never needed his protection, but she was his baby sister, and it was difficult to get that out of his head. He closed the car door and jogged to catch up with her. The air carried a breezy warmth and the smell of the nearby bay. Instead of entering the building, Franny led him around it, and down a path that ended in an outdoor theater-style setup. There was a concrete stage in the middle, and risers built into the surrounding hill looking down on the stage. A group of women were standing in a loose circle on the platform, talking and laughing.

When Clark spotted Nichelle, his heart beat faster, speeding more than from the jog he'd just had. A memory flashed through his thoughts of being in Nichelle's bed, tasting her sweet arousal, losing himself inside her. He wanted to run to her, but she was seated on one of the risers talking to a woman more her age than Franny's. They were bent, their heads together speaking in hushed tones. Franny broke away from him without a parting word and headed to the women on the stage. Clark stood awkwardly to the side, wondering if he should go to Nichelle or sit somewhere else. Maybe she wouldn't want to acknowledge him since her friend was nearby. Clark had always been an embarrassment to girlfriends. He bit his lip, his gaze darting to places of escape, anxiety tingling his skin.

The woman looked his way, then tapped Nichelle on the arm. When she turned, a bright smile split her face, and she stood and waved him over.

Clark was unable to move, his gaze fixed on her. Was she really so happy for him to join her? He willed his feet to move, and when he reached Nichelle, he grabbed her in a tight, relieved embrace, snuggling into her neck. He was both comforted and turned on by her burnt-sugar vanilla smell. Remembering himself, he lifted his head and stared into her eyes, but didn't let go.

"I'm happy to see you too, Clark." She stepped back from his embrace but slid her hand into his. "Meet my line sister and bestie, Amanda."

Amanda stood to shake his hand, but Nichelle hadn't let go, so she waved. "It's nice to finally meet you, Clark."

Finally? Had Nichelle told her friend about him? "It's nice to meet you too." Hopefully that was the right thing to say when meeting your girlfriend's best friend. He'd never been in that position before. He turned to Nichelle for confirmation.

She grinned at him. "Come sit with us. They're just about to start practicing."

"Are we meant to participate in some way?" The sudden thought made him shudder.

Amanda and Nichelle laughed. Amanda said, "Our stepping days are over, I'm afraid." She gazed at the young women center stage and released a small sigh.

Nichelle snuggled closer into his side. "It was fun while it lasted, but I'm only here because they need their grad advisor at events. You and Amanda are here to keep me company."

It amazed Clark how much he'd missed Nichelle considering they'd been in bed together only an hour before. He stared at her, paying little attention to the action going on around them. Perhaps Franny was right. He was in love.

CHAPTER TWENTY-THREE

Nichelle

A N UNEXPECTED RAIN shower tore from the sky and forced Nichelle back into her stifling apartment. She hurried into her shower to strip the wet clothes off before they turned icy in her bedroom. It was always the coldest room in her place, which was great when she was sleeping and could snuggle under the covers, but not so good when she was drenched.

She thought of her birth parents as the spray hit her shoulders. Days had passed since she'd mailed those letters off with no response from either of her parents. Her stomach was in knots.

When she stepped from the shower, the gel on the counter somehow tipped over and spilled on the floor. She scooped up as much as she could and ran a handful through her hair, then wiped up the rest. This day was not going well so far. She dressed and padded into the kitchen for some lunch. While her leftover lasagna was heating in the microwave, she peeked out the sliding glass door blinds at the dreary sky. When she turned to answer the ding of the microwave, the sun broke through behind her, lighting up her whole apartment. *Thank goodness.*

After she finished eating, she checked her phone. The only new emails were spam or from her sorority sisters. Nothing from unfamiliar email addresses that may belong to wayward parents. She huffed and sat on the couch hard. This was beyond maddening, and she was about sick of both of them. She opened her laptop in preparation of doing some research but ended up checking a social media site to mindlessly scroll through. A friend request waited for her.

Holy fuck, it was from Henry Maddox.

She recognized the picture from all the cyberstalking she'd done when trying to identify her father. Once she accepted the friend request, she looked at an inbox notification that greeted her. That was odd because she didn't normally communicate with family or friends that way. She'd trained them long ago to text her if they wanted to engage. She didn't even have the inbox part of the app on her phone. When she opened the two-day old message, she nearly toppled her laptop. A deep inhale, then exhale, and then she read the message from her younger sister, Suzette. She explained that her father, *their* father, received Nichelle's note and asked her to connect because he wasn't great with technology. She asked Nichelle if they could have a call with their other sister, Madeleine.

Nichelle tapped out a response that she'd be happy to

talk with them and promptly sent her phone number. A few minutes later, her phone rang.

With trembling hands, she picked it up and accepted the incoming call, a local phone number flashing on the screen. "Hello?"

"Hi. Is this Nichelle?"

"It is. Hi. How are you?"

"I'm good. This is Suzette. Madeleine's also on."

Madeleine spoke up. "Hi. It's nice to meet you."

Nichelle couldn't believe she was speaking to her actual sisters. She'd pulled their pictures from social media, but there wasn't a whole lot available. From the pictures she did find, she couldn't see much of a resemblance. "It's great to meet you too. I'm happy you reached out."

Suzette said, "We've actually been looking for you for a few years. It's an interesting story because I adopted my son four years ago, and Daddy mentioned you then. He wanted to find you."

"Wow, really? Four years ago?" Tears pricked the back of her eyes.

"Yeah, but he'd been told you were twin boys. So, I'd gone out to all the adoption boards and posted who we were looking for. I even contacted one of those talk shows to see if they'd help. It wasn't until our grandmother died that we realized you were a single baby, and a girl."

She hadn't thought her birth parents cared about her, but at least her father wanted to know what happened to her.

"Well, you can imagine that I was blown away when I received that ring from our grandmother. I had no idea I was adopted."

"Daddy told us. Well, he read your postcard to us." She paused, voice soft. "That's a shame you found out like that."

"I'm just happy I found out. It was a bit of a shock though. I'm still trying to process it."

Except for the initial greeting, Madeleine remained quiet. Nichelle hoped the woman didn't have issues with her. It's not like she put herself up for adoption.

Suzette said, "I bet. We were a little surprised too. Grandma left us all jewelry from her collection and a note that she'd given you the conch ring. Apparently, she'd discovered you a few days before she died. Well, someone discovered you for her. We didn't even know she'd been looking."

"That's interesting. When I read my birth report, it said she was willing to take me, but after Henry said he wouldn't marry my mother, my grandfather said they'd give me up for adoption instead."

"Really? I'm not surprised though. That sounds like Grandma. And Daddy unfortunately. You know you and Madeleine are only a few months apart."

Nichelle sensed some stress in Suzette's voice. Like maybe Henry hadn't been the most ideal father. "I do know. I wondered about that."

"Daddy's being tight-lipped, but apparently after your

mother told him she was pregnant, Momma said she was pregnant. We're still not sure about the timing since there's four months between you." She was quiet for a moment, then continued. "Madeleine, say something."

"What? I'm just listening to you two. You sound just alike. I know when to be quiet and listen."

They both laughed, and Nichelle joined in, but she was so touched. Deeply touched. She was like someone, and that notion was doing strange things to her breathing.

"Madeleine thinks I'm bossy."

Nichelle really laughed then. She never thought of herself as being bossy, but she could see where someone might think that. She never shied away from a conversation, that's for sure.

Suzette asked, "Are you five-nine? I saw that on the Internet."

What a strange detail to be floating around on the Internet. "I am. How tall are you two?"

"I'm about five-eight. Looks like we got Daddy's height. Poor Madeleine took after Momma."

"Hey, not poor Madeleine. I'm just fine with my glorious five foot five inches, thank you very much."

The sisters went on to talk for another hour. They shared details and laughed a lot. They finally got around to how Nichelle would connect with Henry. All agreed on a dinner at Suzette's house the following Saturday, a little over a week out.

When Nichelle hung up, she was buoyed by the phone call. She connected with three of her four siblings, and honestly felt that if she never met her birth parents, she'd be fulfilled. After all, she already had parents. She needed to get them up to speed, but she wanted to wait the full four days that Jamie bargained for. The next day would tell if her birth mother was on board or not.

NOAH'S NEIGHBORHOOD WAS in an older part of town but still had manicured lawns and tidy houses. The ride share pulled up right out front, so Nichelle reached to the floor and removed the two bottles of wine and chocolate she'd brought as her offering for dinner. Hence the ride share. She'd read on the Internet that those were appropriate gifts for Shabbat.

She took a couple of deep breaths before getting out of the car. She hadn't heard from her birth mother, but Jamie gave her a reprieve and agreed to tell Asaf after Nichelle's dinner with Noah if she still hadn't heard. Jamie couldn't confirm if the mail reached Anika or not. Her guess was that her mother-in-law probably got the mail while she and Asaf were at work. She hadn't mentioned anything so far, so odds were she probably wouldn't.

Nichelle walked up the short walkway lined with beautiful flowers and greenery. Someone clearly had a green thumb. Nichelle definitely hadn't inherited that. Her own father always had a vegetable garden, and many flower beds as her mom called them. She loved flowers, especially roses, and her dad cultivated them to perfection. Nichelle couldn't even pull weeds without accidentally dragging out a wanted plant. More flora bordered the underside of the big picture window in the front of the house, lined with white shutters. The house appeared small from the outside but was neat and well taken care of.

Nichelle rang the bell.

Heavy footsteps sounded through the wooden door. Noah opened it wearing jeans and a gingham shirt. "Shabbat Shalom."

"Thank you?"

He smiled, his blue eyes crinkling and nearly closing. "You're welcome. You can say Shabbat Shalom back when someone says it to you if you want." He opened the screen and waved his hand. "Please, come in."

There was a shoe stand next to the door, and Noah wasn't wearing shoes, so Nichelle slipped out of her flats. She was happy she wore socks so walking across the dark hardwood floor would be a little cushier. Once she'd put her shoes in a cubby, she held her offerings out to Noah. "I hope these are appropriate for a Shabbat dinner."

He took the wine and chocolate from her. "Thank you so much. Technically, yesterday was the Shabbat dinner. Shabbat ends at sundown tonight, but we're not traditional around here anyway. Mom and Asaf and Jamie adhere to the customs a little more and they observe Shabbat closer, but not completely either."

"I think Jamie mentioned that before." Nichelle tried to access all the conversations she'd had with Jamie over the years about Jewish traditions, but even though she'd been paying attention, she hadn't really absorbed most of it. She sorely wished she had, but who knew one day she'd all of a sudden be Jewish? She grew up in the Baptist Church with her parents and knew those traditions backward-and-forward although the church-house hadn't seen her in a good long minute.

The cutest little girl ran up and hid behind her dad's leg, holding on to his jeans. Clearly this was his daughter, because she had blond hair and the brightest blue eyes like Noah.

Nichelle bent down to eye level with the child. "Hi. You must be Emma." She hadn't been around many two-year-olds, but that seemed a safe choice in introductions. Did two-year-olds understand? Did they talk yet?

"What do you say, Emma? This is your Aunt Nichelle."

She peeked around her dad's leg just long enough to say one word. "Hi." Then she turned and ran the way she came.

"She's beautiful, Noah."

"Thanks. I think so too, but I may be biased."

"No, she totally is."

"As her aunt, you may be a little biased too." Noah

grinned and opened his arms.

Nichelle willingly stepped into them, absorbing the warmth of her good-natured brother. "Thanks for having me. Did I say that already?" She laughed and stepped back, totally flummoxed. She'd hoped to have Noah's acceptance and ended up receiving so much more. If he was such a great guy, her mother couldn't be too bad since she raised him, right?

"I'm glad you were able to make it on such short notice." He followed the same path his daughter had, along the entryway, and into a dining room.

Nichelle trailed behind. The dining room table was set for three with a booster seat in one of the chairs. There was a steaming platter of brisket, glazed carrots, a bowl of steamed asparagus, and what looked like fresh-baked rolls. The smell of roasted meat was divine along with the yeasty-scented rolls. "Wow, you made all this?"

"I did."

"I'm impressed. It smells delicious."

"Let's hope it tastes as good as it smells. If you want, you can set your purse on the sofa right through there, and if you keep going, there's a bathroom, first door on the right if you want to wash up."

Nichelle turned and followed Noah's directions. The fact that he'd asked her to wash up was a great sign. She usually didn't eat everyone's food unless she really knew them. Of course, she couldn't pass up an opportunity to get to know her brother, so it boded well that he pointed her to the bathroom before she sat down to eat. Hopefully that translated to his own hygiene in the kitchen. At this point, she'd probably eat dirt in order to know more about him and the rest of her maternal family.

Little Emma was perched in her booster seat with her palms pressed together anxiously examining her empty plate. When Nichelle entered the room and took her seat, Emma blushed and covered her face.

Noah grinned. "She can be a little shy around new people."

"Interestingly enough, and nobody ever believes me now, but I was quite shy as a child. It would take me forever to warm up to people, even my cousins who I saw every holiday. But after I did relax, they couldn't shut me up." Nichelle turned to Emma. "I bet you're hungry, huh?"

Emma nodded, eyes bright.

Noah lifted a large serving fork and stabbed a slice of meat. "I think that's my cue." He reached for Emma's plate and loaded her up with meat and asparagus, and half a roll on the side. He glanced at Nichelle while fixing Emma's plate. "Please, help yourself."

Nichelle didn't need to be told twice. The brisket was juicy as she stuck the fork into it. She was excited to try the roasted meat. "Wow, so tender."

"Do you cook?"

"I do, but I've never made a brisket before. My dad used

to on the barbecue pit." Nichelle had a sudden pang of guilt at the mention of her father. It was weird talking to her brother about a dad he hadn't met. She wondered about his own dad. Jamie said they were estranged but didn't really say why. It would definitely not be cool to ask.

"From what Jamie said, seems like you have some great parents."

"They are. They're wonderful and I know they love me. So much, I had no idea I was adopted."

"I'm happy to hear it."

Nichelle blessed her plate once she realized one wouldn't be coming from Noah.

He had started on his roll. "Oh, let me know if you need any butter. I'm not religious, but Emma and I keep kosher."

"I'm sure it's fine. I did wonder about that though. So even though you're not religious, you still follow some of the rules."

He grinned and placed the small bite left of his roll back on his plate. "We prefer to think of them as traditions. Holidays are important as well as Shabbat even though it's more about family gatherings and fun. Sort of like Christmas for a lot of other people. Some people believe 'Jesus is the reason for the season,' but a lot of others use the day to connect with family and friends, exchange gifts, and eat a ton of food."

She nodded. She understood once it was explained that way. "Okay, that makes total sense. What's your favorite holiday?"

"That's a no-brainer. Passover." He picked up one of the bottles of wine Nichelle had brought and poured them both a full glass. "Drinking wine is actually part of the Haggadah, the book we follow for the Passover Seder. There are four times we have to drink." His eyes twinkled as he took a sip of the wine. He looked at the glass, then back at Nichelle. "That's very good."

"It's my favorite." Nichelle looked down at her plate, realizing she'd inhaled everything but a single carrot. "Noah, this food is delicious."

"Please, help yourself."

There was plenty of food left in the serving dishes, but she was absolutely stuffed. She rubbed a hand gently across her stomach. "I don't think I could fit another bite."

"How about you, Emma? Do you want some more?"

Emma glanced at Nichelle, then giggled, shrinking into her shoulders. She shook her head.

Noah's hand hovered near while Emma climbed down from her chair. A minute later, the water turned on in the hallway bathroom.

"She's such a big girl."

"She is." He grinned even wider if that was possible. "Hopefully you'll have a little room left for dessert in a bit." He went into the kitchen and returned with a pie and placed it on the table.

The smell of the buttery crust and spicy apples hit

Nichelle in the face full-on. "Oh my gosh. You better believe I'll make room."

He shrugged, clearly pleased with himself, and sat back down.

"Where did Emma disappear to?"

"The backyard. She has this new discovery wall toy, and she's obsessed with it. She learns too so I let her play with it as much as she wants."

"Does your mother take care of her too? While you're working, I mean."

Noah snorted. "No. She goes to a Jewish preschool. There's one nearby that's diverse so kids of all faiths, or no faith at all, attend."

Based on that snort, looks like they were sailing into the getting-to-know-Anika portion of the night's festivities. "Sounds great. Asaf and Jamie didn't want their kids to go?"

"It's easier for them for Mom to keep the kids. Plus, it gives her something to do."

"Oh, so she doesn't work anymore? Or, I mean, did she work before?"

After taking another drink of his wine, Noah refilled the glass and offered more to Nichelle.

She had only drunk half of the first glass but held it out for Noah to fill, and took a rather large gulp.

"She did. After my parents divorced, she eventually went back to school with our grandmother's help and became a radiation therapist. She did that until Asaf married, then she retired and moved in with them."

"Oh, interesting. Did you get a chance to read my birth report?" Nichelle had emailed it over to him as soon as she got back in her office after their first meeting as siblings.

"I did. Some interesting tidbits in there."

Nichelle leaned forward, reacting to Noah's judgmental tone. "Tidbits?"

"Let's just say, sometimes Mom has an uncomfortable relationship with the truth."

"Oh wow."

"For instance, where she talked about being some great athlete, a swimmer I believe it was, and playing several instruments. To my knowledge, she can swim fine, but she wasn't even on her high school swim team. She dabbles at the piano, but certainly is no virtuoso." He shrugged and put down his glass. "I'm not surprised she said those things though. She wanted whoever adopted you to think she had a lot going for herself."

What could anyone possibly say to that? Obviously, Noah knew their mother, and Nichelle didn't have a clue, but surely there was more to the woman than that. "I'm guessing she has some issues."

Noah spent the greater part of the next two hours filling Nichelle in on what kind of mother birthed her. The selfishness was unimaginable, and all Nichelle kept thinking was that she was so entirely grateful she'd been put up for adoption. The only kinship she felt was Anika had been terrible at romantic relationships. Nichelle felt that in her chest.

It was getting late. Emma had come back inside the hour before, and her dad put her to bed. Nichelle and Noah finished off one bottle of the wine while he spun his memories and made a pretty good dent in the other.

He looked at the nearly empty bottle, puzzled, probably wondering what happened to the rest of the contents. He sighed. "There's probably more I could tell you, but we have plenty of time. One thing is that you're very much like her. Every time you laugh, I look around thinking she's walked in."

"Really? That's nice to hear." Nichelle had wondered who she'd be more like, her mother or father. Maybe a mixture of both. She wasn't sure she'd ever meet her mother, but at least she'd be able to measure herself against her father.

"What's your home life like? I knew of you from work, and you've made some impressive inroads in your career by the way, but I don't know a whole lot else."

Nichelle's breathing quickened, and she twisted the bracelet on her wrist. She was wholly inadequate in this department. "I, uh, well there's not a lot to tell."

"I know your adoptive father from school. What does your mother do?"

"She's retired now. She was an executive at a chemical company for years. They're a bit older than my, uh, birth parents." She stilled her hands after the clasp on her bracelet nearly broke apart.

"Married?"

And there it was. Asaf and Jamie had been married nearly five years and had two kids. Even her baby brother, her youngest sibling by six years, had been married and had a whole daughter. Her sisters were both married with children. She, as the oldest, was the only loser of the bunch. Nichelle was clearly just like her mother. "No, afraid not."

Her neck heated, and not from all the wine she'd poured down her throat. She truly was her mother's daughter. Nurture and nature, and all that nonsense.

"Oh, well I'm sure with your career, you've been busy."

"Yeah. Hey, I better get going and let you turn in. It's getting very late, and I bet that little Emma is an early riser." Suddenly, she couldn't get out of there fast enough. She clicked open the ride share app and scheduled a car, less than five minutes away.

"She is indeed."

They stood, and Nichelle grabbed her purse where she'd left it, then headed to the door and slipped her shoes back on.

Noah opened the door, then leaned in for a hug. "Thank you so much for coming."

Nichelle calmed with the gesture and inhaled Noah's scent of cinnamon and apples. He felt so familiar, like she'd known him her entire life.

When she sat in the car, she said to herself, "This is what it's like to share someone's blood."

The driver pulled away from the curb.

She had a lot to absorb from the evening. Being a failure in love like her mother was only part of it.

CHAPTER TWENTY-FOUR

Clark

THE SUN WAS low over the Bay, indicating Clark had spent a long day at the jewelry store. Weekends were a popular time to shop. Nichelle offered a basketball lesson, and at the time of her proposition, it seemed like a good idea. Now, he was too tired to even pick up a basketball. He wouldn't cancel though because spending time with Nichelle was all he wanted to do. His feelings for her had become impossible to ignore. His stomach twisted into knots every time he thought of her. He loved her, but soon she'd hate him because his analysis of her mother's company was damning.

He went home and quickly changed, then drove back to the park. Even though he was close enough to ride his bike, and still make it there on time, Clark wasn't sure he'd have the energy to bike back home after their game. He was sitting on the bench next to the basketball court when Nichelle eased out of her car nearby.

Clark watched as she slowly made her way over to the

basketball court. She didn't have the usual bounce in her step, especially considering there was a ball in her hands. Normally she would be bouncing it on the grass on the way over, smiling and laughing, in anticipation of combining her two loves—teaching and basketball. At least he hoped she'd be happy to see him.

"Hi." She threw the ball to him, but he wasn't ready, and it hit him in the chest. "Oops. You alright?"

"Fine. I should know better by now."

She shrugged and patted him on the chest where the ball landed. Usually, she would have a snappy comeback. She did give him a chaste kiss though.

"Everything okay? How'd your dinner with your brother go yesterday?" She'd returned so late, he'd only received a quick "I'm home" text.

She shrugged again and sighed. Something was definitely different.

"That good, huh?"

"It went fine. Noah's a great guy, and I'm lucky to have him as a brother. Our mother though…not so much."

Clark sat back on the bench and put the ball on the ground by his feet. "Come sit and tell me about it. If you want."

She wasted no time sitting next to him on the bench and leaning on his chest. "You know how I told you there was something in Suzette's tone that made me think Henry may not have been a great father?"

"I remember. Was it like that with Noah?"

"Ha, no. The stories he told me weren't a subtle indict-ment. She was not a great parent." She bent over and picked up the basketball, and rolled it back and forth over her lap, from one hand to the other. "After leaving their father, they moved in with our grandmother. Anika worked odd jobs but really didn't have any direction for her life."

Clark leaned back on the bench, thinking. To him, that didn't seem like unreasonable behavior. She'd just gone through a divorce. That took some adjustment. "Okay. Do you think she should have done something else?"

"No, not at all. That was fine, but it lasted less than a year. She couldn't get along with her mother, so she moved."

"Oh. They moved without a plan?"

"No. You don't get it. She moved. She left her sons be-hind. They didn't know she was moving, where she went, or if she was ever coming back. Our grandmother was in her seventies, and Anika just left her young sons without a word."

"That's terrible."

"I know, right?"

"But she came back. Eventually."

Nichelle jumped from the bench and bounced the ball onto the court.

Clark felt the loss of her touch to his core.

"Not really. They ran into her at the dentist office one day, but she'd been gone for months. She moved back, and their grandmother sent her to school for radiology or something, and she got back on her feet."

"That's, um, not good."

"I know. That's not all though. Even after she started working and was able to get a place for them, she didn't actually take care of them. Asaf made sure they had breakfast before school, and a lunch packed. Dinners were mostly frozen pre-made stuff or fast food. She went to work, but when she wasn't working, she was in bed in the dark. Usually high from weed."

Clark wasn't sure how to process this information. His own parents were hippie artists and got high all the time. Sometimes on more than marijuana. And although they hadn't paid much attention to him, he'd never starved, and they'd definitely never let Franny fend for herself. "That's terrible."

"It's incredibly selfish. I'm guessing she had some undiagnosed depression maybe. But why not get help especially when your children are suffering?"

"Was your grandmother not able to help?"

"By that time, she was too old and had moved into a senior living residence."

"You have uncles though, right?"

"Yup, two. They fell out with their sister long ago. None of them are on speaking terms. It's a clusterfuck." Nichelle stopped dribbling and sat on the ball, looking off into the park. There were a few families out as the air was cooling. A small group of teens was heading toward the basketball court from across the park.

"You still want to practice? You could do a pick game with those kids coming over."

Nichelle looked up at the sky and shook her head. "Pick-*up* game, Clark. Jeesh. Nah, let's just go."

Worry coursed through Clark. Nichelle never turned down a game. "Sure, no problem." He stood and followed her back to the parking lot.

Nichelle fidgeted with the basketball, biting her lip. "Do you want to follow me back to my place? I have some leftovers."

A small smile played on Clark's lips. She still felt like being together. "Yes, that would be good."

BACK AT NICHELLE'S apartment, Clark pulled down plates while Nichelle removed containers from the refrigerator. "I hope you like pad Thai."

"I love pad Thai. You made it yourself?"

"Yup. I made it for lunch yesterday. I wanted to have something at home in case Noah turned out to be a terrible cook."

Clark chuckled and opened the drawer that housed the flatware, then got two wine glasses out of the cabinet. "You still have plenty of food, so I'm guessing he did okay."

"Whew. Let me tell you, he did better than okay. Everything he served was cooked to perfection. He even made yeast rolls from scratch and apple pie for dessert." She made the chef's kiss sign with her fingers. "We had some wine too. I basically rolled home."

"Oh, I didn't realize you're allowed to have wine on Shabbat."

Nichelle let out a bark of a laugh. "I think I'm going to love Jewish celebrations. They drink a lot of wine. My brother especially."

Clark grinned and nodded. "Looks like that's something you share. Did he mention if your mother was a good cook or not?"

She snorted.

"I mean nowadays." He took an open bottle of wine out of the refrigerator and poured some into the glasses he'd already placed on the counter.

Nichelle put a plate piled high with the pad Thai and broccoli in the microwave and pressed some buttons to start it. "He didn't mention. But he did say he doesn't really like to cook but loves to bake. I guess cooking is a necessity when you're raising a child."

"I guess." That's something neither of them knew a lot about. But he wanted to find out one day. He shook the thought out of his head and moved the remaining plate, the glasses of wine, and the forks to the table.

Nichelle brought over the heated food and dished some

onto Clark's plate. "Bon appétit."

"It looks great." It smelled wonderful too. The scent of the spicy noodles combined with the citrusy smell of the lime made his mouth water. He placed a bite on his tongue and closed his eyes. The slight crunch from the ground peanuts along with the succulent shrimp was a perfect mouthfeel. "Tastes great too. Thanks for inviting me over."

Clark didn't miss Nichelle's posture change. She squirmed in her seat and averted her eyes.

"Is there something else wrong?"

"Well, I was wondering if you wanted to meet my parents." Nichelle turned away, speaking to the wall. "I'm going over for dinner later this week. It'll probably be super awkward, and you probably wouldn't want to. And that's perfectly fine, but I thought I'd ask." She stuck an oversized forkful of pad Thai into her mouth.

Clark took her hand, and when she turned back to him, he studied her face. She was completely serious, and there was a vulnerability lurking just beneath the surface. He didn't like the idea of meeting her parents, especially her mother. Would she be in court when he testified? His stomach tightened, but he also knew he wouldn't deny her. "If that's what you want."

Nichelle threw her arms around his neck, knocking one of the glasses over. "Thank you, Clark. I'm so excited for them to meet—Oh shit."

They both hopped up from the table. Clark righted the

glass while Nichelle ran in the kitchen and came back with a towel.

Once the wine was mopped up, Nichelle wrapped her arms around Clark again. "Seriously, thank you."

He whispered, "You're welcome" into her curls. She smelled of vanilla and burnt sugar, and wine, and all Clark wanted to do was kiss her, and forget about the dread building in his spine.

Pulling back much too soon, Nichelle picked up her fork and took another bite of pad Thai. "So good."

Clark smiled and dug back into his own food. "It really is."

After swallowing another sip of wine, Nichelle cleared her throat. "Can I ask you something, Clark?"

Holding his breath, he nodded. Was this when she confronted him? Did she know?

"How do you identify?"

Clark's insides relaxed but his skin tightened over his forehead, displaying his confusion. "I...I'm not sure what you mean."

"I just mean...well, you know how you want me to research your paternal grandfather's Chinese heritage because that's been a mystery?"

He nodded, not sure he understood where this was going.

"Is that how you identify, though? Asian, because of your last name?"

What she asked seemed obvious now. "I see, you mean racially. No, because I wasn't raised in that culture at all. Lin-Lee is my surname, but I don't even know where it came from."

She nodded and bit her lip. "So, since you were mostly raised by your maternal grandparents, then do you think of yourself as Dutch? As white?" Her gaze was intense, like she was working out a puzzle.

Clark shrugged, not sure how to respond. He was definitely raised with Dutch people, but even his grandparents were more Americanized by the time he came along. They still had certain ways of turning a phrase or food they preferred. He smiled at the memory of meals with them. So much dairy.

"What's funny?"

"I was thinking about how the food was different with them than when I was with my parents. Not completely but some." He searched for the right words. "I am multicultural from an ethnicity point-of-view and when I was with my grandparents, their ways were natural to me, but I didn't identify with them in that way. In school, there was never an instance when I wasn't Black. In society, I'm Black. I've never considered myself anything else."

Nichelle nodded, then took a sip of her wine. "That makes sense."

"Why do you ask?"

She stood. "Give me one sec." She walked to her bedroom and when she returned, the conch pearl ring was on her pointer finger. "I've been having a bit of an identity crisis, I guess. I know I'm still Black, but I spent the day with my white brother yesterday. My white, Jewish brother. And it's kind of weird."

He wasn't sure what to say. He grew up with a white mother and grandparents. It wasn't really something he thought about a lot. "What does that ring mean to you?"

She spun it around her knuckle then twisted it off her finger, handing it to Clark. "You know the Dutch were colonizers, right?"

He frowned but nodded. "I'm aware."

"So what I think of that ring is it was given to my three times great-grandmother who was a free Black woman but maybe had been a slave."

In all the research Clark had done on the original owner, although he figured out the man's name, there was no ready evidence of his relationship with Nichelle's ancestor. "And even if she wasn't, likely her mother was."

"Exactly that. And even though the Dutch didn't colonize Jamaica, they did other islands nearby."

Clark only nodded and absently fingered the ring. His father grew up in the West Indies. He knew that history well.

"And the Jewish side. That's a whole other set of displacement and marginalization. I traced that part of our family back quite a ways, and even though they immigrated to San Francisco from Germany well before the Holocaust, there are so many other pogroms and atrocities before that hardly anyone ever talks about. Stuff I didn't even know about until I started researching my roots." Nichelle scrubbed her hands across her face.

Rocks were Clark's thing. The ring warmed in his palm, and he stared at it, wishing some knowledge would jump from the stone. Something to say that would help Nichelle through her self-described identity crisis. He took a deep breath, then exhaled. "It's really complicated, I know. This is something I've talked about with Franny. Being descended from both slaves and slavers."

Nichelle popped her head up from her hands. "Right, that part. That's what I'm grappling with. I can't make it make sense."

"I don't have answers. As I said, it's complicated, but knowing your genetic makeup doesn't change your lived experience, does it?" For Clark, it hadn't been a huge issue. He loved his grandparents but also knew if he dug into their grandparents, he'd probably find plenty he didn't care to know. It's not that he didn't acknowledge it, but there wasn't more that he could do.

Nichelle held her hand out and Clark dropped the ring onto her palm. "You're right, Clark. I hope to learn more about my heritage, but my lived experience hasn't changed." She stood and kissed him on the cheek. "Thanks for talking it out with me."

CHAPTER TWENTY-FIVE

Nichelle

THE CAMPUS WAS practically empty of students as Nichelle made her way from the parking lot to the political science building. Jamie's car was parked in the lot, and she was anxious for the verdict. Her mother hadn't reached out at all, so she guessed what the deal was, but in the back of her heart, she still held out hope.

The small office was empty, but Jamie's Burberry Weekend perfume lingered in the air. Her messenger bag lay on the floor underneath her desk, and her glasses were on her desk blotter.

Nichelle let out a sigh of relief just as Jamie came through the open door. She offered Nichelle a small smile, but her dimples remained hidden, her shoulders bowed. "Hey."

"Hi. You know that none of this is your fault, right? I don't mean to put you in the middle."

Jamie sighed and sat in her chair and spun around to face Nichelle. "I know, but I'm so sorry."

Nichelle shrugged, but her lip quivered. She took a deep breath to calm herself because although she was severely disappointed, she wanted to spare her friend any grief. It wasn't fair to Jamie how this all worked out. Nor was it fair that she was the messenger. Her mother really sucked. "Thanks, J. So not even Asa?"

"He's being an ass. I think he really would like to know you, but once Anika shut it down, he left it alone. He won't even discuss it with me. They have their little dysfunctional family, and he wants to keep it like that."

"So, he doesn't want another sibling, basically."

"Maybe. I don't know, Nichelle. He and his mother are just alike when it comes to anything unpleasant." She stuck her hand out to Nichelle and waved. "Not that you're unpleasant. They don't know anything about you really."

Nichelle bit her lip, thinking. "Did Anika admit to having a baby at least?"

"She did. I told Asa first, then he asked his mother. She confirmed it but said she didn't want to talk about it. Asa didn't say another word."

"Wow."

"Yeah, I know. Like I said, very dysfunctional."

"And Noah?"

"What about Noah?" Whether coincidence or intentional, Noah walked into their office.

Nichelle hurried and wiped a stray tear before she faced the door, and her brother.

Jamie said, "I was telling Nichelle what happened. I think she was wondering if you would be like the rest of your family and pretend she doesn't exist."

Nichelle whimpered, struggling to keep herself together. She didn't think she'd be so affected by the rejection, but here she was, holding back a hurricane of tears. Hearing the blunt way Jamie phrased it was a little too much for her tender feelings.

Jamie squeezed Nichelle's knee. "I'm sorry. That's not what I meant." She let go and turned to Noah. "I was about to tell her that you weren't like them."

Noah came farther into the room and leaned against the side of Nichelle's desk. "How are you feeling, big sis?"

Nichelle's heart expanded, and she looked up to meet her brother's intense look. "I've had better days but doing okay now. It's disappointing, but I'll live. Thanks for being you."

"Screw them. They're missing out." Jamie smirked and sat back in her chair.

Noah shook his head.

Jamie looked at her phone and stood, picking up her messenger bag. "Sorry to drop a bomb and run, but Noah's here with you, and I have to get to class."

Nichelle stood too and gave her friend a hug. She still had another hour before class. "Thanks. See you later."

Noah took Jamie's seat and watched his sister-in-law as she walked out. He frowned before turning back to Nichelle. "Did she seem different to you?"

Maybe she'd been so tied up in her own misery, but she hadn't paid much attention to Jamie's demeanor. Now that he mentioned it, Jamie was a little off. Too animated. "She did seem a little too cheery."

He leaned forward, putting his forearms on his thighs, and holding his head in his hands. "Asaf's sick." He didn't lift his head but ran his hands across his closely cut hair.

"Will he be okay?"

Noah sat back up and inhaled deeply before letting the breath slowly leak out. "I don't know. You see how they are now. They only said that he was sick and needed surgery. That's all I know."

This news saddened Nichelle to no end. What was worse than being rejected by your own brother? That he may not have a chance to change his mind. That was definitely worse.

"MY MOTHER'S THE worst."

The couple times Nichelle visited Clark's house were rushed, either to pick him up or drop something off. She hadn't really spent any length of time there; they usually hung out at her place. She was excited to be there, to spend time in his comfort zone, but there was so much churning in her head. Her mother's rejection. And her brother's. But also, his mystery illness from which he may or may not recover. Then there was the reckoning with her actual mother. Their dinner was only a couple days away, and she wanted her parents to meet Clark so badly, she hadn't thought it out before asking him. There was so much turmoil between her and her parents right now. What was she thinking adding a boyfriend to the mix? Maybe she was thinking she finally had someone in her life worthy of meeting her parents and she couldn't wait to show him off.

"Your birth mother or adopted mother?"

"Yes."

"Huh?"

"Okay, if I have to pick one, it's my birth mother. Definitely her. I'm so confused these days."

Being around Clark was relaxing, and her body was immediately soothed as soon as she crossed his threshold. He had a calming presence and was always logical about everything, the wheels and gears in his mind forever churning. She'd been anxious ever since Noah gave her the news, on top of the report Jamie gave her, but was more at ease sitting next to Clark on his den sofa. Or maybe it was the surplus of books on every surface. Plus, he had family problems of his own and got past their issues. He didn't go out of his way to be around his parents, but he did visit when necessary. He didn't actively avoid them at all costs like she was doing with hers.

"I think that's understandable. It's only been a few weeks since you found out you're adopted."

"Yeah, but it's more than that. Asaf, that's my other

KELLY CAIN

brother, Jamie's husband."

Clark nodded.

"He's sick. Like really sick, and needs surgery, but I don't know what's wrong with him. Or what his prognosis is."

"I'm really sorry to hear that. Jamie won't tell you?"

Nichelle pulled her sock-covered feet up on the couch and hugged her knees. "Honestly, I'm not sure she even knows. Noah told me about it, and he's not sure. My family has a lot of faults, clearly. And they've certainly held back some important information, but when it comes to something like this, we're open. As soon as my brother..." Her head lolled to the side, and she looked at Clark. "I know this is confusing. So, the brother I grew up with."

"Clifton."

"Right, Clifton." Nichelle grinned to herself, impressed Clark had not only been listening, but remembered. "When he got sick, I'm not sure how much he wanted to share either. But my parents weren't having it. We were in the waiting room when he had surgery, and Mom went with him to all his doctor's appointments. When it got too bad, they set up a hospital bed in his house, and stayed over there with him because he didn't want to leave home. I was over almost every day, mostly to bring food, and run whatever other errands I could. But everyone was completely involved until the end."

"He was fortunate to have you as family."

"Yeah. And I understand it's a personal choice. Everyone

gets to manage their health how they want, but Asaf has a wife and two young boys. Doesn't he owe it to them to be upfront about everything? I just hate this."

Clark moved a hand on top of hers. "Hate what?"

"I guess it's the whole thing about not really knowing my medical history. I know it's selfish, but he has something and I have no idea if it's hereditary because I don't even know what it is."

"That's not selfish at all."

"It kinda is. He could be on the verge of losing his life for all I know, and I'm more worried about how it affects me." She snorted and sat up, putting her feet back on the floor. "That's pretty selfish."

Clark pulled her against him and rested his chin lightly on top of her head. "When faced with death, it's natural to think about our own mortality. And this is a special circumstance."

"Thanks. You're being nice." Nichelle soaked in Clark's smell, his warmth, and kindness.

"Maybe you should give yourself a break. There's a lot to process, and you're doing the best you can. You care about your brother, and what's happening with him. You don't have to beat yourself up about the rest."

"Why not when it's so fun?" She laughed, and stood, bouncing with anxious energy again.

Clark held his hand out, and Nichelle took it, settling back on the sofa next to him. "Your brother is ignoring everything with this new information, but maybe he doesn't have the bandwidth to process it right now. Hopefully he'll come around."

Nichelle leaned into Clark's side and bathed in his words and comfort. Her body relaxed. She loved Clark, but she wasn't sure if the time was right to tell him. He was still holding back a part of himself. A small part, but a part nonetheless.

She sat up straight and gave him a smile. "I should go." If she didn't, she wouldn't be able to hold back her feelings.

"Are you sure? I'm free the rest of the night."

When she'd first met Clark, every moment of his day was planned. Now, he seemed to have extra hours laying around whenever she called. She wondered about that for a moment but decided to shuffle that to the back of her thoughts.

"I guess I could stay awhile." She leaned back into him, resting her hands in his lap.

Clark traced her jawline with his fingertips, his hooded eyes broadcasting his true desires.

That look sent a flash of want through Nichelle. She tilted her head up, and Clark caught her lips with his. Kissing him was satisfying, but her need caressed her core, and she squeezed her legs together to console it. She ran her hands through his strands, pulling him closer, deepening the kiss.

The plush couch they were sitting on was a comfortable dense glacier-gray foam, and Clark laid her back, covering her prone body with his, his breath against her neck. "You feel so good."

"Hmmm." His want was evident against her thigh. She pressed her leg against his dick. "You do too."

"You smell good too." He grinned against her cheek and sat up, pulling her up with him. "Have you seen my bedroom?"

She shook her head, a smile teasing her lips. "You know I haven't." She held on to Clark's strong forearm as he led her down a hallway toward the back of the house. When he flipped the light on inside a large room with a huge bed draped in black in the middle, heat pulsated through her center.

Clark rotated to her with a look in his eyes she hadn't seen before. It was more than lust; his irises glowed with absolute fire. He claimed her mouth and backed her into the wall just inside the entrance to the room.

She tasted his lips, both salty and sweet from their snacks earlier. His tongue was probing and urgent, and she opened for him with abandon, wrapping her hands around his neck, pulling him even closer.

He placed a hand behind her knee and hitched her leg up and around his waist, pressing her cleft firmly against his erection, then rubbed against her. Clark had found a new confidence in initiating the sex between them, and Nichelle was here for it. She spared only a moment of thought as to why. Had he given up on putting a barrier between them? Nichelle certainly hoped so. Before her thoughts could stray

KELLY CAIN

too far, Clark dropped his hands into the pockets on the back of her jeans and cupped her ass. "Is this okay?"

She was more than comfortable with what he was doing. "Yes." But still, she grabbed Clark by the arms and spun him so he was flush against the wall. She backed away from him and slid out of her pants and blouse. She worked on his buckle, because of course he wore a belt, but couldn't get it separated. Her need was urgent, and her fingers wouldn't work properly.

Clark kissed her again while he released the contraption, and allowed his pants to drop to the floor, then pulled her against his hardness.

Nichelle was hot, her nerve endings raw, as Clark trailed kisses down her neck to her breasts, taking his time with each nipple. She scraped her nails across his scalp as he lowered, placing more kisses down her stomach until he found her center. She braced her hands against the wall behind him, while Clark laved her core, dragging his tongue through her folds, then inserting two fingers inside her. "Goodness."

He grinned against her clit before getting back to work.

Clark was turning into a cocky bastard, and she was here for it. He pumped his fingers inside her and swirled his glorious tongue before gently biting her nub. That was her undoing, her orgasm overtaking her, causing her boneless body to slump. He was there to catch her though and spun her around so she was propped against the wall. "Don't move."

When he returned, his dick wrapped and ready, he lifted her so she could circle her legs around him. He placed the head against her entrance and stared into her eyes. "Okay?"

"Yes, definitely okay."

Clark didn't take his time sliding into her. He rooted himself in quickly and pumped earnestly. Nichelle held on for dear life as he ground against her, the friction becoming too much for her already sensitive clit. He slowed, maybe sensing her vulnerability, but she recovered. "Don't you dare stop." He pounded into her against the wall, and she braced herself as her release built and traveled to her core. "Yes, Clark, right there." He grunted into her neck as she came, jerking inside her.

They slid down the wall with exhaustion, crumpling on the floor in pure bliss.

CHAPTER TWENTY-SIX

Nichelle

T HE HOUSE LOOKED sleepy, with its upstairs shutter half closed, and one light shining through the partially open living-room drapes. Nichelle cut the engine to the car and turned to Clark. He was quieter than usual. "Ready?" She gave him a bright smile.

"Are you sure?"

She leaned over and kissed him on the cheek. "Quite. They're going to love you, Clark. Just relax and be yourself."

He huffed but didn't offer another word.

They stepped out and wandered up the walkway. She was anxious for her parents to meet Clark, but she sorely wanted to ignore the other reason for her visit.

Her parents were expecting her. Her mom was probably watching them from somewhere in the house, hidden behind a blind.

She used her key to unlock the door. "Anyone home?"

"In here." Her mom's voice rang out from the kitchen, and Nichelle and Clark followed the delicious smell of fried fish.

"Hi, Mom." Nichelle stooped and wrapped an arm around her mother's slender neck and kissed the side of her face. "This is Clark. My boyfriend." She gave Clark an encouraging smile.

He reached out a stiff hand. "It's nice to meet you, Mrs. Sampson."

Her mom appraised him from head to toe before accepting the handshake. "Please call me Betty. You are a handsome fellow, aren't you?"

Clark opened his mouth to respond, but Nichelle nudged him. He bit his lip. "Thank you."

"Have we met, Clark? Your name seems familiar for some reason."

Clark looked down and pulled at his ear. "I don't believe so."

"Where's Dad?"

"He's upstairs in the bedroom, changing. Just got back from tennis with Marlin." Her dad had played tennis with Nichelle's older cousin for as long as she could remember. Since most of her cousins were older, her memories usually went back far.

"Dinner smells good." She sat her purse on a stool and pulled Clark over to the kitchen sink to wash their hands.

"Thanks, baby. It's almost ready."

Nichelle circled around to the stove and looked inside a boiling pot. Greens, ugh. Not her favorite. She peeked into the oven where a pan of macaroni and cheese was browning, the gooey dairy bubbling to the top. Next to it was a cast iron skillet filled with cornbread. Those were much more appealing. "Great, because I'm starved."

Her mom chuckled. "When are you not?" She turned to a silent Clark. "Are you hungry, son?"

He nodded. After a beat, he cleared his throat and spoke. "I am. It all looks so good."

"Hey there, little girl." Her dad walked in from the hallway and wrapped her in a big hug.

She let out a smothered, "Hi, Dad."

He released Nichelle and turned to Clark with an outstretched hand. "You must be the boyfriend. I'm Robert."

Clark reached for Robert's hand, more relaxed than he'd been with Betty. "Yes. I'm Clark Lin-Lee. It's nice to meet you."

Nichelle leaned into Clark's side as they stood in the kitchen, offering her support. She asked her dad, "How was tennis?"

He grinned. "I beat Marlin all over the court. It was glorious." Her dad was super competitive when it came to sports. He'd coached her at home for basketball, then when she'd surpassed his skills, he and the father of one of her teammates had hired someone for private lessons. He intended her to be the best. She'd never quite lived up to that particular expectation though. She was good enough to play at the collegiate level but wasn't the best by far. She was happy enough making the team.

"That's awesome. Sounds like you had a great time."

"I always do. You should come out sometimes." He patted Clark on the shoulder and led him over to the kitchen table. "Do you play, Clark?"

Nichelle snorted. Clark could barely catch a huge basketball. She couldn't imagine what he'd do with a small tennis ball.

"No, sir, I don't." He stiffened back up just a bit.

Her dad eyed Clark closer before they sat. "You work out?"

"Actually, I cycle. And do some home calisthenics."

"Dad, Clark rides his bike like hundreds of miles at a time. With a bunch of other people. Can you imagine?"

That brought a small smile to Clark's lips. Nichelle imagined he remembered her expressing that sentiment a few times when he first mentioned it to her. "Not hundreds usually, but a fair number."

Since Clark appeared to lighten and become comfortable, Nichelle left them to their conversation and took some plates down from a cabinet. She set the table while her mom pulled the finished food out of the oven.

When they sat down to eat, there was a tension in the air. They were being a little too polite with *pass the fish please*. And *here, let me pour that for you*. That's not normally how they operated at dinner, and she didn't believe it had anything to do with Clark's presence.

Nichelle spooned a bit of hot macaroni and cheese into her mouth and immediately regretted it, pushing some back on the spoon and airing her mouth.

"Be careful, baby."

"Yeah, tell me about it. Good though."

Clark said, "This fish is delicious. We ate some similar in Texas, but this is far superior."

Her mom said, "Thank you, Clark."

Nichelle squeezed Clark's thigh under the table, and the tips of his ears turned pink.

As hungry as she was, Nichelle set her spoon down. "Listen, I need to go ahead and get this out."

"Okay." Her dad balanced a forkful of greens primed for biting but set it back on his plate.

Her mom looked at her, her expression completely neutral. "We have company, dear."

"None of this is new to Clark. We haven't discussed it much, but obviously we can't just ignore the elephant in the room. I'm hurt because you didn't tell me about being adopted. I'm embarrassed that everyone knew except me."

"Yes, but—"

"No buts, Mom. Please let me finish." Nichelle waited until she felt she could talk coherently, without crying again, and definitely without yelling. She wanted to yell at both her parents for their betrayal, but that was never her way. And especially with Clifton's death so new, she wouldn't do that to them. She loved them both completely; they were her parents. And always would be. But still, they needed to hear her truth whether they wanted to or not.

Clark scooted closer and held her hand.

Her mom said, "Go ahead. You let me know when it's okay to say something."

This was not starting out like she hoped, but her mom's defensiveness was not a surprise. She softened her tone, while still keeping it firm. "I want you to know that I love you both. You'll always be my parents. Even though you didn't give birth to me, that won't change." Nichelle looked at an encouraging Clark, shoring up her resolve, his warm hand in hers an anchor. "I feel strongly about that, but I also want to know the people who did birth me. I want to know my siblings and see how we're alike. What we share."

Her mom's lips thinned into a straight line.

Her dad cleared his throat. "That's reasonable. What are you going to do to find them?" He looked at his wife's stern face, but she didn't return his stare. "We don't have any documents other than the one I shared with you already."

"I've already found them, Dad."

Her mom stood, the chair scraping across the tile floor under her. She walked over to the sink and inexplicably turned on the water. She stood there watching the stream disappear down the drain.

"I'm not doing this to hurt either of you. Nobody will take your place." She squeezed Clark's hand and released it and stood. She walked over to the sink, turning off the water.

"You understand that, right, Mom?"

"Oh, is it my turn to talk?"

Nichelle rolled her eyes and went back to sit next to Clark. "You're being petty. You withheld this from me my whole life. But go off then." Clark wrapped his arm around her shoulder. A comfort, but also a reminder to keep her cool.

"I'm only making certain I can speak." She, too, went back to the table but didn't sit. "Those people didn't want you. I'm not being cruel, only stating a fact. Why would you track them down? If they wanted you, they would have looked for you. Or better yet, they wouldn't have given you up to begin with."

Nichelle's eyes widened. "Wow, that is cruel actually. My sister—that's right I have a sister, two incidentally—my sister says they have tried looking for me. But their father was given faulty information. His mutual friend with the mother said I was twin boys." Nichelle couldn't bring herself to claim her birth father or mother. Not in front of her actual mother and father. "They didn't know I was a single girl until after the grandmother died. She told them in a note and that she'd left me the ring."

"I'm sure they'll be wanting that back."

"Why are you being so negative? Nobody has asked me for anything."

"Yet."

Clark tightened his grip on Nichelle's shoulders. His

touch transformed from comfort to outrage although the expression on his face remained unchanged. He watched her closely.

Her dad put his hand over her mom's. "It's a bit of a shock, and we're only trying to process it."

"Seriously, Dad? You're shocked. You've known for thirty-two years. Imagine if you'd just found out a few weeks ago."

"That's not what I meant, honey. We've given you everything in the world and have been good parents to you."

"No doubt. You've been the best parents, but you still lied. You can't erase that. Maybe if I'd grown up knowing I was adopted, I wouldn't have the urge to know these people. But you took that choice away from me, so here we are."

Gathering her second wind, her mom spoke up. "You'll have to excuse all this family dirty laundry, Clark, but apparently Nichelle couldn't wait." She redirected her energy to Nichelle. "All that may be true, and we've already apologized to you, but they still gave you up for adoption. Do you not care about that?"

"Sure, I care. But I also know young people make mistakes." She looked back and forth between her parents. "Apparently, not-so-young people do too. I'm willing to at least hear them out."

"There's no excuse for just giving away your own flesh and blood. If it were me, I wouldn't give those people the time of day."

"Well, it's not you, Mom. And what about my siblings? I have two sisters on one side, and two brothers on the other. What did they do in all of this? How is it their fault? I should be able to know my siblings. We've already wasted all this time being apart." Nichelle's stomach gripped at the thought.

Her mom only shrugged and slumped back into her chair. The fight hadn't left her completely, but she didn't have an answer for that. Maybe she thought about mentioning the brother Nichelle grew up with, but even their own mother knew they didn't have much in common. They never sought each other out, and only interacted when pushed together. Bringing Clifton into the conversation wouldn't move the needle in her mother's direction.

"Well, anyway, I already knew one of my siblings. He works on campus, and the other is Jamie's husband." She swung her gaze around to her father.

"Jamie? You mean Professor Perkins?"

Nichelle nodded. "Can you believe it? My officemate has been my sister-in-law this whole time. She talked about her family, and it was my family too."

"That's quite the coincidence."

Her mom suddenly decided to remain completely quiet. She didn't even stir in her seat.

Clark was perfectly still as well.

"And who works on campus? Do I know him?"

"I'm not sure. His name is Noah Perkins. He's one of the

IT managers."

"Yes, I know of him. I don't think we've ever met though."

"I was literally in his office a month ago and he fixed my laptop. There was something familiar about him, but I never would have guessed we were siblings. Do you see why I need to know who these people are? This town is way too small to be free-balling it like we have been."

He nodded. "I take your point. What about the other side?"

She patted Clark's knee. "We're meeting them tomorrow. They're having a dinner for me. Turns out, I went to high school with one of my sisters. She's only four months younger than me but was a year behind because of the school age cut-offs. Otherwise, who knows, we may have been friends. I have a picture of her, and she doesn't look familiar, but I bet she will when I see her in person."

He picked his fork up and took a bite, nodding his head.

"And my other sister is four years younger, but it wouldn't have mattered anyway because she went to Catholic school. I have nieces and nephews even. I never thought I'd have any of that."

Her mom woke up then. "You never once mentioned anything about wanting any of that. We've been wondering if you even wanted children of your own since until now you never seemed to be serious about anyone."

Clark squirmed in his seat, but Nichelle settled her hand

on his leg.

"I do want children someday. That's one of the reasons I went looking for my birth family. I certainly wouldn't want to bring a child into the world without knowing my medical history."

"What do you mean? There was medical information in your birth records."

"Sure, okay. Anika had acne, and Henry overproduced calcium. Big whoop. They were teenagers. How much medical history do you think there was at that age? Not enough to do me any good."

"If I recall, your grandfather died of cancer."

"He sure did. My brother says he smoked and didn't eat well. After he was blinded, he walked a lot, but that was basically the only exercise he got, and he had to be careful. They all believe he got cancer from his lifestyle choices rather than any genetic reasons. Nobody else in his family had it. That's good information to have."

She huffed but didn't give up. "There's genetic counseling. You could have solved all this taking that route instead of tracking down these people."

"Listen, Mom, I know you don't approve, but this is what it is. You can't change it even though you really tried to head it off beforehand. I'm trying to keep you and Dad up-to-date with what's going on in my life. If you don't want to know, just say the word."

Of course her mom was quiet then. She was too nosy not

to want to know what was happening, and she couldn't trust her husband to stay inside the loop with office gossip.

"I'll take your silence as an affirmation." She looked at her dad who had just forked a big bite of greens in his mouth, his hand poised with a chunk of cornbread to go in next.

He nodded, his mouth too full to do anything else.

Clark moved his hand to grasp hers under the table and squeezed.

Nichelle squeezed back and picked at her food, her appetite nearly gone. Her expectations hadn't been high on how all this new family information would go over with her mother, but she'd held out hope that she was wrong. Betty Sampson would get over it. Or she wouldn't. Nichelle didn't have the spoons to care. She was still too angry with both her parents for lying to her so many years.

They ate the rest of their food in silence, and when they finished, Nichelle and Clark went home.

CHAPTER TWENTY-SEVEN

Nichelle

"**A**RE YOU NERVOUS?" Clark asked.

"Well, I wasn't. Should I be?" Nichelle jumped into Clark's SUV and put her seatbelt on.

He slid into the driver's side. "I have no idea. You're meeting a lot of family for the first time. You eased into the other side with Noah."

"I guess I hadn't thought about it like that. But no, I'm not nervous because I have you. Have I thanked you lately for going with me? Especially after that disaster with my parents."

He glanced at her, but since he was driving, he didn't look at her long, his hands on ten and two as usual. Clark was nothing if not predictable. Predictable and steady. "It's my pleasure. I'm interested to see the similarities with you and your family." Nichelle couldn't help but notice how Clark's posture was so much more relaxed than when she took him to meet her parents. He was also being chatty where he hadn't spoken more than a handful of words on the way to the previous dinner.

"Really? I didn't think you liked doing the family thing. Or the people thing, really."

He stilled for a moment, listening to the GPS, then turned right at the stoplight. "I don't mind people as much as you think I do. I have a limited capacity, otherwise I'm tired. I can give more, but it's taxing."

"Do you and Francesca ever hang out?"

He grinned. Something he'd been doing a lot lately. It looked good on him. "Sometimes, but she's pretty busy with school and your sorority. We catch a meal when our schedules line up, but we mostly see each other at the store when she's working."

"Oh, that's right. I guess you do see a lot of her considering you work together."

"Some. When she's working, she's out front helping customers unless it's slow. Then she's doing business-related tasks for the store. You'd be surprised how much it takes to keep a jewelry store open. I certainly was."

"I probably would. That's way outside my purview. I barely keep my checking account balanced." And that was only because her mom drilled in fiscal responsibility her entire life.

A few minutes later, they drove across a bridge that let them into the quaint beach town of Benicia. Neither of her sisters lived in the same town where they all grew up, but they both lived in the general area. Madeleine lived with her husband and son in the valley about an hour and a half away while Suzette lived in the opposite direction, but a little closer. More like a half hour.

Even though Nichelle grew up right down the road, she'd never had a reason to visit this particular town. "Have you been here before?"

"Hmmm, it's been a while, but yes. I think I debated here in high school."

"Of course you were on the debate team."

He only shrugged and made another turn, then pulled to a stop on a nice street with manicured lawns. "Looks like quite a few cars in their driveway and on the street, so I passed the house to park. We can walk back."

Nichelle looked behind them to the house Clark indicated. There were cars parked everywhere. They parked four houses away. "Jesus."

"Exactly how many people are in your family? I thought it was just your father, sisters, and their husbands."

"Well, Suzette mentioned my aunt may come over from Sacramento, but she wasn't sure. And her daughter, my cousin, who lives in the city. And I think one of her sons. Those were all maybes though."

Clark arched an eyebrow. "We'll see soon enough."

As they walked down the sidewalk, heading for her sister's house, Nichelle lagged a bit behind to sneak a look at Clark's backside. He had a fresh haircut, precision lines bordering his neck, soft waves falling just so. His dark-gray pressed pants hung perfectly on his trim waist and hips, highlighting a delectable butt she couldn't wait to get her hands on again. Nichelle swung her gaze to a passing car. This was the worst time to get distracted by Clark's hot body. She had a whole family to meet. Then again, lusting after Clark certainly calmed her nerves.

He turned his head and slowed his pace. "Everything okay back there? You still want to go?"

"I'm fine." She giggled to herself.

The house was built into the side of a hill so only a small part was visible from the front. There was a compact but nicely landscaped yard out front with beautiful fuchsia roses in full bloom. Two men stood on the steps, joking and laughing with one another.

One of the men turned to her and smiled. He was tall, well over six feet, and lean. His head was shaved but the stubble on his chin was black mixed heavily with gray. "You have the look of your mother."

"You must be Henry."

He opened his arms, and Nichelle stepped into them. "I sure am, babe. I'm your dad, and I love you."

Tears pricked the back of her eyes. She only had one dad, but she was touched by his outreach. She patted his back and stepped away. "Thank you." She reached for Clark's hand and pulled him closer. "I'd like you to meet Clark. Clark Lin-Lee. Clark, meet my father, Henry Maddox."

Henry reached out to shake Clark's hand. "Nice to meet

you, fella. Now who are you to my daughter?"

"He's my boyfriend." She grinned and shrugged. She loved calling him that.

"It's nice to meet you." He pumped Clark's hand.

The young man standing next to Henry cleared his throat.

"Yeah, man. I've lost all my manners. This is your cousin, Alex. He's my sister's son. His mama's inside."

Nichelle took Alex's proffered hand and shook it. "Good to meet you."

She turned to her father. "I'm sorry for your loss. I wish I could have known her."

Henry nodded, face somber. "I wish you could have too." He opened the screen door. "Come on in so everyone else can meet you."

Clark cupped the small of Nichelle's back and followed her through the opened door. Where they connected, Nichelle felt a warming sensation. She relished Clark's touch, and she was happy he was sharing meeting her family for the first time.

Inside was a bustle of people moving about through the house. The entryway was open, bordering the living room. A huge sectional couch lined two walls, and people crowded the seats. More folks were clustered in groups standing in the middle of the room which connected to the dining room where platters of food filled the dining room table. To their immediate right, the kitchen held two people unwrapping desserts and placing drinks on the kitchen table. One of those people was her sister because she was Henry's twin. "Suzette?"

"Oh wow, hello. I didn't see you come in." She walked right up to Nichelle and gave her a hug, then stepped back smiling. "It's so good to see you." She reached past Nichelle to shake Clark's hand. "Hi, I'm Suzette."

"I'm Clark."

Behind her, Henry spoke up. "And that other lady in there is my girlfriend, Johnnie."

"Oh my goodness. Aren't you the prettiest thing?" Johnnie was slim and had an open, friendly face.

"Thank you."

The crowd overwhelmed Nichelle as she was shuffled through the house, introductions galore for both her and Clark. She met her aunt who was about Nichelle's height, thin with a pretty face. She was a couple of years younger than Henry. They had two younger brothers, but neither were there. Nichelle sensed another rift in this family too.

She met cousins and smaller nephews and a niece and her two brothers-in-law. Nichelle was beginning to think her other sister changed her mind about meeting when the sliding glass door opened and in walked Madeleine. She was noticeably shorter than Nichelle and Suzette, and wore her hair cropped close almost identical to Clark's. Hers may have been an inch longer on top and was curled instead of Clark's waves. The short haircut really complemented her pretty face.

Nichelle headed to her sister, and they met somewhere in the middle.

Madeleine's hug was strong and warm. "There's my sister."

If Nichelle still held any reservations about Madeleine, they completely disappeared. Apparently, her sister preferred in-person interaction rather than telephone conversations. And now her birth family was almost complete.

THE AIR ON the little beach community was cooler than across the bridge. The three couples sat out in the back on the deck with full bellies and glasses of wine in their hands.

Most people had left, although a few remained inside. Henry had to work so he and his girlfriend left too. Clark and Nichelle sat close to each other, Clark's arm effortlessly slung across her shoulders, and her hand resting in his lap.

Clark stroked Nichelle's upper arm absently. "It beautiful out here." He groaned as he adjusted in his seat, rubbing his taut stomach. "I can't remember being so full."

Suzette grinned. "You two are so cute together. I'm happy we had something for you to eat."

"I know. I should have mentioned he was pescatarian. Totally my fault." She couldn't believe she hadn't remembered something as important as her boyfriend's dietary restrictions.

The squeeze of her arm let her know she'd been forgiven.

"It all worked out. And it was nice having everyone together for once." Madeleine leaned back against her husband on the chaise lounge they were sharing.

The frown on Suzette's face told a story, but Nichelle hadn't quite figured out what yet. "Do you not normally have family dinners?"

"Girl, not at all. My family and Suzette's get together for Christmas some years, but we have in-laws too, so we have to split our time. You see your father keeps a girlfriend, so he usually stays busy."

Nichelle worried for Suzette's teeth. She seemed to be grinding them as she listened to their sister. "Oh. That's too bad."

"Do you mostly spend time with your parents or Clark's? Or do you split the time?" Apparently, Madeleine was a fountain of conversation when face-to-face, unlike their brief phone talks.

Nichelle stiffened at the inquiry, but Clark answered without hesitation. "I spent more time with my grandparents growing up, and they passed away a few years ago. I have a sister, and we see her often."

She worried he would stumble over his relationship with his parents. Maybe he was used to answering those types of questions. "Matter-of-fact, his sister is my sorority sister. She's a few years younger and goes to undergrad at the university. I'm the chapter's graduate advisor."

"Is that how you two met?" Madeleine asked.

She wasn't sure if it was the best time to mention the ring and that whole drama. "We met through Francesca." She turned to Suzette to draw her into the conversation. "How long have you two been married?"

"Almost eight years." She looked at her smiling husband. "Can you believe it?"

Eight years? And she was Nichelle's youngest sister with four years separating them. "Wow, were you like high school sweethearts?" Nichelle really was a relationship loser.

A giggle bubbled up from Suzette, and her husband joined in. "Not at all. I was working at the bank a couple years after high school, and he was doing security work as a side job. He's a sheriff's deputy."

Nichelle smiled but lifted her brow. "What am I missing. That doesn't sound like a funny story."

"We're laughing because he's nearly ten years older than me. He wishes we were high school sweethearts."

"Hey, obviously I look good if your sister thought that."

"Sure, baby. You look very good."

Everyone laughed, including Clark, although it was more of a polite chuckle. She'd come to realize that most times, he didn't actually get the joke, but he'd learned enough social cues to laugh when it seemed appropriate. Nichelle hated that he didn't feel like he could just be himself. It wasn't necessary to always know what people were joking around about. She squeezed his thigh and allowed her gaze to fall on him and linger a bit. She couldn't help herself. She liked all the touching.

Nichelle rotated back to her sister. "Well, you two look great together." Then she circled to Madeleine and her husband. "What about you?"

Madeleine took a sip of her wine. "Hmmm, well, we weren't high school sweethearts either." She chortled. "We've actually only been married a couple of years. My son is from a previous relationship."

Clark leaned back in his chair, taking Nichelle with him. He was relaxed, and her head rested on his hard chest. His arm came across her stomach, holding her in place. Somehow, he knew she needed the extra strength, and he offered it willingly. He really was too good to be true.

It's not like she hadn't suspected that all along.

CHAPTER TWENTY-EIGHT

Nichelle

WHAT IF SHE'D grown up with her brothers and mother? Ever since she'd left her sister's house, Nichelle thought about scenarios where that would be possible. As she sat in her car in the parking lot of her apartment, she pondered it again. Sure, it would have been wonderful to share her childhood with siblings, something she missed out on with her adoptive family. Her brother was already an adult when she was born and that contributed to them not being close. There were other reasons. But then again, growing up with her brothers would also mean she would have dealt with her birth mother's neglect. Her inability to offer love and support. Her selfishness.

And then there was her birth father. Again, her sisters were incredible and so well-adjusted. If events happened the way her paternal grandmother wished, she would have been raised by her, not Anika. Nor Henry because he was busy with his women and being as neglectful as her birth mother, allowing his daughters to be bounced back and forth between their grandmothers.

She pulled her cell phone out of her purse and stared at the name long and hard before tapping the icon.

Her mom answered before it rang on Nichelle's end. "Hello?"

Nichelle breathed in deep. The thing she realized is that her parents saved her. She could have languished away in the system instead of being adopted at three months old—too young to ever know anything other than immense love. They bestowed on her a good life. A great life. They never gave her a reason to think they didn't love her wholeheartedly. That's why she'd been so blindsided when the pearl ring came and when she read the accompanying note from her grandmother.

Her mom's voice came through again, clear and strong but strained. "Nichelle?"

"Hi, Mom. Can I come over?"

"Sure, baby."

When Nichelle approached her childhood home this time around, she didn't feel the dread she'd felt the last few times. She was at peace with her life, and the decisions she'd made. She had amazing friends; she enjoyed her career no matter how she came into it. So what if she and her father didn't share blood. He'd shared his passion for political science, and it soon became her passion too. And she loved her sorority. Yes, her mother's sorority, but hers as well. She'd formed unbreakable bonds and she was glad of it.

Nichelle used her key to unlock the door and was met by her mother coming into the entry hall. "Hi, Mom."

She wrapped Nichelle up in a warm hug and held her there for a long while. Eventually, her dad joined them. So much was conveyed through that hug. Her parents told her she was their daughter, and they were sorry they hadn't told her. She told them she was glad, and that she'd forgiven them.

When they finally released each other, Nichelle wiped the errant tears leaking out of her burning eyes. She had a great cry and put her anger behind her for good. Honestly, she'd held onto it too long. She didn't mean to cause suffering to her parents, but at the same time, working through her crisis of identity took a minute. "What's for dinner?"

Her dad roared with laughter and pulled her in for another hug, walking down the long hallway to the kitchen. "There's my girl."

"We have some leftover chicken and dumplings." Her mom clucked behind her. "And before you say it's too hot for soup, I say it's never too hot for my chicken and dumplings."

"I'm not even trying to argue with that logic, Mom." She washed her hands and pulled down a large bowl while her mother pulled the soup from the refrigerator. The pieces of her life were finally falling together. She'd made peace with her identity and was excited to learn about those new portions. Relationships with three of her four siblings were kickstarted, and she still held out hope for the fourth.

Then there was Clark. She was in love, and she was mostly certain he was too. She grinned to herself as she punched the buttons on the microwave.

"Where's that boyfriend of yours?"

Nichelle rotated to her mom with her brows raised. Had she said something out loud?

"Don't look at me like that. Your smile is powering that microwave without you having to turn it on." She took the glass of water her husband handed her. "I know you see it, Robert."

Her dad grunted, kissed Nichelle on the cheek, and walked out toward his office.

Nichelle rolled her eyes. "He's at work."

"Oh, okay. He seems like a nice young man. A little quiet, but nice. Very handsome."

"Yeah, you really have to get to know him before he speaks much." The microwave dinged, and Nichelle removed her bowl of goodness and set it on the table. "Hmmm, this smells delicious, Mom."

"You said he works at a jewelry store?"

Nichelle was certain she hadn't mentioned where Clark worked. More than likely, her mom dragged that bit of info from Amanda. "He and his sister own that jewelry store down on Bancroft. Their grandparents left it to them."

"Oh yes, I know the store. Does he like it? Working there?"

"Not really. I think he tolerates it more than anything. Mostly he works in the back in a lab he built." Nichelle blew on her spoon and deposited some soup in her mouth. "Hmmm, so good."

Her mom's eyebrows knitted together. "In a lab, you say. What exactly does he do in the lab?"

Something in her tone had Nichelle forgetting about her soup. "He's a geochemist."

Her mom's eyebrows flew up to her hairline. "I think I know where I've heard his name before." She raced down the hall to her husband's office.

Nichelle followed and when she got there, her mom was rifling through a stack of folders on top of a filing cabinet. Since she'd retired, she'd turned her home office into a workout room. Looks like she'd kept any needed paperwork in her husband's office although he couldn't be too happy about it.

"What's going on, Betty?"

"Give me a moment, and I'll tell you." She finally pulled out a clipped stack of legal-sized paper. "Here it is. Clark's name was so familiar because I'd seen it in these case files. He's on the witness list."

A churning started in Nichelle's stomach, and she ran her hands through her curls. "Witness? Witness for which side?" She asked the question but already knew the answer. But did Clark know?

"For the prosecution, honey."

Nichelle sat down hard on the couch, her breath caught in her throat. Surely, he couldn't have known. He'd mentioned a couple of cases he was testifying on, but obviously nothing about her mother's company. And Nichelle definitely told him, so he was aware. He had to be.

For the second time today, tears flowed from her eyes. An eerie premonition gripped her heart. Maybe trusting Clark so easily hadn't been the right decision after all. Maybe loving him was even worse.

CHAPTER TWENTY-NINE

Clark

MEETING NICHELLE'S SISTERS and family with her was the best time Clark had experienced in a while. Probably since their road trip. He loved being with Nichelle. He loved Nichelle.

The plain truth was he wanted to be with her. Period. He'd testified this morning, and thankfully her mother wasn't in the courtroom. Now he would tell her the whole sordid mess and prostrate himself before her. She was a reasonable person, and surely she'd recognize he was only doing his job—securing his reputation and following the law.

He wasn't sure, and maybe she was a better actress than he realized, but he sensed love seeping through her touch whenever they were together. He could see a future with Nichelle. He'd never been so clear about someone in his entire life. He tilted his head back and smiled at the ceiling, then picked up his phone and texted her.

Clark: *I know we're supposed to meet later, but if you're free for lunch, can we have a picnic?*
Nichelle: *What's this about?*

WHAT AN UNUSUAL response from her. He'd expected some playful retort, but there was stiffness in those three words. She normally didn't respond that way.

Clark: *I need to tell you something.*
Nichelle: *So tell me.*

THIS WAS CERTAINLY not what he expected.

Clark: *Is there something wrong?*
Nichelle: *When and where?*
Clark: *Would you mind picking me up? Around 1?*
Nichelle: *K.*

HER RIGIDITY DIDN'T bode well for the news he needed to share with her. He cared for her deeply and didn't want to lose her.

He didn't have a picnic basket but found a canvas bucket Franny gave him with a flower inside. The plant died long ago so he washed it out and set it outside to dry although there was no way it would dry in the next hour. He'd have to line it with a trash bag before placing the food inside. He worked his hands into and out of a fist several times to calm his nerves. This was why he planned ahead.

Clark made shrimp salad sandwiches on croissants. He removed grapes from the refrigerator and searched for anything else he could bring. He had a large bottle of sparkling water, but other than that, nothing portable. Oh, cheese. There was some soft gooey cheese, but no baguette to accompany it. The grapes would have to do. Hopefully Nichelle would appreciate the thought because he'd been around her enough during meals to know she'd prefer some salty chips or some sort of creamy potato concoction. He threw in almonds for good measure.

Nichelle texted him from the driveway, so he picked up the filled bucket and a tote bag packed with a blanket, cups, hand sanitizer, and his refillable water bottle, and headed out the door with a lighter step. The thought of telling the truth buoyed him. But he stopped short when he saw her. She had the top down, something she normally spared him from.

He eyed the small car, danger lurking in its exposed core. "Can we put the top up?"

"Nope." She leaned over the passenger seat and pushed the door open. "We're going less than five miles. You'll live."

He sighed, then slipped into the car. "You know I hate the top down."

"Yup, and you know I hate not having the top down. We're not going far. Live a little."

What was that supposed to mean? He lived plenty. It was dying he was worried about.

"Stop pouting, Clark."

"I'm a thirty-four-year-old adult. I do not pout. I'm merely concerned of wayward debris removing my head from my body. Or getting into an accident with an eighteen-wheeler, and again, having my head removed from my body."

Nichelle sniggered and reversed out the driveway. To her credit, she eased onto the street and drove reasonably to the park. It was the same park where they'd played basketball but on the opposite end away from the sports fields.

He couldn't get out of the car fast enough.

"You forgot something." Nichelle leaned over and picked his water bottle off the floor and tossed it to him. It had fallen out of the tote.

His reflexes had improved considerably over the past couple of months being around Nichelle. She kept him on his toes. He seized the bottle out of the air and stuck it back in the bag, surveying the area for a good spot to spread the blanket.

She lagged behind him, uncharacteristically quiet.

"Is something wrong?"

"No."

Clark was never one for taking a hint, or picking up on context clues, but even he understood Nichelle wasn't her normal self. Perhaps she hadn't worked her issues out with her parents. Last he'd spoken to her, she was headed their way. That was more than likely the root of her mood.

Although she ought not take it out on him. The roof down seemed entirely ungenerous. He wasn't exactly mad, but he was a bit miffed at her concerning the whole car roof situation. "If you're upset, you shouldn't project. Share with me what's wrong?"

"Why do you think something's wrong? Because you're a baby who's afraid to drive a couple of blocks with the top down?"

"It wasn't a couple of blocks. And I wasn't afraid. It's unsafe, and I have a right to not feel unsafe."

Nichelle huffed and lowered herself to the blanket Clark laid out. "You were the one who wanted to meet. I dropped everything. And by everything, I mean watching *Matchmaker Paradise*."

Clark shook his head and pulled food from the bucket. He'd texted her. He wanted to talk to her. To explain his secrecy. To plead with her and make her see he was a good person. Someone she could trust and share her life with. This decidedly was not the best way to start off. "You're right. We made it safely. Let's just eat." He unpacked the tote.

"Croissants. What's inside?" She picked up the bottle of hand sanitizer and squirted a glob in her hands, then set the bottle back on the blanket.

Nichelle was normally good-natured. She was usually easy to forgive, and he hoped that would serve him today, although her mood was decidedly sour. More than a couple months had passed, and it would appear she still hadn't forgiven her mother. Clark would have to take his chances. "Shrimp salad. I hope you like."

"Okay." She leaned over to pour herself water into a cup, and Clark admired her from his vantage point. Her curls were in two French braids and tied together in the back, revealing her long, elegant neck. Her smooth skin was dewy from the slight exertion of walking across the park. She was wearing blue shorts, which revealed her long, toned legs. Her silver tank top accentuated thin but strong shoulders.

Clark wanted to pull her up into his arms and kiss her right there. But that would have to wait until after they'd hashed it out. He would reveal his secret, beg her to under-stand if needed, then declare his feelings. All of his feelings, including his love. He was sick of keeping it bottled up. He wanted the ease of relaxing together in someone's backyard, couples enjoying good wine and conversation. He'd never felt the need for sharing time with others before, but Nichelle brought that side out of him. He wanted that permanently, and he trusted Nichelle wanted it too.

She dipped a grape in the cheese and popped it into her mouth. "Good." She mostly said that to herself.

Clark's skin cooled. Something was terribly wrong, and it was more than the rift between Nichelle and her parents. She was upset with him. "Tell me what's wrong."

"What do you mean?"

"You haven't said much since we sat down."

"You asked me here, remember?"

He sighed.

She rolled her eyes, and stood, waving her arms about. "I could live the rest of my life without hearing another one of your long-suffering sighs. I swear to God."

He stilled. Nichelle never spoke to him in such hateful tones. She never spoke to anyone in that manner. "What happened?"

She paced around their pristine blanket, creating wider circles with each pass. "What happened? Hmmm, okay, Mr. Innocent. What happened is that you testified against my mother's former company and failed to mention it."

Clark gasped and stood. "Wait, I was—"

She stood right in his face, pointing her finger. "No, you don't get to talk now. You had all the time in the world to speak, and never said a word. How could you?" Nichelle's face was flushed red, and a vein throbbed in her neck.

He opened his mouth but thought better of it. She'd asked him a question, but also said not to speak. He scratched his head in confusion, unsure how to proceed, and a sudden mist stung his eyes. She wouldn't forgive him.

She bit her fist, then let out a heavy breath. "When did you know? This whole time you've known me, did you think you were coming for my mother?"

"No, no, not at all. I didn't realize she even worked for the company until we were almost home from Texas. You mentioned she worked for the chemical company."

"And that's why you got all cagey, and said you had a secret and couldn't talk about it."

Clark nodded his head vigorously. "Exactly. I really liked you a lot, but this case was an unfortunate coincidence."

"And you didn't feel you could trust me to give me this explanation. You thought, what? That I'd run to my mother? The one who's retired and just assisting. She wasn't even involved with the incident. It was one bad apple siphoning money from the company and covering it up."

"Yes, we know that now, but you didn't mention Betty was retired."

Nichelle stopped her pacing to stare daggers into Clark's eyes. "That's Mrs. Sampson to you. And I spoke in the past tense about her job. After working for the company for thirty years, she retired after my brother got sick."

"I didn't realize."

"No, Clark, you didn't realize. That's why communication is so important."

Clark made a tactical error, but he couldn't tamp down the words bubbling up his throat. He wasn't wrong, just mistaken. It was an honest mistake. And Nichelle hadn't been completely forthcoming. "I told you I had a conflict. But you should have told me your mother was retired."

"You're seriously turning this shit on me now? Seriously? Well, that's a…choice, I guess." She picked up her purse and walked toward the car.

Clark called after her. "What I mean is we wouldn't have any issues if you only told me."

Nichelle jumped in her car and left the parking lot, tires squealing.

He glanced around and tensed. One quick check of his pocket revealed he'd left his phone in Nichelle's car. He'd have to walk home with the half-eaten food, which was probably good, because he needed to reevaluate his life choices. He couldn't believe he'd fallen in love with someone so stubborn and unreasonable.

CHAPTER THIRTY

Nichelle

NICHELLE SAT IN her car in the parking lot of her apartment building, fuming. Her hands shook so hard, she put them under her armpits to keep them still. How dare he testify against her mother? Or at least think he was. And the whole trust thing was an even bigger issue than she knew.

She hit the steering wheel. He screwed her knowing all of this. Their whole relationship was based on a complete lie. And she trusted him. They'd become so close on the road trip, and that night in Barstow… He told her he wanted a future with her even knowing he was betraying her family. Why was she always making the same mistake in love?

That's exactly why she'd put all her energy in her career. By the time she got her undergrad degree, she realized guys would rather hang out for one-on-one games on the court instead of in a restaurant. She thought they were a thing, when in reality, they were just a pick-up game teammate.

She looked down at his phone in the console. Maybe she

could give it to Francesca later. Of course, at that moment, Amanda's call was a harsh reminder that she couldn't put Clark's sister in the middle of them. Her friend warned her, but she didn't listen.

"Hello."

"Hey, girl. What bee's in your bonnet?"

She picked up Clark's phone and tucked it in her purse. He was definitely the bee in her bonnet.

"Nothing." She put a smile on her face, hoping it would convey through the phone. Her friend was visiting her parents for a week, and Nichelle didn't want to sour her trip with her issues. "How are you? What's going on down there in all that humidity?"

"Whew, chile. You haven't said nothing but a word. I can't even begin to describe it but thank goodness for air conditioning. That's all I can say. What's going on out there? Have you watered my plants?"

Shit. Not only had she not watered Amanda's plants, she'd forgotten to go over there and check on her house. "Ummm, I haven't had the chance?"

"Are you asking me or telling me?"

"Sorry, A."

"I already knew you hadn't. My alarm hasn't been touched."

"I know I'm a terrible friend. I'll go over there now."

"You don't have to go right this minute. What's going on? Your voice sounds strained."

She could never hold anything back from Amanda. Nichelle told her bestie about the argument she had with Clark. How she'd fallen in love with him. And how he'd thrown that love in the gutter with the rest of her past loves.

"Man, how long have I been gone?" Amanda's voice rose octaves as she asked the rhetorical question. "A lot has happened. Why didn't you tell me when we talked after your thing with your parents the other night?"

"Because the thing with my parents was enough. I didn't want to throw Clark in the mix."

"Okay, so have you worked out the thing?"

"With my parents? Yeah. We're great."

"And Clark?"

Nichelle dug out his phone and stared at the black screen. "I can forgive him. But I don't know if I could be with him. I'm definitely gonna need an apology though. And from what I've learned of Clark Lin-Lee, he never thinks he's wrong. Let him tell it, he knows everything."

"Do you plan on apologizing for leaving him stranded at the park?"

She rolled her eyes and was grateful her friend couldn't see her. She didn't like admitting when she was wrong either. "We'll see."

"That didn't sound too convicted."

"Yes, okay. I'm going to apologize for leaving his sorry ass in the park."

"Girl." She laughed, and Nichelle couldn't help but join

in. "I hope you work on that apology before you see him."

"Yeah, I guess. An apology for leaving him is one thing. Forgiving him for his lies is quite another."

They disconnected the call, and Nichelle sat there a moment longer gathering her thoughts. She'd return the phone to Clark and apologize for abandoning him. Hopefully he'd have one for her too. Then she'd go water Amanda's dang plants.

Clark was sitting on the steps in front of his house when Nichelle pulled up. The door behind him was open, illuminated by the porch light. He didn't move even as Nichelle turned off her car.

She breathed a sigh of relief that he hadn't left his keys somewhere in the car too. She picked up his phone and got out of the car, walking at a leisurely pace up the walkway. Laying eyes on him rose her pressure again, but she couldn't ignore the warmth in her belly seeing him gave her too.

It wasn't like Clark to be so still when she was around, and he only looked up when she was right up on him. "Hi."

He looked up, sadness marking his otherwise beautiful face. "Hi."

Nichelle extended her hand with the phone and took a deep breath. "I apologize for leaving you at the park."

He nodded and took the phone from her, sliding it in the pocket of his sweatpants. "Okay, I accept your apology."

"Okay, thanks. And you…apologize for…"

His head whipped up, a confused crease in his brow.

"Apologize? What did I do?"

"Wow, you're serious right now?"

"Tell me why you're getting upset again. I can't read your mind."

She placed her hands on her hips. Her mom used to say, "...on her imagination." She wasn't sure why a quote from her mother popped in her head at that moment, but it reminded her that this wasn't her personality. She didn't pop off in anger without working through her feelings. "Listen, Clark. You hurt me. You lied to me. We had something, and you didn't trust me with the truth."

"I get why you're upset, but please try to see it from my point of view. My reputation means a lot to me, and it was unethical for me to tell you about the case, no matter how much I wanted to. Also, I didn't want to put you in that position—choosing between me and keeping a secret from your mother."

"Yeah, except it doesn't really involve my mother. And if you'd trusted me enough to tell me, you would have found that out." She turned to leave, then circled back around. "At least I know where I stand in the grand scheme of things with you. Way lower than your reputation. Good to know."

Clark put his head in his hands and scrubbed them across his face.

Nichelle knew exactly how he felt. They were no closer to resolving this issue because even though she was ready to forgive him, he wasn't ready to ask for forgiveness. "You're a very stubborn man. I've gotta go water my friend's plants, so call me when you're ready to apologize." She wasn't sure that would mean anything in terms of their relationship, but at least it would be a start.

She turned on her heel and strolled down the pathway back to her car. She may want a deep relationship with Clark, and he may reciprocate those feelings, but he was going to have to own his part in all of this. She didn't mind apologizing for her stuff—well she did, but she apologized anyway—but she refused to go forward in a relationship with someone who couldn't see the error of his ways. And as errors go, this was a pretty big one as far as she was concerned.

By the time she returned home from Clark's house, she'd come to a realization. She needed to move on and put Clark out of her mind.

CHAPTER THIRTY-ONE

Clark

WHEN NICHELLE LEFT him, Clark picked himself up, and lumbered back into the house. He hoped she would be able to see his point of view, but it was useless. She called him stubborn, but that's an adjective he reserved for her. Only she couldn't see it.

He pulled a beer out of the refrigerator and took it to his den. The real estate agent called it a family room, but with no family to speak of, he'd renamed it. One day, it may go back to its original purpose, but unless he could make things right with Nichelle, he didn't know if that day would ever come. His life had turned into such a mess.

Nichelle's obstinance was mind-boggling. He stayed in his lab for a reason. Maybe it was time to get back there and accept his fate in life.

When Clark awoke the next day, he wasn't feeling any better. He'd dreamed about Nichelle all night. He tried to see it from her point of view, and he understood why she would need an apology, but he wasn't sure he could give her one when he didn't feel it in his heart. They were so different, and it was difficult to accept that and move forward, but he also realized that his love for her wasn't dissipating anytime soon either. Moving forward without her seemed like the worse option, but did he have a choice?

Clark shifted to the floor of his bedroom and did what he always did when he needed to find a solution. He rose, straightening his arms, and carried his weight, up and down.

After twenty push-ups, he realized he wasn't the most patient person in the world and was easily thrust back into his shell. Up and down, up and down.

By fifty, the epiphany occurred that maybe he wouldn't always fall in line, but that's okay as long as he fit with the person he loved. He and Nichelle matched even though they were different. She understood him and put up with him no matter how awkward he was, and clueless about social situations. More than that, she didn't just put up with him, she embraced his idiosyncrasies and even though she occasionally teased him, it was through the prism of her good nature. Even Franny warned him to try to conform, and not embarrass her. Nichelle never did that.

By the time Clark was straining at almost a hundred push-ups, his arms were jelly. And he was no closer to figuring out what to do about Nichelle. He simply wasn't wrong. It was an impossible situation, and he could have trusted her, but he hadn't known her that long. He trusted others. Well, maybe not trusted, but listened when others said they really liked him and wanted to be with him. Turned out that wasn't true. Nichelle wasn't like that though.

There existed a big world outside his lab. And all those people out there, some were more interesting than he suspected. Spending the afternoon with Nichelle's paternal birth family taught him that. Being with Nichelle taught him that far more. Turned out, he could learn a thing or two from others. He was ready to learn, but not apologize. He wasn't wrong. Hopefully she could accept that and move forward.

He checked the time. It was still early, and Nichelle liked to sleep in. He needed to be at the jewelry store in a couple of hours but felt he couldn't wait to talk to her. He showered, then completed his morning routine, dressing in dark gray pants. Next, he texted Nichelle, hoping she would be up.

She didn't text back, and that concerned him. Was she so upset that she would never return his messages? He would accept her decision, but he wouldn't be happy about it.

Clark opened the door to the garage, but before he could settle into his SUV, his phone pinged. It wasn't Nichelle though, and his heart dropped. Franny wanted to know if he would be at the store today. He typed out a quick reply and sat behind the steering wheel. He wasn't due there for another two hours and going early was useless because he didn't have a current case. Instead, he drove to the park where he'd enjoyed so much time with Nichelle. He'd sit in the air conditioning and watch the players, but it would occupy his time and still give him a closeness to the woman he loved. If he never heard from her again, he would come back to the court for a pick-up game occasionally and remember their time together with fondness.

There were ten people playing a full-court game. The rhythm of the bounce of the basketball lulled Clark into a melancholy peace. He watched the mix of men and women run up and down the court and marveled at his ability to enjoy the game he'd never cared about before. Playing basketball would never replace cycling, but he made room for it to spend time with Nichelle and ended up really appreciating it. One of the women lifted from the ground, and spiraled through the air, laying the ball perfectly in the hoop. He recognized the grace of that basketball player. On her way down, a man was parked underneath her, and they both went down hard, in a tangle of legs and arms. Before Clark could think, he turned off the engine and raced through the early dew of the wet grass, forgetting all about his store-ready shoes. He'd go home and get another pair if necessary, but all he could think about was getting to Nichelle.

Before he could reach her, she righted herself and held out a hand to help the man up.

Clark wanted to sorely injure the other player for being reckless and placing Nichelle in danger, but she simply laughed and high-fived the man.

He stopped at the edge of the court, unsure how to proceed since she was fine, and they were still playing.

Nichelle spotted him, doing a double take, as she ran down the length of the court, getting back on defense.

A damp breeze reminded him he was standing in wet grass. He moved over to the bench and sat, hoping she would have time to talk to him before he had to leave. It was his responsibility to open this morning, and he couldn't be late.

Ten minutes later, someone called game, and Nichelle trudged over to the bench to retrieve a towel out of a sports bag laying near his feet. Others followed, some talking of beat downs they would deliver next time, others gloating over their win. Nichelle quieted and stared at Clark as she wiped down her face, chest, and arms. Her hair was in a high ponytail, but curls escaped and stuck to her neck.

Clark fidgeted in his seat on the bench. "I'm glad you didn't get hurt."

"Me too." She stuffed the towel back in her bag and slung it over her shoulder. "You're a little overdressed for a game."

"Yeah." Clark looked around. Some players hung back, clearly surveying what was happening. Considering how overdressed Clark was, he couldn't blame them. "I've got to get to the store, but do you have a minute? It won't take long."

Nichelle crossed her arms over her chest and frowned. "There's only one thing I want to hear from you. Otherwise, you're wasting my time."

"But I—"

"But you nothing, Clark. Not unless it's an apology." Her posture stiffened, and she walked toward the parking lot.

Clark fell in step beside her. "Nichelle, I hoped we could get past this. To move forward and build on what we have."

They reached Nichelle's car and she opened it, throwing her bag inside. "All we have are lies, Clark. Lies and distrust. Hardly a strong foundation."

"I explained why I couldn't tell you."

"And I explained why that isn't good enough." She stood, staring at him, fists clenched.

The muscle under Clark's eye involuntarily contracted, jumping in an unusual rhythm. He cleared his throat. "You're being—"

She held up her hand and shook her head, then slid into her car. She closed the door with just enough force for the mechanism to click in place, then drove out of the parking lot, and Clark's life.

Clark's phone rang. Franny calling again, this time a video call. "Hello." Clark let out a deep sigh.

"What's that for? I was just calling to see if you're on your way."

He slid into his car and frowned at Franny. "Yes, but…"

He sighed again.

"Nichelle?"

"Yes."

His sister bit the side of her lip, clearly contemplating releasing some odd bit of information or the other.

"What is it, Franny?"

"I. Um. Well, I called Nichelle about some sorority business, but when I mentioned you, she shut me down."

Clark's heart clenched. She really was done with him. He understood it on a surface level, but this drove the point home. "She's upset with me and wants me to apologize. I don't believe I was wrong." He shrugged. "An impasse."

"After getting to know her these past couple years, I felt you two would be perfect for each other. You're so different, but in a complementary way. Know what I mean?"

He nodded.

"She's so good-natured, and easygoing. I wouldn't ask you to apologize if you didn't mean it. I know you wouldn't, but are you sure you're not wrong?"

Clark explained all the details of what went wrong. Starting from realizing Nichelle's mother's involvement to fighting against his feelings knowing he couldn't tell her the truth to their last fight and her refusal to understand or forgive him.

"Oh, Clark."

He blinked. "What?"

"I get why you felt your integrity was on the line. But do

you understand why you should have left her alone until all that mess was over? You didn't have to date her."

"I—" What Franny said was completely true. He warred with himself plenty of times about that very issue, hadn't he? "Yes, I understand. Not being around her wasn't an option. I tried, but I couldn't."

"Because you love her."

"Exactly."

"Yeah, but you see where you're wrong." Franny narrowed her eyes and crinkled her nose. "Right?"

Clark inhaled slowly and let it out. That much was true. Every stolen touch blurred the line. Or a kiss was crossing the line. By the time they'd joined, he was so far past the line, he forgot there was a line to begin with. "Yes, I see now."

"What're you going to do about it?"

"I need to call her."

Franny shook her head. "Not now, and not over the phone. Make her understand how sorry you are. Really drive it home."

Besides apologizing, Clark wasn't sure what else would be required. His instinct said Franny wouldn't be able to help him. He needed to figure it out for himself. But she was right; over the phone wasn't the correct direction. He'd go to work, then sleep on it, and plan tomorrow.

CHAPTER THIRTY-TWO

Nichelle

"WELCOME TO THE first day of the second summer term. This is Contemporary Political Ideologies. If you did not sign up for Contemporary Political Ideologies, this would probably be a great time to find the class you actually did sign up for."

Two students packed up and left, sheepishly slinking out the door and into the hallway. There was a glass window set in the wooden door, so they were visible speaking with each other, heads bent over a phone.

Nichelle waited a few beats before smiling at the remaining twenty-odd students, the familiar first-day optimism blooming in her belly. It wouldn't last though; it never did. "I'm Professor Sampson and will be your hostess for the next month. You should have already received the syllabus. If you didn't, please shoot me an email after class. In the meantime…" She went on to explain the objectives of the course, highlighting that although they would hit on the historic ideologies—liberalism, conservatism, libertarianism, and populism—they would explore a variety of provocative writers and thinkers who would expand (hopefully) their political world views.

Summer school wasn't ideal because of the compactness of the coursework. Because of that, she condensed assignments to make it easier on herself. Endless grading was enough to make her rethink her life choices, so she didn't even put herself in that position during the summer. She still had final papers from the first summer term waiting for her in the office when she finished up class.

When Nichelle did make it back to the office she shared with Jamie, she put her feet on the desk and released a hard breath.

Jamie touched her hand to her chest.

"What?" She cracked the door and peeked out to ensure nobody was coming. Her father would not be happy at her casual display.

"You better be careful. If Professor Sampson comes in, I don't know you."

It was a little awkward with Jamie and her father, but they'd been mostly ignoring the new relationship. "How's my brother anyway. Has the surgery been scheduled?" Nichelle casually threw the question out there, but it wouldn't be casually caught. Jamie did everything in her power to not talk about Asaf's illness. Any information Nichelle picked up was from Noah.

Jamie closed her eyes, and sighed, then turned to

Nichelle. "It's tomorrow morning at eight-thirty."

"Oh wow. So soon? How do you feel?"

"The love of my life and the father of my children is having major surgery tomorrow. How do you think I'm feeling?" Jamie wiped at her eyes and shook her head. "I'm sorry. Truly. It's just so hard. I don't mean to take it out on you."

Nichelle scooted closer to her friend cum sister-in-law and placed a hand on her shoulder. "It's okay. You beat up on me all you want. I can take it. I pray he'll be okay."

"Thanks. I do appreciate it."

"Is there anything I can do? I should call Noah and see if he wants me to babysit Emma." Nichelle cringed at the thought. What did she know about two-year-olds? Absolutely nothing, that's what.

"Anika is watching the boys so she can keep Emma too if Noah wants."

"She's not going to the hospital?"

Jamie shook her head and searched her purse. "I can never find a tissue when I need it."

Nichelle removed one from the dispenser on Jamie's desk and handed it to the clearly discombobulated woman.

"Thanks. I know I'm a mess."

"Totally understandable, J. I just wish there was more I could do."

"Yeah. I think the surgery will turn out okay, but it's still so scary."

"I know." And she did know. This was not the first brother who had gone under the knife. Clifton made it through the surgery fine, but it was a tough cancer, not easily removed. By the time the surgeon came out to tell her and her parents it went well, they'd researched enough to understand that it wouldn't matter. And sure enough, a little over a year later, he was gone. According to Jamie, even though she didn't say exactly what was wrong with him, Asaf didn't suffer from the same ailment, and she was glad, but it was still upsetting. She was selfish enough to want her brother to hang around longer in case he changed his mind about having a relationship with her. She shook herself and patted Jamie's back. Obviously, more importantly, she wanted him to be okay for the family he already had.

Jamie blew her nose, then threw the tissue in the wastepaper basket. "Thanks for everything. I'm going to head out. We have an early morning."

"No problem. Like I said, I'll be praying for him."

She looked at the photos on Jamie's desk, and her stomach flipped. Having this new family was great, but that also meant more people were added to the mix. More people for Nichelle to care about. More people to possibly break her heart. She took a breath and fired up her laptop. As her mother always said, no reason to borrow trouble. Everything would work out fine. Asaf would pull through, and Jamie and the boys, and Noah, would have him for many years to come.

NICHELLE'S PHONE BUZZED, and she frowned at the device on her coffee table. With raised eyebrows, she looked over at Amanda eating waffles and drinking English breakfast tea. They were reviewing notes from the final practice the night before. The sorors were ready and would probably win it all. The step show was later that evening, so time would tell, and it wouldn't be long.

The phone buzzed again. "Who could that be?"

"Why don't you look at the phone and see, silly?"

The past few days, Nichelle jumped whenever the phone buzzed. It was never who she hoped.

She stood and walked over to the coffee table. A couple texts from Noah flashed across the screen. Shit, she'd forgotten all about Asaf's surgery. Clearly, she was already officially the worst sister ever. She strode back to the dining room table and showed Amanda. "It's Noah. Asaf's surgery was this morning."

"Is everything okay?"

She read the couple of texts, then read them again. She blinked a few times, then read again. "He's out of surgery, and it went well. Everything's fine, but…"

Amanda looked up, worry creasing her brow. "But?"

"He asked if I'd come to the hospital. He wants to see me."

"Oh. Well, that's good news, right?"

Nichelle shrugged. "I mean, yeah. I guess so. I just… I don't know. I wish it were under different circumstances. I'm not sure how I feel meeting him for the first time in the hospital. Don't you think that's weird?"

"You should do what you're comfortable with. If he wants to see you now, he'll want to see you once he's home from the hospital."

"Hmmm, then that brings on a whole new set of problems."

She looked up at her, brows drawn together. "Oh, you mean your birth mother. Because she lives with them."

"Got it in one."

"Let them worry about that. Concentrate on your brother wanting to see you."

"Yeah." She looked around, for what, she wasn't sure. "Everything's such a mess."

Amanda stood and put an arm around Nichelle's shoulders. "This is a good thing, love. Just go with it."

"I know." Then she surprised herself by letting out a huge sigh. Clark had truly rubbed off on her. She burst into tears.

"Girl, what's wrong with you?" Amanda moved her other arm around Nichelle and drew her into a tight hug.

Nichelle cried some more, then drew down to a sniffle. "I miss Clark."

"I figured. This thing with your brother is obviously emotional, but that was serious waterworks for someone who *wants* to see you." She dragged Nichelle over to the couch, then went back into the kitchen for a glass of water.

Nichelle pulled a tissue out of the box on the end table and dabbed at her eyes. "Why did I let this happen to me again?"

"*Let* this happen? *To* you? Girl, you better take some responsibility and make some big-girl decisions."

"Amanda." Nichelle bucked her eyes, and her face heated.

"Amanda nothing. You love the man. He loves you. He made a mistake. You know it. He knows it. Just move ahead."

"But he won't apologize." With shaky hands, Nichelle took a sip of the water Amanda left on table then placed it back.

"You sound like a broken record. You're both stubborn, but someone has to give in. Or I guess you could just regret it the rest of your lives. Your choice."

"But—"

The water on the table nearly toppled when Amanda bumped it before sitting next to Nichelle on the sofa. She reached out and righted it before it could fall and spill everywhere. "He admitted he used bad judgment. Maybe that's not an apology, but it does show that he understands how he hurt you. Now, if you can't live with that, it's totally up to you. Your feelings are absolutely valid. Forget about it. Forget about him and move on." She lifted the glass from the table and handed it to her friend. "But if you can live with it, have some grace and forgive him even if he didn't ask."

Nichelle nodded and drank the water.

THE HOSPITAL WAS located one town over, close to where Jamie and Asaf lived. Nichelle had never been to their place, even before when she and Jamie were only coworkers, but she always knew basically where their house was located. She hadn't actually spent much time in the town. Thank goodness for GPS.

When she came off the elevator, Noah was waiting in the hallway, a stern crease to his brow.

Nichelle tensed at first, but the expression on her brother's face was pretty much his default. He seemed to always be worried about something. They met halfway and hugged. "Hi."

"Hi." Noah rotated and walked down the hallway, not waiting for Nichelle to follow. His clip was speedy, his usual pace.

Nichelle trotted to keep up. When they got to Asaf's room, they stopped outside the door which was barely cracked. They couldn't see inside, but Jamie's voice floated out to them. She was relieved, almost giddy.

Noah placed his hand on the door. "Are you ready?"

"As I'll ever be." Nichelle followed Noah into the room.

Jamie was sitting in a chair that was pulled up to the bed. She was speaking to her husband with a smile plastered on her face, although the evidence of her worry was etched in the lines around her mouth and the dark circles under her eyes.

Nichelle had seen photos of Asaf, both on Jamie's desk at work and in Noah's house. With him lying in the hospital bed, a couple of hours removed from surgery, he basically looked the same. She hadn't known exactly what to expect, but there were no tubes down his throat or even oxygen in his nose. He did have the little chute thing in the back of his hand where an IV tube could connect, but otherwise, he looked like a darker version of Noah. He had black hair and dark eyes, but the brothers had the exact same face shape and smile, which Asaf was currently pointing Nichelle's way.

She waved at Jamie, then moved closer to the bed, but didn't crowd it. Noah was at her back, providing silent encouragement. "You look good."

Asaf laughed. "Thanks. It's good to meet you."

"I'm happy to meet you too."

Jamie stood and gave Nichelle a side hug, then grabbed Noah's hand. "Let's give these two a minute." They left the room and shut the door behind them.

Nichelle fidgeted, and suddenly didn't know what to do with her hands. She glanced around the room, thinking of something to say.

"Do you want to sit?"

She stared at the chair Jamie just vacated. Did she want to sit? Vulnerability skittered across her skin, even in a way she hadn't felt when she met Noah. She took a deep breath to steady herself and sat in the chair.

"I want to apologize for making this difficult for you."

Nichelle shrugged. "I understand. It was a bit of a shock for me too."

"Noah says you had no clue you were adopted. You really didn't know?"

"I really didn't. I have amazing parents, and they've loved me like I was their own. I suppose I am."

Asaf nodded and pushed himself up in the bed. Nichelle stood to help, but he waved her off. "I'm happy to hear it. Jamie's been telling me more about your dad. She's always had kind words about him as her boss. It is such a coincidence. Almost unbelievable."

She nodded because what could she say? These were conversations she'd been having for weeks, and now he wanted to start all over. Maybe she was a little resentful. "I know I said I understand, and I do, but I'm also a little hurt. I don't expect you to say anything, but I wanted you to know. And I hope this isn't a one-time thing."

"You mean because I was feeling my mortality?" He chortled. "Yeah, that's part of it, but I hope we'll be able to build a relationship from this now. If you're still interested."

Nichelle stood and moved closer to the bed, grabbing the

handrail. "You're my brother, Asaf. That means everything to me."

He nodded, a slight mist in his eyes.

"I'll go get the others."

Nichelle chatted with her new family. Her birth mother was missing, and that was okay with her. This venture was more about her siblings and finding a sense of belonging than her birth parents. After all, she had wonderful parents who loved and cherished her. She'd worked hard for a rewarding career. And even though she'd all but given up, she hoped a certain caring man would be a welcome addition to her complete life. Family meant the world to her, and as far as she was concerned, she had it all.

CHAPTER THIRTY-THREE

Nichelle

THE CAFÉ WAS minutes from campus, which was good because Nichelle was late. She'd finally decided to check out the group Francesca recommended all those weeks ago when she first discovered her adoption. She had a good grasp on her life as far as her parents were concerned, both adopted and birth. Relationships with all her siblings were progressing so she couldn't be happier. But there was still that niggling thought in the back of her head that she'd missed out. She forgave her parents for not telling her she was adopted but still had a bit of a thorn in her side about her birth parents and the ease with which they were able to throw her away.

Henry called her every couple of days but only stayed on the phone for a minute or two at a time, so it was difficult getting to know him on anything but a surface level. She hadn't been able to pin him down on his feelings leading up to the time before her birth. He was cagey, and Nichelle struggled with navigating this new relationship.

Then there was Anika. Even though Nichelle was able to meet Asaf, she wasn't sure how their relationship would progress either considering their mother lived with her brother. When would they have time to get to know each other? What about Asaf and Jamie's kids? Would their mother continue to pretend she didn't exist even though Nichelle had dealings with everyone in her household?

So she found herself outside the café to talk it out with other people in her same boat. She'd give it a chance and see how she liked it. Fresh baked bread hit her nose as she walked through the front of the little sandwich shop, but she was already late so would have to pick up something to eat on her way out. She pulled open the door leading to the back room where a group of people were seated around tables set up in a circle. The room was nearly full, but she spotted a seat on the other side and squeezed between an older white woman and a middle-aged man with thick black hair.

"Should I continue or..." Another woman about Nichelle's age looked at a man directly seated across from Nichelle.

Nichelle squinted her eyes because the woman looked familiar, but she was having trouble placing her.

The man smiled. "Since you were just getting started, why don't we let the newbie introduce herself. If that's okay, Lauren."

The woman shrugged. "Sure, that's fine."

He then turned his gaze to Nichelle whose face was already heating up. She didn't mind speaking in front of people but hated that she'd interrupted by being late. "Welcome. My name is Carl and I officially lead this group, however, we all work together. Please introduce yourself and share as much or as little as you like on what brings you here." Carl gave Nichelle an encouraging smile.

She cleared her throat, wishing for a bottle of water. "Hi, everyone. So sorry I interrupted. My name is Nichelle and I recently found out I'm adopted. I'm still learning how to navigate this new space with siblings and birth parents, yet want to honor the parents who raised me too. So that's why I'm here. Hoping to gain some insight from people who are in my same boat." She smiled and shrugged, looking around the table. "Thanks for having me."

"We're happy you're here, Nichelle. Thanks for sharing." Carl then turned back to Lauren, inclining his head.

While Lauren spoke, Nichelle got a good look at the woman with the luminescent brown skin. She was sure she'd seen her before. This Lauren with thick, dark hair hanging past her shoulders, stick straight, and intelligent brown eyes.

Once the meeting was over, some people broke into smaller groups to talk while others headed to the exit. Lauren was one of the latter and although Nichelle hadn't placed her yet, she was sure she knew her from somewhere, so she followed her out through the shop and onto the sidewalk. "Hi, Lauren, right?"

The woman stopped and turned, a cautious smile on her

face. "Hi, yes, that's right. I'm Lauren."

"I'm Nichelle. Sorry to stop you but I feel like we know each other. Do we?"

Lauren nodded. "Not really know each other, but I was in the grad program under your um…" She faltered and grimaced.

Nichelle ignored the misstep. She couldn't blame Lauren, considering Nichelle was just getting used to all her family changes herself. However, Robert Sampson would always be her dad. "Oh, that's right. I knew you looked familiar. I remember you had classes with my dad. Professor Gray was your thesis advisor, I think."

The muscles in Lauren's shoulders relaxed. "Good memory." She smiled again, this time much friendlier. "It was nice seeing you, but I have to run. I'm a florist and need to get back to the shop. It's just down the street, but a busy day for us."

"Totally understand. Oh, is that Steele Florist? They're wonderful."

"Yes, thanks so much. It was my parents' shop, but they've retired so it's mostly mine now."

Nichelle wasn't sure she was misinterpreting Lauren's tone, but it sounded like the florist wasn't happy about inheriting the store. "Ah gotcha. Well, don't let me hold you up. I hope to see you next time." She gave Lauren one last wave then headed back to campus.

It was a clear, sunny day with a warm breeze. Her steps

were light as she walked, and she was happy with her decision to join the adoption group. As she had listened to those who shared, she realized she wasn't alone in this journey. Lauren shared that she had no intention of looking for her birth parents and probably wouldn't respond if they ever came looking for her. Nichelle could respect that, but her path was different. She relished her new relationships.

Which was good because it looked like her relationship with Clark was heading toward an old one.

THE BREEZE FROM the extra fans brought in for the show was a relief to Nichelle. Bodies were crammed together in the auditorium, factions cordoned off in their own areas, flashing their hand signs and wearing their colors, greeting each other with their signature sounds.

When the MC came onto the stage, all those sounds blended to a cheer. This party was about to get started. Nichelle turned to her seatmate on the right and grinned at her bestie. "This is gonna be lit." She then rotated to her mother on her left, who wouldn't miss a step show unless she was in the hospital. ICU at that. "Eep, our sorors are gonna take the whole thing. Watch."

Her mom shushed her and looked toward the stage.

First up were some graduate Delta Sigma Theta sorors from Oakland. The lights went down in the auditorium, and they were plunged into complete silence. A video played on the big screen behind the stage with a woman speaking as though welcoming passengers on a tour bus. One of the Deltas came out dressed as a tour guide, in red and white, a cute hat perched on her head. She mimicked greeting the passengers on board as the video-speaker shuffled actual passengers aboard the bus. She exited, and the lights came up on the stage. Several members were grouped together. Then the music started. "Oo oop," broke through the crowd, and the yelling from the masses began in full force. Those sisters danced and stepped like it was going out of style, red scarves flying. Old heads weren't up for the prize money, but they sure stepped like they were.

Nichelle stomped her feet right along with them, grinning and laughing, alternating between slapping Amanda's arm and shoving her mom's shoulder.

More graduate groups performed, including the gentlemen of Kappa Alpha Psi, defying gravity with their canes. It was a thing of beauty, and Nichelle marveled at their talent.

Her mom leaned over and spoke close to her ear. "That's what you should have got you, a Kappa man."

Nichelle ignored her and kept watching the stage, but her words stung. Even if Nichelle chose to forgive Clark, her mother was still hot about the betrayal. Family dinners wouldn't be as comfortable with Clark at the table. She couldn't think about that now, because her younger sorors were up next.

Sorors came out in all black with large sparkling letters of Psi Gamma across their chests, foregoing their usual colors of blue and silver. They wore one-piece body suits and two-inch heeled boots, dressed as secret agents.

Amanda sat up on the edge of her seat, giving Nichelle's arm several pats. "They look good."

All Nichelle could do was nod. They did look good, and they were ready. She could feel it in her bones.

The team snapped their heads up, and put a hand to their ear, as if listening to a device. A man spoke over the loudspeaker, telling them of a serious matter. All nodded and moved into position.

Nichelle held her breath.

The stepping began, with them chanting, "This is a…serious, serious, serious matter," along with their choreo-graphed steps. They ended the sequence with a head-roll and snapped to attention with their hands out at their sides. They broke into a dance routine, more stepping, then strolled off the stage.

Nichelle finally released her breath. Not a step was missed, or a gesture forgotten. They'd perfected their routine and executed it perfectly.

Intermission came, and people all around stood up to go into the foyer to hit the concession stands. The only food item allowed in the auditorium was water, and Nichelle had forgotten to bring some. She stood, wiping sweat from the back of her neck.

Francesca bounded over with her line sister, Tasha, and hugged Nichelle's wet neck. "Oh my gosh, did you see them?"

Laughing, Nichelle patted the girl on the back. "They were incredible. Definitely winning tonight."

Francesca grinned and looked over Nichelle's shoulder, then elbowed Tasha, and left.

Nichelle whirled around to a touch on her arm. Her eyes widened in disbelief, but she took the cold bottle from Clark's hand, and sat down hard. She looked at a grinning Amanda, then shifted to glance at her glaring Mom. She took a breath and turned back to Clark, cold droplets running the length of her arm. "What are you doing here?"

The buzz of the audience died down to a low roar. The seats behind her were empty of their patrons, probably taking advantage of the intermission. Clark sat and leaned forward.

Amanda and her mom leaned forward as well.

Clark stilled, then took a large breath, and held it.

Nichelle knew all of his quirks and movements. He was probably taking a calming breath.

She, herself, tried calming gestures unsuccessfully. Her stomach rolled, and her heartbeat increased.

Clark released the breath. "I apologize."

Her mom shifted in her seat. "You can keep that apology. What you did—"

Nichelle put up a stilling hand. "Maybe you and Amanda should go get something to eat. I think your blood sugar may be low."

Amanda stood, and her mom huffed. "Anything he has to say to you ought to be able to be said in front of us."

Clark's face reddened under the scrutiny, but he didn't back down. "I understand now why you were upset." He turned to her mom. "Perhaps I can explain my thought process to you."

Nichelle shook her head. "Here we go."

"No, I was wrong. And I'm apologizing. I thought maybe your mother wanted further explanation."

"Why were you wrong, Clark?" Nichelle leaned in closer.

"I could have maintained my integrity and protected your trust by simply staying away. By not pursuing a relationship with you until the case was over."

Nichelle nodded, a small smile creasing her face. "But it wasn't simple, was it?"

"No. Because…" He glanced at Amanda and peeked at her mom, then examined Nichelle, a mist glowing in his eyes. "No, it wasn't simple because I love you."

Her heart beat so fast, Nichelle had to take some breaths. She stood and reached for Clark's hands, pulling him into an awkward hug over the chairs. An apology is all she was waiting for and had pretty much given up on, but it was wonderful to hear anyway. "Good thing because I love you too."

They held each other, as her mom and Amanda, and the

other audience members faded into the background. Nichelle wasn't sure how long they stood like that, but as far as she was concerned, it wasn't long enough. Unfortunately, the folks whose seats Clark was occupying didn't feel the same.

She held on to his hand as he made his way to the end of the row, their tight grip never faltering over the rush of people coming back inside to both rows. When they got to the end, they embraced once more. "I wish we could leave."

Clark pulled back, biting his lip. "Franny would kill us, especially you."

"Not to mention Mom."

"What are we—"

"We'll worry about Mom later. She'll get over it. It's not like she doesn't owe me one."

Clark's lipped curled into a grin. A real, genuine, happy smile.

Nichelle's eyes pricked with his happiness. He deserved to be happy. And so did she. "She may owe me one, but let's not push her." She led him to another row nearer the college-aged onlookers. They sat as close as they could considering the seat divider, but arms and legs entangled through the remainder of the show.

When Psi Gamma was announced as first place runners-up, both Nichelle and Clark jumped to their feet, cheering in excitement. Maybe the sorors didn't win the grand prize, but first place was nothing to sneeze at. It carried a hefty prize, as well as bragging rights. As far as Nichelle was concerned, it was a perfect night.

THE BED WAS warm and comfortable even with Clark's big body taking up half the space. Although her eyes were still closed, it was clear to her he was awake, probably watching her sleep. He was still. Too still. She peeked an eye open. "Creeper."

His eyes widened, and the tips of his ears turned pink. "I, uh."

"I'm just joking around, Clark. Come here."

He turned a relieved smile on her and inched closer.

She wrapped her arms around his neck, pulling him near, and kissed his sumptuous lips. "Morning."

He grinned against her mouth and kissed her deeper until they were both panting. "Good morning."

"Do you need to be anywhere? Like the store or…"

He breathed in deeply and laid on his back, stretching his arms above his head. "Describe need? I have so much to do, and I cannot wait until Franny graduates."

"So not need but should." It's not like she didn't have some grades to upload into the system herself.

Nichelle's phone buzzed. She swung her feet to the floor, and when she looked at the screen, she groaned. "Mom wants us over for breakfast."

Clark's face tightened, then relaxed. He got up and walked to her side of the bed, sank to the floor near her feet, and rubbed her calves. "We have to face them at some point."

Nichelle slid off the bed into Clark's lap. "I don't know what to do."

"We could stay in bed all day and forget the world exists."

Nichelle's head snapped back. "Who are you and what'd you do with my boyfriend?"

Clark nipped at her chin and kissed down her neck, stopping just short of her naked breasts. "He's still here. Only now it's the sexed-up version." He ran his thumb across her cheek. "What do you say?"

She leaned her forehead against his. With Clark hard and ready, and her own arousal tingling all through her veins, the decision shouldn't be that hard. She sighed, and Clark fell back, placing his arm over his face, knowing he'd lost the battle. "We may as well get it over with, right? The longer we wait, the more your mom will work herself up."

He didn't move his arm or open his eyes, but mumbled a grumpy, "Yes, of course."

Nichelle tapped out a reply to her mom and set the phone down, then slinked across the floor to Clark and positioned herself over his stretched-out legs. His erection was down to half-mast, but she meant to do something about that.

Clark lifted his arm and looked at Nichelle hovering over his dick. He watched as she lowered her mouth and licked up the length. "I thought—"

"Shh, we have a little time."

He started to lift up on his elbows, but she put a hand on his chest. "Not that much time."

She took him in her mouth, and his length grew to full strength nearly gagging her. The groan Clark released had Nichelle redoubling her efforts. She stroked him and swirled her tongue around the head.

He bucked his hips and dug his fingers into her hair. "God, that's perfect." She moved her hands under his firm ass and let him fuck her mouth. "Yes, right there. Oh God. I'm coming."

Nichelle released his dick and watched while he spilled all over his stomach.

"You ready for a shower?" She was trying for levity because visiting her parents this morning wouldn't be easy. She moved to stand, but he held out his hand, still prone on the floor. "What, you need help?"

He grinned. "So much help."

Nichelle couldn't wait to show him how much more help he may need in the near future, but first, they had a breakfast date to make.

EPILOGUE

Eight months later

"V'HI SHE'AMDAH LA'AVOTEINU v'lanu." Everyone was singing-ish, most were mispronouncing, especially her sisters and parents—not Clark because he studied. Nichelle looked ahead to the next pages. Noah put sticky-notes throughout her Haggadah marked with who was saying what part. Unfortunately, they were nowhere near the break for dinner. She groaned because even though she had been warned there would be a lot of wine drinking during the Seder, she was already feeling it. She probably should have taken sips instead of gulps. This was a marathon, not a sprint, and she'd made a rookie mistake.

Her mom read the passage about the ten plagues, and everyone took small tastes of wine after each individual plague was read. Noah had explained they were non-traditional in this way because technically they were supposed to only spill out a drop of wine for each plague. Clearly, Nichelle wasn't the only one who felt the effects of those blessings. And then without warning, Emma dumped a basketful of ping-pong balls all over the table. The balls landed on plates of matzah, in wine glasses, and everywhere else imaginable. The non-Jewish people in the room were stunned, including Nichelle who was Jew-ish and still learning; Noah, Jamie, Asaf, and their boys nearly fell out of their chairs laughing.

Emma giggled. "It's hail."

Their unconstrained joy was contagious and soon everyone joined in the mirth.

Madeleine swiped at her eyes from laughing so hard. "Scared the shit out of me."

Nichelle and her mother's gazes locked for a quick second. She cursed sometimes, but never in front of her parents.

Then they launched into how different things would have been enough: Taken out of Egypt, *Dayeinu;* Killed the oppressors' first born, *Dayeinu;* Split the sea, *Dayeinu,* etc.

Nichelle took a couple of breaths. *Dayeinu.* Having a relationship with her adopted family would have been enough. She was beyond blessed as she looked around the table at both old and new family members. Her birth mother still refused to acknowledge her, but this was enough. Her birth father couldn't make it because he had a prior engagement, but this was enough. *Dayeinu.*

Noah did a symbolic washing of his hands, bitter herbs were swirled in salt water and eaten, and then they made tiny sandwiches of the matzah and charoset. Nichelle and Noah grinned at each other.

Asaf took a bite, then studied Noah. "This is really good

charoset this year. Did you do something different?"

"Wow, low blow. Your sister made it this time."

Nichelle had made the charoset with Noah's guidance, and it came out perfect. She couldn't be prouder.

Asaf looked at Nichelle. "Great job, sister."

Jamie smiled at her with watery eyes.

Hearing her siblings call her sister never got old.

Finally, it was time for dinner. Nichelle sat near the kitchen entry, to Noah's right, so she jumped up to help ferry the food.

Her brother and Clark followed her in to get the various dishes they'd prepared. Well, mostly Noah, but he did allow Nichelle to make some of the simpler food like steamed asparagus and roasted potatoes. Noah picked up the platter of roast beef and took it out into the dining room.

Nichelle handed Clark the large bowl of soup. "This is great, right?"

"It really is. I've never enjoyed a holiday more."

"I know, right? Noah says it's his favorite." Nichelle dished asparagus onto a plate. "He says it's because of all the drinking. I can't believe we have more 'blessings' and then whisky for after dinner. I'm glad we rode with Mom and Dad."

Clark smiled and set down the bowl. He adjusted the kippah Noah bought for her. It was made of a beautiful gold cloth and matched her blouse perfectly.

Then he kissed her so deep, her toes numbed.

"Whoa, what was that for?"

"You're glowing, and so beautiful. I couldn't resist."

Noah walked back in. "Guys, where's the rest of the food?" He looked between Nichelle and Clark, and rolled his eyes, then picked up the forgotten bowl of soup, and walked it into the dining room.

"We better get this food out there before my brother melts. He's running a tight ship, and I don't want to be the one to get us off course."

Clark ignored her and leaned in again.

Nichelle met him halfway because who was she fooling—a kiss from Clark was worth it.

They were spared her brother's stern look because he didn't come back in, so they took in the asparagus, extra barbecue sauce for the beef, and roasted potatoes. Dessert was a lemon cake that Noah made. He wasn't happy with the overall look of it although Nichelle thought it was fine. They'd cut it into slices and placed them on individual plates which satisfied her perfectionist brother.

The remainder of the program went by with more wine drinking, then the kids were turned loose in the house to look for the Afikoman. The boys led Emma around, clearly allowing their younger cousin to "find" it. They looked under couch cushions, in bureau drawers, and even Suzette's purse. She laughed at the intrusion of those small hands. It wasn't there though.

While the kids searched, Nichelle gave Clark a look, and

stood up and headed to the bathroom. She waited inside, and he came in a minute or two later. More than likely, everyone would realize they disappeared, but she didn't care. She loved Clark, and when the mood struck to show him, she always went with it. They'd wasted too much time wondering about the other.

She pulled him into a tight hug and breathed in his jasmine and vanilla scent. She briefly wondered how long the scent would take to leave him. Franny was graduating the next month and had decided to take over the store. With his new semi-freedom, Clark and Nichelle planned a summer getaway to the Caribbean. Nichelle wanted to explore more of her roots on Henry's side, and maybe track down exactly where the ring originated. The ring had started all this in her life. That ring brought her sisters and brothers she could cherish. A new father and mother she could appreciate for giving her life, as well as even more appreciation for the parents she already had who gave her a wonderful, love-filled life. And it also brought her the sexy, beautiful, caring man in her arms. She said a silent prayer for her grandmother who'd sent her that ring.

"I love you, dearest."

"And I you. I was just thinking about how lucky we are."

Nichelle squeezed him and looked up into his eyes. "So was I."

He nodded and kissed her temple. "A year ago, I'd given up on being happy. I was existing. Sure, I got some joy out of my work and cycling, and of course Franny. But today, I still have all that, and I've repaired my relationship with my parents which I thought was irreparable. And most of all, I have a family. You're my family, and I'm truly happy."

Nichelle glanced at the engagement ring Clark had given her the month before. She'd been shocked when she opened the jewelry box with the yellow diamond. It was emerald cut, set East-West, four carats. She stood on her tippy toes and captured his lips with hers, closing her eyes, and losing herself in him for just the moment. She was warm with wine and love and wouldn't have it any other way. "We better get back before someone comes to get us."

The kids were still turning the house upside down. Finally, Asaf strolled around the room and stood next to the china closet, and kicked at the bottom enough to get the kid's attention. They flew to where he was standing, nearly knocking him over. Emma raised the matzah in triumph, and everyone clapped for her.

Nichelle leaned over to Noah. "We don't actually have to eat that, do we?" It may have been wrapped in a paper napkin, but Nichelle could imagine the look on her mom's face if the thing were split into equal pieces, and she was asked to eat it. Nichelle wasn't looking forward to that either.

"Absolutely not." He laughed, then cringed, and laughed again.

Lastly, the boys opened a door to let in Elijah. His cup of

wine was waiting for him near the Seder plate, but when Jamie picked it up, she turned the empty cup for all to see. "He's been here everyone. He's had his wine."

Nichelle glanced at Clark who raised a brow. They hadn't seen anyone drink from Elijah's cup. She looked at her dad, who was nearest the wine.

He shrugged and schooled his face to his most innocent look.

Nichelle's heart squeezed. All of her family was included. Seriously, she couldn't ask for anything more.

Dayeinu.

The End

Want more? Don't miss the next book in the Secret Ties series, *Two Sides of a Secret*!

Join Tule Publishing's newsletter for more great reads and weekly deals!

Acknowledgements

This story, so personal to me, took many iterations before getting to this final version. Through name changes of the main characters, title changes, and different POVs. What remained consistent were my Book Besties, Jamie McLachlan, Amanda Linsmeier, Bianca M. Schwarz, and C.H. (Cathie) Armstrong. Their names were always included as characters because I wanted a way to honor what their support means to me. This was the first book I wrote from start to finish with the Wordmakers community. I wrote a fourth of the book during the week of my first #20Kin5Days then finished it within the community sprints. I can't express how much Wordmakers inspire me. The support from my publishing siblings, Denise N. Wheatley, Fortune Whelan, Mia Heintzelman, Stacey Agdern, Heather Novak, Janine Amesta, and Lisa Lin means so much. Navigating this Tule journey with you has been amazing. The Romance Schmooze discord was a game changer for me. I've learned so much from you and appreciate you allowing me to soak up culture I missed out on for so long.

Thanks so much to A.R. Vishny for the insightful sensitivity read. I can promise you if anything is wrong in this book concerning Jewish culture, it's on me for muffing up her wonderful feedback. I wrote this book how I experienced my Jewish discovery. Thank you to my sister-in-law, Rebecca, for stamping approval on an early draft.

My agent, Amy Brewer, is truly the best. I don't have words for what her support and guidance has meant and continues to mean. One day I'll figure out how to string some together to capture my appreciation of her. Thank you to my amazing editor, Sinclair Sawhney, and all of the staff at Tule Publishing for your insight and guidance. Having a second series with you was a no-brainer.

Visit Kelly's website at kellycainauthor.com and connect with her on BookBub. Join Kelly's newsletter for inside info and exclusive content—Between The Sheets.

If you enjoyed *A Kiss From the Past*,
you'll love the next book in the…

Secret Ties series

Book 1: *A Kiss From the Past*

Book 2: *Two Sides of a Secret*
Coming in July 2023

Available now at your favorite online retailer!

More Books by Kelly Cain

The Everheart Brothers of Texas series

Book 1: *An Acquired Taste*

Book 2: *A Tasty Dish*

Book 3: *Tastes So Sweet*

Available now at your favorite online retailer!

About the Author

Kelly Cain is a native Californian but has spent the last couple of decades in Texas, currently residing in the live music capital of the world, Austin. Consequently, most of her books are set somewhere between those two locations.

Kelly writes multicultural romance with determined women directing their own fates, and the swoon-worthy men who adore them. She loves reading most genres but please don't ask her to pick just one. However, she can pick her favorite book boyfriend – Will Herondale.

When she isn't reading or writing, Kelly is most likely using a genealogy site to research her extended family, both old and new. Or cooking/baking something delightful.

She has two adult daughters, and a new granddaughter. Visit her website kellycainauthor.com for more info.

Thank you for reading

A Kiss From the Past

If you enjoyed this book, you can find more from all our great authors at TulePublishing.com, or from your favorite online retailer.

TULE
PUBLISHING

9 781959 988038